THE CURSE OF THE CHERRY PIE

Also by Amy Patricia Meade

The Marjorie McClelland mysteries

MILLION DOLLAR BABY
GHOST OF A CHANCE
SHADOW WALTZ
BLACK MOONLIGHT

The Tish Tarragon series

COOKIN' THE BOOKS *
THE GARDEN CLUB MURDER *
THE CHRISTMAS FAIR KILLER *

The Vermont mystery series

WELL-OFFED IN VERMONT
SHORT-CIRCUITED IN CHARLOTTE

* *available from Severn House*

THE CURSE OF THE CHERRY PIE

Amy Patricia Meade

SEVERN
HOUSE

First world edition published in Great Britain and the USA in 2021
by Severn House, an imprint of Canongate Books Ltd,
14 High Street, Edinburgh EH1 1TE.

Trade paperback edition first published in Great Britain and the USA in 2022
by Severn House, an imprint of Canongate Books Ltd.

severnhouse.com

Copyright © Amy Patricia Meade, 2021

British Library Cataloguing-in-Publication Data
A CIP catalogue record for this title is available from the British Library.

ISBN-13: 978-0-7278-9055-9 (cased)
ISBN-13: 978-1-78029-771-2 (trade paper)
ISBN-13: 978-1-4483-0509-4 (e-book)

This is a work of fiction. Names, characters, places and incidents are either the
product of the author's imagination or are used fictitiously. Except where actual
historical events and characters are being described for the storyline of this novel,
all situations in this publication are fictitious and any resemblance to actual
persons, living or dead, business establishments, events or locales is purely
coincidental.

All Severn House titles are printed on acid-free paper.

Typeset by Palimpsest Book
Falkirk, Stirlingshire, Scotla
Printed and bound in Great F
TJ Books Limited, Padstow,

ONE

'**O**ur Father, who art in heaven, hallowed be thy name,' the minister of the First Baptist Church led in prayer. It was an unseasonably warm day in mid-March and a summery breeze swirled through the blossoming cherry trees and magnolias of the Hobson Glen Memorial Cemetery, sending a shower of pink and white petals cascading down upon the crowd gathered beside the open grave.

'Amen.' The minister closed the prayer and gestured for the mourners to step forward and pay their last respects.

Dressed in a floral-printed black chiffon dress and a pair of leather pumps, Tish Tarragon, the owner of Cookin' the Books Café, and her well-tailored attorney boyfriend, Schuyler Thompson, stepped from the crowd hand in hand, placed a pair of white carnations upon the cloth-covered casket, and moved aside. Single mother, Mary Jo Okensholt, and Channel Ten weatherman, Julian Jefferson Davis – dear friends of Tish's since the days they attended the University of Virginia together – followed suit, each laying a single flower upon the casket before joining Tish and Schuyler in the nearby clearing.

The foursome watched as other friends and townsfolk said their farewells: romance writer Opal Schaffer, library board president Augusta May Wilson and her husband, Edwin, library executive director Daryl Dufour, and last, but certainly not least, town eccentric Enid Kemper.

The elderly Enid, wearing a ragged cardigan over a navy-blue housedress, presented a white carnation and gave the casket several gentle pats as Langhorne, her green conure companion, rested upon her shoulder. 'You were a good man, Lloyd Rufus, and a helluva a good plumber. You always made sure Langhorne and I had heat and hot water, oftentimes without sending us a bill. Should be me in that coffin, not you, but God always does take the good ones. Rest easy.'

At Enid's words, Lloyd Rufus's widow, Celestine, let out a

mighty wail. Tish, her wavy blonde hair blowing gently in the breeze, rushed to the woman's aid. In the months since Cookin' the Books opened, Celestine Rufus had proven herself to be not just a loyal employee and an excellent baker, but a treasured friend.

Taking over for Celestine's eldest daughter – who herself was in tears and being propped up by her husband – Tish wrapped a consoling arm around the baker's shoulders.

'Oh, Tish.' Celestine sobbed as she took the younger woman's free hand in hers. 'I can't believe he's gone. We were supposed to grow old together.'

Tish pulled Celestine's bright-red head close to hers and did her best to silently soothe her as she cried. There were no words adequate to quell the grief and shock Celestine and her family had experienced. Only the previous week, a jubilant Celestine announced to Tish and Mary Jo that Lloyd's newest employee was competent enough to start taking over some of the more difficult jobs at Lloyd's plumbing and heating business. The news not only meant less crawling around on the ground and less heavy lifting for Lloyd, but also two free Saturdays a month – Saturdays to be spent with grandchildren, shopping in Richmond, roaming the quaint streets of Colonial Williamsburg, or enjoying a leisurely weekend in Washington, DC.

And now Lloyd Rufus was dead, having suffered a massive stroke mere weeks before his sixty-first birthday. Dead, in his favorite chair, while watching late-night television. Dead, without a chance to say goodbye to his family or give his wife a parting kiss. Dead, before he could spend a newly free Saturday morning doing whatever he wished.

The Rufus children and their spouses had paid their final respects. Now it was Celestine's turn to say goodbye. 'Come with me,' she begged as she clutched Tish's hand ever tighter.

Tish nodded and escorted Celestine to Lloyd's casket. 'Oh, Lloyd,' the older woman sobbed. 'Just when we thought we were finally comin' out on top. That was always the way with us, wasn't it, hon? Still, I have no regrets. Not a one. I fell in love with you the minute I saw you. The boy on the green, with that leather jacket and that grin. You were the prettiest boy I'd ever seen. You're still that boy, in my mind. Always have been, despite babies and grandbabies and fights and unkind words. I'll keep watchin' over our family, Lloyd, like I've always done, but our family won't ever stop wishin' you were here.'

Celestine placed a red carnation on her husband's casket and stepped away from the open grave, leaning on Tish as she was escorted back to the waiting arms of her children.

'That was rough,' Julian noted as Tish returned to the clearing.

'Poor Celestine,' Mary Jo lamented. 'There must be something we can do for her.'

'We'll figure it out,' Tish vowed. 'In the meantime, we have a funeral luncheon to pull together, so we'd best get back to the café.'

'Yes, I need to put some ice in my punch,' Julian stated. He often took charge of beverages at Tish's catered events. 'Who'd have guessed it was going to be so warm today?'

'Um, you, possibly?' Tish quickly pointed out.

'Yeah, Channel Ten pays you for your weather forecasts, don't they?' Mary Jo rejoined.

'Yes. And no. The forecasts come from the National Weather Service. I'm simply the messenger. The fabulous-looking messenger.' Jules ran a well-manicured hand through his meticulously coiffed and gelled chestnut hair as Tish, Schuyler, and Mary Jo rolled their eyes.

'As much as I'd like to join y'all for the luncheon, I'm scheduled to give a talk at the assisted-living center in twenty minutes,' Schuyler announced as he smoothed his close-cropped flaxen hair. He had entered Hobson Glen's mayoral race at the start of the year, but now – with only three polling points standing between him and the opposition and less than six weeks remaining until election day – sticking to the campaign trail was of the utmost importance.

Tish gave him a kiss goodbye. 'I'd save you some food, but we're packing up the leftovers to give to Celestine and her family.'

'That's OK,' he replied. 'Someone always brings sandwiches or pizza into campaign headquarters. I won't go hungry.'

'Sandwiches? From where?'

'Oh, the convenience store around the corner.'

'Convenience store?' Tish allowed her jaw to drop in mock horror.

'I know,' Schuyler sang. 'I know.'

'Tomorrow I'll try to stop by with some decent food,' she promised before giving him another kiss. 'Will you be home for dinner?'

'No, I have a planning meeting with staff and then a dinner interview with a reporter from the *Richmond Times-Dispatch*.'

'Ah, well, I'll see you whenever you get home.'

'I promise I won't be too, too late,' he offered as an apology before turning on one heel and heading toward his silver BMW 3 Series sedan.

As Schuyler made his departure, Mary Jo, her curvaceous figure draped in a navy-blue pantsuit and her highlighted brown hair done up in a French knot, led Jules and Tish to her black Chevrolet Traverse. Seeing that Enid was about to embark back to town on foot – as was her wont – she invited the woman to join them. 'Ms Kemper, why don't you ride with us?'

Enid, as usual, declined. 'Nah. I'm not going to the café. I'm taking Langhorne for a walk and then getting him home for some lunch and a conditioning bath and blow-dry. This warm spell has sent him into an early molt.'

Tish and Mary Jo knew better than to interfere with Langhorne's demanding grooming schedule.

'I understand.' Tish smiled. 'Will we see you both for Sunday lunch tomorrow?'

'Usual time,' Enid confirmed.

'Good. I'll add some extra seeds to Langhorne's pasta. You know, to help with the molt.'

'It *is* a stressful time,' Enid acknowledged while looking at the bird on her shoulder. 'But Langhorne seldom complains.'

'He's a trooper,' Jules noted.

Enid Kemper nodded in agreement and shuffled away down the main path that led to the cemetery gate.

In the meantime, Opal Schaffer had come along, wheeling her bicycle beside her. Her long silver hair was pulled into an elegant side braid, and her ankle-length black maxi-dress with floral embroidery was redolent of cigarette smoke and incense. 'Mind if I catch a lift with y'all? As nice as the weather is for a bike ride, I'd like to get to the luncheon before the Rufuses do.'

'Of course. Hop in,' Mary Jo welcomed as Jules hoisted Opal's bike into the tailgate of the Traverse and slid into the backseat.

With a quick 'Thank you,' Opal climbed into the seat next to Jules, leaving Tish to ride shotgun. Her passengers safely belted in, Mary Jo started the ignition and drove the SUV toward the cemetery gates, taking care not to come too close to Enid Kemper as she passed.

Tish gave a heavy sigh. 'Sounds as if Lloyd Rufus was the only thing standing between Enid and no heat or hot water.'

'You think that's why she's rushing home?' Mary Jo suggested. 'To take advantage of the hot water while she has it?'

'Could be,' Tish allowed. 'Although she's not exactly known for being overly sociable.'

'I never knew Lloyd Rufus well,' Opal admitted, 'but he was always a fair and honest businessman.'

'I didn't know Lloyd Rufus well at all, either,' Jules added, 'but what we heard today was quite a testimony to his character.'

'Poor Celestine,' Opal remarked. 'Having lost a husband myself, I can tell you she has a long, tough road ahead.'

'I keep wishing there was something we could do,' Mary Jo said aloud.

'We'll think of something,' Tish reassured her. 'As Opal said, there's plenty of time to do things to help Celestine through the grieving process.'

'Tish is right,' Opal agreed from the backseat. 'The best thing you can do right now is to be there and listen.'

'And do what we do best – provide a tasty luncheon and send Celestine and her family home with the leftovers,' Tish added.

'What are we having?' Jules asked. 'I'm starving.'

'A variety of sandwiches on different breads – including a few vegetarian and gluten-free choices,' Tish directed toward Opal. 'And a selection of cold salads. I didn't do hot food because I didn't want Celestine and her family to have to reheat the leftovers. A bunch of sandwiches and salads in the refrigerator means that she and her family can help themselves at any time.'

'Good thinking,' Opal approved. 'What about dessert? What do you bake for a great baker?'

'I kept it simple and seasonal with strawberry and rhubarb tarts.'

'You may not know this, but Tish is a pretty great baker in her own right,' Mary Jo proclaimed from the driver's seat.

'Oh, I know,' Opal replied. 'Her gluten-free seeded sourdough is my favorite.'

'Tish's baking goes far beyond bread,' Jules explained. 'She came in first place in our university baking contest.'

'Second place,' Tish corrected.

'Nuh-uh,' Jules refuted. 'Don't you remember? The guys from Alpha Epsilon Pi came in first, but they were disqualified when the judges discovered the flecks of green in their carrot cake weren't pistachios but marijuana.'

'Yes, but that doesn't negate the fact I came in second.'

'Of course it does. The judges were stoned out of their minds, mistakenly gave the trophy to the frat boys, and when they realized they'd been doped, gave the award to you.'

'Jules is right,' Mary Jo agreed. 'If the judges hadn't ingested that marijuana, you'd have easily won. But they were all so high. I remember one of them had such a serious case of the munchies, he took that disgusting Bisquick crust and purple ketchup pepperoni pizza—'

'Oh my God, I remember that thing,' Tish exclaimed.

'—back to the judges' chambers and ate the whole pie in one sitting.'

'Ewww,' Tish and Jules cried in unison.

'I never heard of purple ketchup,' Opal confessed.

'It was a weird nineties trend,' Jules explained, while undoing his gunmetal-gray silk tie and loosening the top two buttons of his white dress shirt.

'For children,' Mary Jo added. 'But some sorority decided to use it because they thought it looked cool.'

'Ah, what was your prize-winning recipe, Tish?' Opal asked.

'Chocolate chip cookies,' Tish answered.

'Not just chocolate chip cookies, but the *best* chocolate chip cookies,' Jules amended.

'I don't think you've made them for the café, have you, Tish?' Opal inquired.

'No, I haven't. I typically leave the sweets to Celestine while I get on with the bread and entrees. She and I discuss what's selling and what isn't, of course, but I leave it to her to decide what to bake because she has such an innate sense of what people will like. It's been incredible to have her by my side for the start of my business. It wouldn't have been half as successful without her. I suppose, however,' Tish added, 'that I'm about to find out just how much Celestine's helped my business, since she's taking some personal time for the next week or so.'

'Sounds like you'd better put your baking apron on,' Opal suggested.

'And bake some chocolate chip cookies,' Jules added. 'I can guarantee you'll sell the first batch before the café is even open. I have the fifty-dollar bill to prove it.'

Mary Jo brought the SUV to a halt in the Cookin' the Books parking lot, in a spot directly in front of the café's side garden, where her son Gregory, aged seventeen, and her daughter Kayla, fifteen, were playing a game of tag with Jules's beloved Bichon Frise, Biscuit, and the Rufus grandchildren deemed too young to attend the funeral service.

Mary Jo removed the key from the vehicle's ignition and stepped out of the driver's side door. 'Hey, how is everyone?'

'Fine,' Kayla replied as she approached her mother and gave her a hug. Biscuit followed closely at her heels. At the sight of his owner, he gave a small, excited yip.

'Biscuit,' Jules greeted, scooping the dog into his arms. 'Have you been a good boy?'

'He was a very good boy, Uncle Jules,' Kayla explained as Gregory chased the handful of giggling children around the garden. She was the spitting image of her mother, and nearly as tall. 'Even when one of the kids made him a bonnet out of paper napkins. Fortunately for Biscuit, they lost interest in dressing him pretty quickly. We've been out here playing tag almost the entire time.'

'Aw, well, thanks for looking after him. After all that exercise,

I think someone deserves some water and a cookie.' Jules carried Biscuit off toward the café.

'Thank you, sweetie. I appreciate you and your brother doing this.' Mary Jo smoothed her daughter's long dark hair.

'No worries. How's Miss Celestine?'

'Not too good, chicken. It's going to take some time before she's her old self again.'

Tish joined the pair and thanked Kayla for her babysitting services. 'We should probably round up the kids and get them inside for some lunch. This way, they're happy and fed when the rest of the family arrives.'

'Good idea,' Mary Jo agreed. 'The last thing anybody needs today is a meltdown.'

Kayla, Mary Jo, Tish, Opal, and Gregory rounded up the children and brought them inside where they served them milk, juice, fruit, and sandwiches. The plan was a success, as the children were happily – and quietly – eating their lunches when their parents and grandmother arrived, followed by a sizable group of mourners.

While the funeral group filled their plates with sandwiches and salads from the counter buffet and Celestine's family took turns monitoring the grandchildren, the café became filled with the sounds of quiet conversation and gentle laughter.

Confident that all the guests were engrossed in their lunch, Tish fixed herself a small plate of food to be consumed surreptitiously behind the counter, where she was at the ready should someone require extra condiments, napkins, or a second serving. Instead, she was greeted not by a guest but by a rather rotund middle-aged man in a khaki-colored uniform.

'I'm sorry, sir, but the café is closed for a private event,' she explained.

'I didn't see a sign.'

'There's one on the door.'

The man swiveled around to spy the sheet of printer paper upon which Tish had scrawled in black magic marker: *CAFÉ CLOSED. PRIVATE EVENT.*

'An eight-and-a-half-by-eleven-inch sheet of paper hardly constitutes a sign,' the man said derisively as Jules wandered over from his place near the punch bowl. 'Town zoning regulations dictate that temporary signage should measure at least two feet square but must not exceed seven square feet in area.'

'Who is this guy?' Jules demanded.

'I was just about to ask,' Tish replied.

'Wade Lightbody.' The man introduced himself. 'I'm Hobson Glen's new sheriff. I'm filling in for Clemson Reade until y'all elect someone else for the position.'

At the mention of Reade's name, Tish felt her breath catch. After they had solved three cases together, the former sheriff left town on Christmas Eve without a single word of goodbye.

'Just because it's a temporary position,' Lightbody went on, 'don't think I'll be resting on my laurels. I mean to clean up this town. In the past year, three people have been murdered in Hobson Glen and another man killed in a neighboring community, amateur sleuths have gotten involved where they don't belong, and a civilian has been shot. That all points to a police force that's disorganized and weak on crime. Problems like that come from the top.'

Tish felt her face go red with anger. 'As the amateur sleuth and wounded civilian in question, I can assure you that Sheriff Reade and his team were both highly methodical and balanced in their actions.'

Mary Jo and Celestine, who had until now been engaged in conversation, approached the counter, their curiosity fueled by what they could sense was a less-than-friendly confrontation.

'In your simplistic view perhaps, Ms . . .?' Lightbody prompted.

Tish folded her arms across her chest defiantly. 'Tarragon.'

'Ah, yes, Mizz Tarragon.' He chuckled. 'How could I forget a name like that? From your simplistic layperson's viewpoint, Sheriff Reade may have seemed competent, but an experienced lawman recognizes slipshod leadership when he sees it.'

Tish opened her mouth to argue, but Jules intervened in an attempt to defuse the situation. 'Exactly what brings you here, Sheriff?'

'Coffee. I heard this place serves the best in town, so I thought I'd give it a try.'

Mary Jo stepped behind the counter, filled a cardboard cup

of coffee, and slid it toward the new sheriff. 'There you go. Two dollars and twenty-five cents, please.'

'Where I come from, restaurant and store owners don't charge on-duty police officers for food or services. It's called respect for law enforcement,' Lightbody announced.

'Where I come from, respect is earned, not automatically given,' Tish countered. 'Considering you've crashed a funeral luncheon in order to badmouth your predecessor and strong-arm me into giving you free food, you'll forgive me if that respect isn't immediately forthcoming. However, since the till is closed for the day, this cup is on the house.'

Lightbody took the cup and turned on one heel, but not before issuing a warning. 'I'll keep this conversation to myself, Mizz Tarragon. Mind you, if other members of the force were to learn of your attitude, it could be detrimental to your business.' With that, he strolled out of the front door of the café and into the parking lot where his white Ram pickup truck was parked – illegally – in a disabled spot.

'Was he threatening you?' Mary Jo asked as Lightbody pulled out of the parking lot. 'That sounded like a threat.'

'It might have been if there was anywhere else in town to get coffee in the morning,' Tish stated. 'With the Bar and Grill closed, the closest place to get breakfast and lunch is ten miles away in Staunton. Besides, I know Sheriff Reade's team. Most of them are regular customers. They wouldn't boycott the café on the word of a man like Lightbody.'

'Maybe not, but remember they're no longer Sheriff Reade's team,' Celestine pointed out with a frown.

'Ugh, I can't comprehend how anyone could replace Reade with a blowhard like that,' Jules complained. 'It's like Boss Hogg from *The Dukes of Hazzard* and Sheriff J.W. Pepper from *Live and Let Die* had a baby. And he's the baby. Still, I suppose I'd be bitter too if I had a name like Wade Lightbody. Wade? Weighed? Lightbody? His parents had a terrible sense of humor.'

'Whatever the cause for his abrasive personality, I shouldn't have reacted the way I did,' Tish said with remorse.

'Don't be sorry. He was totally trying to provoke you.'

'Yeah, well, I shouldn't have taken the bait.'

Celestine spoke up. 'I hope you're not saying that on account of Lloyd, because he wouldn't have suffered through that fool's behavior. Neither would I.'

'Is everything OK over here?' Celestine's eldest daughter, Lacey, approached the group. She was in her mid-thirties, blonde, and dressed head to toe in black: three-quarter-sleeve sweater, capris, and kitten-heeled sandals.

'We're fine, darlin'.' Celestine draped an arm around Lacey's shoulders. 'The new sheriff just came by to introduce himself.'

'Here? Right now?' Lacey questioned. 'The sign on the door says "Closed."'

'Precisely,' Jules replied.

'He's a bully, barging in here like that,' Mary Jo explained.

'I should have done more to defuse the situation. I hope you didn't find his presence too intrusive?' Tish apologized to Lacey.

'Not at all. For a minute there, I thought he was here to pay his respects, then I saw the scowl on his face and realized my daddy would never have hung out with a man like that.' She smiled.

'That's what I was just tellin' 'em,' Celestine rejoined with a chuckle.

'You have no reason to apologize, Tish,' Lacey went on. 'This lunch was mighty kind of you. You saved us all kinds of money, and although it's a sad day, it's been nice to talk to the aunts and uncles before they all drive back home.'

'Well, when the going gets tough, the tough get cooking,' Tish quipped. 'I just wish there was something more I could do to help.'

'You've done plenty. And we seem to have things under control at the moment. I've made all the necessary phone calls to the bank, social security, the mortgage company, and credit card companies, and Mama's staying with me, Jeff, and the kids for a spell while she gets her bearings.'

'Lacey's always been the organized one in the family,' Celestine praised.

'Thanks, Mama. I'm just trying to make things easier for you. Heaven knows they're tough enough right now. Oh' – Lacey gasped as she drew her hand to her mouth – 'I forgot to cancel your dentist appointment for tomorrow.'

'That's OK. I took care of it.'

'I'm glad you did, but I wish you didn't have to. I should have remembered.'

'Nonsense, honey. You've been doin' a lot. Callin' all those people, makin' arrangements. I wasn't doin' a thing at the time, so I made the call. Easy. What won't be so easy is callin' the bake-off people and tellin' them I have to cancel.'

'The bake-off. That's next week, isn't it?' Tish asked, recalling how excited Celestine had been to earn a spot in the Virginia Commonwealth Bake-Off.

'Yeah, I can't do it, though. Much as I wanted to, I just can't.'

'I know how much it meant for you to compete, Celestine,' Tish said gently. 'You've dreamed of winning that trophy since you were a little girl. You're dealing with a lot right now. Why don't you take a few days and see how you're feeling before making a final decision?'

'Nope, my mind's made up. I couldn't hardly stand the pressure when Lloyd was here. Now that he's gone . . . though I've gotta say the $15,000 prize money sure would come in handy right about now. Lloyd's life insurance policy didn't even cover the whole funeral and until I can either sell his business or liquidize his equipment, I'm livin' on my income from the café.'

Tish shifted her weight from side to side uncomfortably as she glanced at Mary Jo and Jules in turn and contemplated her next move. She couldn't afford to loan Celestine the cash she needed – although business at the café had begun to boom, Tish was still in debt herself. Nor could she afford to give Celestine more hours, but there was something she could do. 'I'm not the caliber of baker you are and I'm uncertain what the bake-off rules are regarding substitutions, but I'd be willing to compete in the bake-off on your behalf.'

Celestine broke into a broad smile. 'You'd do that for me?'

'Of course. But don't thank me yet. You haven't tasted much of my baking.' She laughed.

'You'll do just fine, sugar.'

'Thanks, I'll certainly try my best. I mean, so long as it's OK with the bake-off judges and I can find someone to fill in here at the café.'

'I can cover for you,' Mary Jo offered. 'I'll talk to Augusta May about doing some of my admin work from here when it's quiet. I'm sure she won't mind, given the circumstances.'

'That would be awesome.' Tish thanked her friend.

'And I can take over the morning bake,' Celestine suggested.

'Um, thanks, but don't you think you should be taking some time off?' Tish urged.

'I will be. I won't be servin'. I can't face people's questions about Lloyd right now, but I do enjoy bakin'. It's therapy for me and I've missed it these past couple of days. Besides, I can never sleep in the mornin's anyway. Sleepin' even less now. Be good for me to have somethin' else to do to keep me from thinkin'.'

'Are you sure?' Mary Jo confirmed. 'I can easily do the morning bake. I live just upstairs.' Having split from her husband and finding the home she'd shared with him too expensive to maintain on her own, Mary Jo and her children had moved into the two-bedroom apartment above the café which had been occupied by Tish prior to her moving in with Schuyler.

'I'm positive. You have to get your kids off to school in the mornin'.'

'Well, if there's a morning you feel like staying in bed, just let me know. Until then, I'll make sure to have your coffee waiting for you. One cream, two sugars.'

'Just the way I like it,' Celestine verified.

'This is perfect,' Jules exclaimed. 'I'm off the weather desk and on the human interest beat next week, so I'll be at the civic center, covering the bake-off for Channel Ten. I'll make sure to feature you in a couple of my segments.'

'Did you hear that, Tish? That should be good for business,' Celestine rejoiced.

'Good for business and very well deserved,' Lacey echoed. 'I can't believe you're willing to do this for Mama.'

Neither can I, Tish thought to herself as she reflected upon her lackluster cake decorating skills. *Neither can I.*

TWO

The week after Lloyd Rufus's funeral saw Tish standing in the red-carpeted main lobby of the Henrico County Civic Center. Gone were the dress and heels, replaced by her usual work uniform of black T-shirt, fitted black jeans, leopard-print loafers, and apron. In this case, however, the apron bore the logo not of the café but of the Virginia Commonwealth Bake-Off.

'Hey, honey,' Julian Jefferson Davis greeted as he cradled Biscuit in his left arm and hugged the caterer with his right. 'How are things?'

'So far, so good,' she said with a smile. 'I'm registered for the event and my booth is ready to go. I'm just waiting for the start signal. The judges were kind enough to allow me to compete with my own recipes, even though it meant some last-minute ingredient orders on their part.'

'That's wonderful news. I know you practiced Celestine's recipes just in case, but you'll be far more comfortable working with your own. I know we're not allowed to help with the baking, but Biscuit and I are here extra early to lend you our moral support.'

Jules was dressed for broadcast in a dark-blue suit, white button-down shirt, and a pink silk tie, the fabric of which had also been used to fashion a bowtie for Biscuit.

'I appreciate the support – I'm as nervous as can be! But is Biscuit allowed on the floor of the competition? I mean, with all that food, the exhibition hall might be limited to service animals.'

'The rules don't apply to Biscuit. He's a bona fide – get it, bone-a-fide? – journalist.' Jules pulled a lanyard from beneath the Bichon Frise's bowtie and presented the card attached.

'Oh my goodness, he has his own little press pass. "Biscuit Wellington Davis, Channel Ten News,"' Tish read aloud. 'Wellington?'

'I had absolutely no say in Biscuit's first name, so I wanted him to give him a middle name that had a bit of panache and style.'

'Biscuit Wellington. He sounds like a menu item.' She laughed as she scratched the dog beneath his chin. 'Is Daddy going to cook you?'

'Bite your tongue!' Jules scolded. 'By the way, while we're on the subject of middle names, I'm going to be changing mine.'

'You are? What happened?'

'Maurice happened. He's the new editor of the *Times-Dispatch* culture column. He's sweet and intelligent and looks like Lenny Kravitz.'

'Lenny Kravitz. Wow!'

'Back up there, girlfriend. You already got yourself a man. So does Maurice. And a brand-new baby boy.'

'So, how did Maurice change you?'

'Well, he and I were both covering the opening of that new downtown theater and we got to chatting and he's just so wonderful and articulate and . . . well, I felt like an absolute jerk. Here I am talking to this beautiful soul I consider to be a friend while bearing the name of a man who fought to keep Maurice's ancestors enslaved. I never felt so damned ashamed of myself, Tish. Monuments have fallen, mindsets are changing, laws are changing. It's time for me to change, too. Maurice's baby boy shouldn't have to live with that shadow hanging over him. It's bad enough his father has.'

Tish presented Jules with a kiss on the cheek. 'I think it's a wonderful idea. However, as your friend, I want you to know that I love you no matter what you call yourself.'

'Thanks. And, as a Northerner, you're wondering why the hell it took me forty-two years to come to this conclusion.' He laughed.

'Nah. I was born in a city that still hosts a Columbus Day parade. We all could do better. We all *need* to do better. So, what's your plan?'

'Effective immediately, I'm using Julian Davis, without my middle name, for broadcast. I'll issue a statement as to my reasons at a later date. In the meantime, I'm going to legally change my middle name.'

'Have you told your mother yet?'

'No, I'm afraid to. She's a proud Southerner – former Miss Alabama – and the one who named me. She watches my broadcasts just to see my name on the lower third. That's going to be a tough conversation.'

'I'm sure you'll find the courage to tell her when the time is right. Have you chosen a new name yet?'

'No, I've been brainstorming, but nothing quite fits.'

'Well, take Biscuit's name as a lesson and don't brainstorm while watching the Cooking Channel.'

'I don't know. Jules Bananas Foster has a nice ring to it.' He smirked. 'Speaking of food, what are you making for the competition?'

'For today's savory bake, I have Anna Karenina's Tarragon Chicken—'

'Oh, I adore your tarragon chicken! Can I have that for my birthday dinner next week?'

'Of course,' she agreed before describing the rest of her bake-off dishes. 'For the showstopper bake – which takes place over the next two days – I've decided to bake Miss Havisham's wedding cake.'

'Miss Who's what?' Jules raised a well-tweezed eyebrow.

'Miss Havisham from Dickens's *Great Expectations*. Remember her?'

'No,' he answered bluntly.

'She was left at the altar as a young woman, so she becomes a recluse, locking herself away in her mansion, blocking out the sun, never removing her wedding dress, leaving the wedding feast and cake uneaten on the table, and even stopping the clocks in her home at twenty minutes to nine – the time she received her fiancé's fateful letter.'

'And you're baking her wedding cake.'

'Yes, complete with cobwebs, mold, and a few tunnels where the mice have nibbled through,' Tish replied, delighted with her idea.

'That sounds . . . appetizing,' he deadpanned.

'Despite the description, it will be. The cake will be pink champagne with raspberry mousse filling and vanilla buttercream. The cobwebs will be made of spun sugar and the mold will be nothing more than a dusting of pulverized mint leaves and icing sugar. The brilliant part, however, is that the mold and heavy cobwebs will disguise the fact that I'm terrible at piping frosting. If I don't pipe a perfect flourish or a straight line, I can cover it up with a cobweb.'

'I admit pink champagne in a cake does sound rather delicious.'

'It is. And it's the most delicate shade of pink. Perfect for a wedding cake, although not a wedding cake of that time.'

'Mmm, that might have to be my birthday cake. Minus the cobwebs and icky bits.'

'Got it,' she agreed. 'When I was planning my contest entries, little did I know I was also planning your birthday dinner.'

'Haven't you learned by now that it's always about me?' he teased.

'You're right, I should have known better.' She sighed.

'So, what's the last item for the contest?'

'For the signature bake? You tell me,' she joked. 'So far everything has wound up on your birthday menu.'

'Chocolate chip cookies?'

'Sorry, no. Although the way the ladies at the registration booth reacted, maybe I should bake those instead.'

'Well, what *are* you baking?'

'I'm going to make my "Champion" Frangipane Cherry Pie.'

'Champion? That's the spirit! You won't win if you don't have the attitude. That's probably why they reacted the way they did. Not everyone reacts kindly to confidence.'

'Jules, it's called "Champion" because that's how it's described in the book.'

'Which book?'

'*In Cold Blood.* Nancy Clutter is known for baking a "champion" cherry pie. It's the last thing she bakes before her brutal murder.'

Jules's jaw dropped. 'Good Lord, honey. No wonder those ladies reacted poorly. You named your signature bake after a mass murder! I know you're a natural-born detective and all, but you need to keep that under wraps for now. This bake-off is one of the oldest in the country. It's a time-honored tradition that's taken very, very seriously. We're talking old-school

Southern-belle stuff going on here. Just take a look around you. See all the floral-print dresses, seersucker suits, and wide-brimmed hats? And let's not even start on all the big hair. Honey, there's enough Aquanet hair spray in this building to deplete the ozone layer of three planet Earths.'

Tish disregarded Jules's exaggerations. 'I didn't tell them the pie was inspired by *In Cold Blood*. I left that part out as I knew some people might find it upsetting.'

'You did? So, then, why did they seem so disapproving?'

'I have no idea. It was just a wall of silence, frowns, and blank stares. I was going to ask you if you knew anything until you started likening the bake-off to a barbecue at Twelve Oaks.'

'Me? I don't know anything. I mean, I know the history of the bake-off – how the contest started and by whom and when – but nothing I read mentioned anything about cherry pie.' He pulled a face. 'Maybe one of the judges is allergic?'

'Then why not tell me that? Why act as if I'd registered to bake a meat pie inspired by *Sweeney Todd*?'

'Yuck.' Jules wrinkled his nose. 'Listen, I'm not doubting you experienced what you did, honey, but is there a chance you may have misread the situation? You're incredibly astute at gauging human behavior, but maybe you saw those women's reactions as negative just out of plain nervousness.'

Tish gave some thought to Jules's statement and it did make sense. 'I am more than a bit anxious about the bake-off,' she confessed.

'I know how badly you want to bring the trophy home to Celestine.'

'I do. It would mean so much if I could win that prize money for her. Yet at the same time I'm not a fan of competition itself. My mother's side of the family was all female and highly competitive. It seemed my cousins and I were always in a contest to see who was the prettiest, the thinnest, the smartest, the most successful. When we got older, the competitiveness focused on our personal lives: who had children first, who had the nicest home, the best husband. After years of feeling like I didn't measure up, I just don't have the wherewithal to view life as a contest any longer. I believe there's room for everyone to achieve their dreams and be happy.'

'Amen, sister,' Jules commiserated as he slung an arm around his friend's shoulders. 'Try being a gay journalism major in a family of Southern Baptist 'Bama fans. If my family wasn't shouting "Praise the Lord," they were hollering "Roll Tide!" Every year, I was mocked for not joining the other men in the family at Bama games and stripping off my shirt and painting my body red and white. Think about that for a minute. I was teased by my relatives for not going out half naked in a beer-fueled frenzy, on a cold winter day, looking like a human stop sign. Thank heavens my mama understood me; otherwise, I would have felt like a complete misfit.'

'Families.' Tish sighed as she linked arms with Jules and led him into the civic center's exhibition hall.

Boasting eighteen-thousand square feet of floor space, thirty-foot-high ceilings, and situated within an easy drive of downtown Richmond, the civic center was the perfect venue to host the bake-off. The great expanse of floor space had been divided into ten rows of ten contestant booths, to accommodate a contest of one hundred bakers. Each row was separated by a five-foot-wide aisle so both judges and bake-off volunteers could easily monitor contestants, and so that ticket-holding members of the public could watch their favorite bakers in action.

Each of the one hundred booths had been fitted with marble countertops, an electric range, two electric ovens, a dishwasher, and a miniature refrigerator. Shelving beneath the counters contained a variety of kitchen implements: whisks, spatulas, rolling pins, baking pans, measuring spoons and cups, a digital food scale, and cooling racks. Any equipment not found beneath the counter was located on racks in the civic center storage room and was available for sign-out on a first-come basis. Other smaller appliances, such as mixers and food processors were to be provided by staff the morning they were needed.

'It's smaller than your kitchen at the café,' Jules noted upon his arrival at the booth fitted out for contestant number fifty-nine, Tish Tarragon, 'but it looks like a nice workspace.'

'Yes, supposedly the bake-off hires a kitchen designer to help with the booth layouts. They allow us a five-minute inspection upon check-in to ensure everything's working and to get the "lay of the land," so to speak, then we're banned from entering the booth until the starting buzzer sounds.' As Tish described the schedule for the day, a woman in her late fifties approached.

She was perfectly turned-out in a designer navy-blue skirt and blazer, with matching pumps; her chin-length dark-blonde hair had been blown dry into soft waves, and her makeup, replete with a set of false eyelashes, had been professionally applied.

A good-looking, dark-haired young man in a black pinstripe suit trailed closely behind her. He was in his mid-twenties, his suit close-fitting as was the trend, thus showing off a lean and muscular physique, and his sole task appeared to be smiling and glancing anxiously between the woman and his iPad.

'Kitty Flournoy.' She extended a set of pink-polished fingers toward Tish. 'Chair of the Virginia Commonwealth Bake-Off Foundation.'

Tish accepted the tepid handshake and introduced herself while Jules took a step forward. 'Julian Davis. Channel Ten News.'

'Mr Davis, everyone in the Richmond area within range of your station's broadcast signal knows who you are. I hope you don't end up in a fracas with a crème caramel,' she quipped, alluding to Jules's on-camera history of being swept off his feet by a snowplow during a winter storm two years earlier and unwittingly igniting his elf's hat on a Christmas lantern at the town holiday fair the past December.

Jules took the remarks in his stride. 'Don't worry. The station has outfitted me with rubber soles and an asbestos suit.'

'Very good. I'm busy today, but I'll have Desmond make an appointment for tomorrow should you care for an interview.'

'That would be terrific. Thank you.'

Kitty gestured to the young man behind her and he dutifully began typing into the iPad. 'So, Ms Tarragon, what dishes are you preparing for the competition?'

'Tarragon chicken for starters,' Tish replied.

'Named for the herb or is this your own special recipe?' Kitty punctuated the sentence with a loud 'ha.'

'Yes, I see what you mean,' Tish acknowledged, echoing the laugh. 'I'm making the classic French recipe, but mixing it up by baking it and adding roasted spring vegetables.'

'Lovely.' It was clear from the expression on Kitty's face

that she wasn't genuinely interested, but ticking off the boxes on some imaginary checklist. 'And the showstopper bake?'

'Miss Havisham's wedding cake.'

'Hmm, I don't believe anyone's ever done that before. Desmond.' She gestured to her young assistant who rapidly typed something into the iPad and then blushed crimson.

'W–w–which spreadsheet would I find that on, Miss Flournoy?' Desmond stammered.

Kitty heaved an exasperated sigh. 'Never mind, Desmond. Never mind. I'll check with Willadeane Scott when she gets here. She probably doesn't even need the spreadsheet. Woman has a face like a foot, but she's damned efficient. Did she say when she'd be here?'

'Ms Scott said she had some work issues to deal with first thing this morning, but she'd be here before the start of the competition,' Desmond replied.

'Well, sorry I can't immediately validate that yours is the first Miss Havisham cake, Ms Tarragon,' Kitty apologized, 'but our organization relies upon volunteer help. Desmond and I and a few marketing people are the only ones on the payroll. However, if memory serves, I do believe your idea is a unique one. Originality is valued here at the bake-off. Just remember your work needs to taste as good as it looks.'

Tish nodded, still irritated by Kitty's scathing comment about the missing volunteer, Willadeane.

'And for your signature bake?' Kitty pressed.

'Frangipane cherry pie.'

At the mention of the pie, Kitty's face blanched. 'Cherry?'

'Yes, with a layer of almond batter and nestled in a golden, slightly sweet pastry case.'

'Surely rhubarb or strawberries would have been more seasonal,' Kitty snapped before summoning Desmond and rushing off to speak to the next contestant.

When she'd gone, Tish turned to Jules. 'Still think I may have misinterpreted what happened at the registration table?'

Jules shook his head. 'Not for a heartbeat, honey. I'm sorry I doubted you in the first place.'

'No worries; I wondered myself there for a time. But Kitty's face just now eliminated any shred of doubt in my mind.'

'Mine, too. Kitty looked downright shaken. For a woman as cold as she is to be frightened, something big has to be at the root of this. I'll do some nosing around and see what I can find.'

THREE

With forty-five minutes to go until the official start of the competition, Tish went to the large kitchen that had been designated as the hospitality suite to pick up a bottle of water and settle her nerves. As she refilled her travel mug with the complimentary coffee on offer, she was approached by three of her fellow contestants.

'Hey, I think you're in the booth next to mine,' the older of the two women in the group stated upon drawing near. She was in her late sixties, with salt-and-pepper hair and a deep tan. 'I'm number fifty-eight.'

'Fifty-nine,' Tish introduced herself and extended her hand. 'Tish Tarragon.'

'Dolly Pritchard. And this here is Riya Patel.' She gestured to a dark-skinned woman in her late thirties, who wore her apron over a traditional sari in a brilliant shade of turquoise.

Riya leaned forward and shook Tish's hand. 'Pleased to meet you. I'm on the other side of Dolly in booth fifty-seven.'

'Nice to meet you too, Riya.' Tish returned the handshake and slid her eyes toward the male of the group who looked to be of the same age as Dolly.

'Gordon Quinn,' he announced and extended his hand. 'One of only two men in the bake-off. One of those men is a grumpy old coot. The other's a handsome college kid. I'll let you guess which one you're talking to.'

'You aren't grumpy,' Riya dismissed.

'But I *am* an old coot, apparently,' Gordon teased.

Dolly gave Gordon a playful slap on the arm. 'Stop giving Riya a tough time. Ya coot,' she added, much to her companions' amusement. 'Gordon's booth is in a different row from ours this year, unfortunately.'

'I'm in booth sixty-three,' he declared. 'Someone decided we rabble-rousers needed to be separated.'

'Probably because we were having too much fun,' Riya remarked.

'The three of us have been competing for years,' Dolly explained. 'This is Riya's fifth bake-off, Gordon's sixth, and my tenth.'

'Wow, you all must be terrific bakers to have qualified so many times,' Tish said. 'Have any of you won?'

'Dolly came in second place two years ago. That's the closest any of us have gotten,' Riya stated.

'Dolly should have taken first prize that year,' Gordon opined.

'It's true. Your "Under the Sea" showstopper cake was magnificently decorated, Dolly.'

'And you should have taken first *last* year, Riya,' Dolly added. 'Third place, my foot. Your samosas are the absolute bomb.'

'I don't think the spices I use are for everyone,' Riya lamented. 'It's a risk I take at baking contests, but I like to stay true to the recipes I ate as a child and that I feed my own children.'

'The problem isn't either of you or your recipes.' Gordon spoke up. 'It's Whitney Liddell. She has the judges and everyone involved in the bake-off hoodwinked into believing she's some sort of domestic goddess.'

'Who's Whitney Liddell?' Tish asked.

'She's been the bake-off champion three years running. She's here today to try to make it four.'

'Even though she's not all that great a baker,' Dolly sniped. 'I know that might sound like sour grapes, but it isn't. Whitney Liddell is a *good* baker, but she's not three-time-champion good.'

Gordon and Riya nodded their heads in agreement.

'So how does she keep winning?' Tish questioned.

'For starters, she's a nice-looking woman,' Gordon replied. 'And charming – when she wants to be. She's not very nice to her fellow contestants. She's stuck-up and snobby and won't even look at you when you say "hello." But when the judges are around, butter doesn't melt in her mouth.'

'She thinks she's some kind of celebrity. She goes on the internet and shares photos of her perfect house, perfect kids, perfect recipes, perfect everything,' Dolly explained. 'And people think if they drive the same car she does and wear the same clothes, they'll live the same life. A whole bunch of her "followers" come down here to watch her compete.'

'Whitney's a social media influencer,' Riya clarified. 'She runs a lifestyle blog and has a hundred thousand followers on her Instagram account. When she won the bake-off the first time, she covered the whole experience on social media. As a result, the bake-off received extra publicity, as did the companies who provide the flour, bakeware, and other supplies for the event. Some of them probably paid Whitney for an endorsement as well.'

'Is that permitted? The winner accepting payments from bake-off suppliers?' Tish queried.

'We all wondered the same thing, so someone asked Kitty Flournoy about it. Apparently, the bake-off has no rule against winners using their prize for monetary gain, so long as they represent the bake-off in a positive manner.'

'Which Whitney does, perfectly,' Dolly stated. 'She's precisely what Kitty has wanted in a champion all these years: a modern-day, web-savvy Betty Crocker, complete with the hair, makeup, feminine outfits, and fans. Kitty's not going to give that up if she can help it.'

'Are you suggesting the contest might be skewed in Whitney's favor?' Tish was skeptical.

'I wouldn't say that, no. None of us would be here if we thought we couldn't win. It's just that, well . . .'

'There were some odd circumstances surrounding the past few contests. Circumstances that contributed to Whitney being named the winner.' Gordon completed Dolly's thought with a grave expression on his face. 'We think there are a few people around here who wouldn't mind if Whitney won again this year. What they'd be willing to do to guarantee that, who knows? All we know is we're here to take the trophy away from her.'

'That's why it's so nice to have a new face around here.' Dolly smiled. 'Beginner's luck, you know.'

'Thanks, I, um, I hope so.' Tish was set to ask about the odd circumstances Gordon had mentioned when the shrill Mid-Atlantic accent of Kitty Flournoy came booming through the civic center's public address system, directing all contestants to return to the exhibition hall floor.

Tish wished her new friends the best of luck as they departed the hospitality room and then splashed some milk into her coffee before hastening back to her booth. Once there, a woman bearing a clipboard greeted her. She was approximately forty-five years of age, exceedingly tall and, despite the shapeless nature of her waistless shirtdress, quite slender. On her feet were a pair of well-worn Birkenstocks and her mousy brown hair had been pulled into a sloppy ponytail at the back of her head. The badge that hung from a lanyard around her neck identified her as Willadeane Scott, Kitty Flournoy's absentee volunteer.

'Contestant number fifty-nine. Ms Tish Tarragon,' she greeted, her voice a question.

'Yes, that's me.'

'Hi, Miss Tarragon. I'm Willadeane, the monitor for this section of the hall. I'll be watching you and the contestants in the adjacent booths during the competition to certify adherence to bake-off rules and standards, but also to ensure that you remain comfortable over the next four days. Before the competition starts, can I help you in any way?'

'No, I think I'm set,' Tish answered nervously.

'Good. Now, just to review the schedule, there will be a forty-five-minute lunch break at noon and then another fifteen-minute break at three o'clock. You're also entitled to two ten-minute personal breaks at any time during the day. To use them, just raise your hand and I'll log you out. When you return, just check back with me, so I can log you in again. Should you need any additional equipment, again, just raise your hand and I'll log you out so you can visit the storage room. When you're finished, come to me so that I can log you in again and mark the equipment as being in use. Do you have any questions?'

Tish shook her head. 'No, I think it's clear.'

Willadeane gazed at Tish over the top of her cat-eye reading glasses and down the length of her prominent Roman nose. 'Good. Should you need anything during the competition – a glass of water, tea, coffee, anything at all – don't hesitate to ask.'

As Kitty mentioned, Willadeane Scott was remarkably efficient – reassuringly so, thus making Kitty's later comments about the woman's plain appearance seem that much more cruel.

'Thank you,' Tish replied with a smile.

'You're welcome. Good luck.' The cool efficiency of Willadeane Scott was quickly replaced by the frantic figure of Julian Davis. He was clutching Biscuit tightly to his chest and his hazel eyes had a wild, haunted look to them.

'Are you OK?' she asked.

'I'm fine, but you're not.'

'You know, I'm actually feeling a lot better than I was. I talked to some of my fellow contestants and my nerves have settled quite a bit. You, however, look as if you're about to jump out of your skin.'

'Because you're in danger, Tish. You need to change your bake-off entry.'

'Change my—? I can't do that Jules. There are just three minutes until showtime.'

'But you have to. You can't bake that cherry pie. You just can't. Bake some chocolate chip cookies instead,' he suggested. 'I'm sure you have the recipe memorized.'

'I can't switch now, Jules. I don't have the supplies. The bake-off people were already kind enough to accommodate me taking Celestine's place, even though it meant last-minute recipe changes. I can't do that again just because of the reactions of a few people.'

'Yes, you most certainly can. I just found out why those few people reacted the way they did, Tish. It's because the last two contestants to enter a cherry pie in the bake-off are dead,' Jules nearly shouted.

'What?' She couldn't believe what she was hearing. 'Dead? How?'

'That's what I'm trying to tell you, honey. It's the cherry pie. It's cursed!'

FOUR

Despite Jules's prophecies of doom, Tish survived the first three hours of the competition and, upon breaking for lunch, found herself approximately twenty minutes ahead of schedule due to her homemade chicken stock (no convenience foods were permitted at the bake-off) cooling faster than usual in the climate-controlled environment of the civic center.

Stepping outside the booth, Tish was soon joined by Dolly and Riya, and the trio made their way to the hospitality suite where a modest, yet filling, lunch buffet had been arranged. Tish grabbed a wrap of chickpeas, tahini, red bell pepper and spinach and sat down at one of several round tables erected there.

Gordon Quinn, his plate boasting a chicken salad sandwich and a bag of chips, plopped down beside her. 'How's your very first bake coming along?'

'So far, so good,' she answered, as Riya, carrying the same wrap as Tish and chocolate brownie on the side, and Dolly, toting a plate of tuna salad and cottage cheese, filled out the rest of the table. 'The chicken stock for my tarragon chicken dish cooled more quickly than usual, so after lunch, I can get to work on making the sauce, browning the chicken, assembling the vegetables, and baking. How about you? What are you making?'

'*Maiale al Latte*,' Gordon replied, his blue eyes sparkling. 'Pork Braised in Milk. I learned it from a local woman when I was stationed in Caserma Ederle – Camp Ederle – outside Vicenza in Italy decades ago. It isn't the prettiest thing to look at, but nothing else tastes quite like it. I got the prep work finished this morning, so now, all I have to do is put the Dutch oven in and prepare some polenta for serving.'

'Cooking meat in milk. Sounds intriguing,' Dolly acknowledged. 'I'm cooking a vegan moussaka. My mother was Greek, so I've always cooked traditional moussaka for my children, but with everyone going vegetarian these days and my husband having high cholesterol, I decided to cut out the meat and substitute it with red lentils and add zucchini to the sliced potatoes. It's more labor-intensive than the original in that you need to cook the lentils separately before adding them to the sauce, but I'm pretty sure I'll finish in time, so long as the oven temp cooperates.'

'Oh, those pesky oven temps,' Riya commiserated. 'I made tandoori chicken my first bake-off, and had difficulties getting the oven hot enough.'

'I remember that.' Gordon nodded while chewing a bite of sandwich. 'But you persevered and the tandoori turned out excellent.'

'Thanks, Gordon. Just the same, I hope I don't have the opposite problem today. I'm making Hyderabadi chicken biryani – the signature biryani from my family's home in India. I've fried the onions, marinated the chicken in spices, and soaked the rice. After lunch, I need to partially cook the rice, strain it, layer it in a pot with the meat, onions, and vegetables and let it steam at three hundred and fifty degrees for about an hour and a half. If the oven is too hot, it will turn out too dry. There's not much that can be done to a dry biryani.'

'I did a little test run with the oven in my booth by baking a potato and the temp seems accurate, although the top element seems to burn a bit hotter than the bottom,' Gordon explained.

'That's good to know, Gordon. Thank you. I'll be sure to put the biryani on the lower rack.'

'Same with my moussaka,' Dolly rejoined. 'Wouldn't do to let the cheese get too brown on top.'

Tish had been quietly munching her wrap, wondering if she should ask the group about the 'curse' Jules had mentioned earlier. This seemed as good a time as any. 'I'll have to keep that in mind when I bake my cherry frangipane pie later this week.'

Her statement had the anticipated effect. At once, her tablemates stopped eating and stared at her in silence. 'Yes, I'm baking a cherry pie. A decision I made before I knew about the alleged "curse." I only just learned about that this morning.'

Riya was the first to speak. 'It's not so much a curse as a bad-luck recipe.'

'Bad luck?' Dolly disputed. 'Two women died, Riya. I'd say that's a bit more than just plain ol' bad luck.'

'There's no such thing as luck or curses,' Gordon reasoned. 'People use those words to explain things that they can't understand.'

'Then how would you explain those two deaths?' Dolly asked.

He shrugged. 'Unfortunate coincidence. Happens all the time.'

'What do you think, Tish?' Riya asked.

Not one to believe in curses, Tish was naturally inclined to agree with Gordon, but she withheld comment. 'I honestly don't know enough about the situation to make a judgment.'

'I'll fill you in.' Dolly plunged a fork into her cottage cheese, ate a bite, and hunched over the table eagerly. 'Two years ago,' she started in a near-whisper, 'a woman named Lillian Harwood participated in the bake-off for the very first time. She was my age, maybe a little older. A widow and a retired schoolteacher. Ate lunch with us every day she was here. Her savory bake was a meat pie that was simply to die for.'

Gordon cringed at Dolly's poor choice of words. 'Really, Dolls?'

Dolly quickly apologized.

Riya intervened. 'The pie was exceedingly delicious. My booth was beside hers and the smell was incredible. Lillian cooked the filling in a Dutch oven for hours before baking it in homemade pastry. It went over very well with the judges.'

'Lillian's second bake,' Dolly continued, 'the showstopper, was a mountain scene. She baked a three-layer cake and decorated each layer to resemble a level on the mountain – the bottom was green and loaded with trees and wildlife, the second was flecked with gray to resemble rock and scattered with smaller trees and mountain goats, and then the top resembled a snowcap.'

'And her signature bake? The cherry pie?' Tish prompted.

'She never baked it. She died before she could compete. Heart attack.'

'Which isn't unusual for a woman her age,' Gordon noted.

'No,' Riya allowed, 'but it was shocking.'

'Especially as it seemed she was on course to take the prize trophy away from Whitney Liddell,' Dolly observed.

'You said this was two years ago. Was that the year you came in second place?' Tish questioned.

'It was. I thought I could snag the top spot, but Whitney scored slightly higher in the signature bake.'

'The competition was that close?'

'Yep, I was actually ahead of Whitney until the very last round, when the judges awarded her a practically perfect score. She wound up beating me by a point and a half. That's it. A point and a half.'

'No two ways about it. You were robbed,' Gordon stated blandly.

'Your showstopper cake alone should have won you first place,' Riya asserted before breaking off a corner of brownie and popping it into her mouth.

'What about the second woman?' Tish asked. 'Who was she and what happened to her?'

'Penelope Purdue,' Riya answered and broke off yet another corner of brownie. 'But she liked everyone to call her Pen. She thought it was funny, you know, Pen Purdue – like *pain perdu*, the French term for French toast.'

Tish smiled. 'Gotta love a good food-based pun. Unless, of course, that pun is your name.'

'Pen didn't seem to mind at all. She had a very good sense of humor. Always smiling, cracking jokes. Pen competed the year prior and had become friends with Lillian, so last year she decided to pay tribute to her friend by baking the cherry pie that Lillian never got to bake.'

'The exact same recipe?'

Riya nodded. 'Pen wanted to win the bake-off in Lillian's honor. And she came close to doing it, too. She made some Moroccan chicken dish for her savory bake and a beautiful peacock cake for her showstopper.'

'And the cherry pie?'

'She didn't get to bake it, either. Pen left here the afternoon of the showstopper bake not feeling well. Since she'd finished her cake and submitted it, the monitors allowed her to leave early rather than forcing her to stick around for the judges' tasting. Pen died later that evening in the hospital of an apparent allergic reaction.'

'A reaction to what?'

Riya shrugged. 'We were never told.'

'With all the ingredients in this place, it could have been anything,' Dolly speculated.

'Yes, you're probably right.' Tish frowned and reorganized the contents of her wrap sandwich with her fork.

'Are you still going ahead with your pie?'

'I don't have much choice. I can't change it now.'

'Yes, but now you know about the curse and everything that happened to Lillian and Pen. Had you known earlier, you wouldn't have chosen that dish for your signature bake.'

'Probably not, but I've already made the commitment. A couple of coincidental deaths isn't sufficient grounds for putting a whole bunch of people to a lot of trouble.' Tish refolded the wrap and took a bite.

'I don't think Kitty would take very kindly to you rehashing the whole curse thing, either,' Riya ventured.

'But if Tish is baking the cherry pie, it's already being rehashed,' Dolly argued. 'Once people see that a cherry pie is her signature bake, that's all anyone will be talking about.'

'So, let them talk. Look, I feel bad about Lillian and Pen, but I think the whole "curse" theory needs to be put to bed once and for all. It's complete nonsense. This isn't some mystical spell. Maybe Tish is the one to prove that.' Gordon finished his statement by chomping noisily on a chip.

'But what if Tish doesn't get a chance to prove it? What if' – Riya's voice lowered – 'what if she *doesn't* survive?'

Tish left the hospitality suite before the end of lunch break so she could clear her head before the start of the next round of the competition. She genuinely didn't believe in curses and unlucky recipes, but Riya's final question and the unusual timing of the deaths of both Lillian Harwood and Penelope Purdue had left Tish shaken. So shaken, in fact, that when Jules tapped Tish on the arm as she walked past him on the way back to her booth, she jumped.

'You OK?' he inquired. 'I've been looking for you all over the place.'

'I was at lunch, like everyone else competing in the bake-off.'

'Lunch? How can you eat at a time like this?'

Tish raised her eyebrows. Jules was the poster child for stress eating. 'Hey, that's my line, isn't it?'

'Usually, yes, but I haven't eaten a bite all day. I've been too busy interviewing contestants. Speaking of which, I found out that the two women who died did so before they even baked their cherry pies.'

'I know,' Tish acknowledged. 'I talked to some of the other bake-off contestants during lunch. Both Lillian Harwood and Penelope Purdue died after the second day of competition.'

'So, what are you going to do?' Jules prodded.

'Nothing. What is there for me to do?'

'Talk to the judges about changing your menu, that's what.'

'We've been through this already, Jules. It's far too late in the competition to change my last entry. Besides, what excuse would I give? That I believe that there's a curse on anyone who bakes a cherry pie? It's utterly ridiculous.'

'But what about the dead women? Don't you find it strange that both of them died when they did?'

'Of course I do, but strange things happen. Things we can't always explain. Am I completely at ease baking the cherry pie after learning what I have? No, but I need to remain calm and clear-headed and focus on bringing that prize money home to Celestine. That's my reason for being here.'

'I suppose you're right. I'm just worried about you, Tish.'

'I appreciate that, Jules, but I'll be fine. I didn't survive a bullet wound only to be taken down by a pie.'

Jules laughed softly. 'When you put it that way, it is kinda ridiculous.'

'Kinda?' Tish glanced around. In the time she'd been talking to Jules, the majority of her fellow contestants had returned to their booths. 'Looks like I'd better get back.'

'I'll walk with you and give you a hug for luck,' Jules proposed as he followed closely behind his friend. 'Then *I'm* getting lunch. The smell of all this cooking is making me hungry.'

'Everything makes you hungry,' she teased before stepping into her bake-off kitchen.

'It does, but being around this food is particularly challenging. I'll probably gain twenty pounds over the next four days. I'd better get my fat pants dry cleaned.' Jules snorted.

Tish didn't smile in return. She was staring, open-mouthed, at a sheet of paper that had been left atop the warm stove during her absence.

'What is it, honey?' he asked.

'It's a note.' She held the paper aloft. Upon it had been scrawled in red ink: *DROP OUT OF THE BAKE-OFF OR YOU'LL BE NEXT.*

'What did I tell you? It's the curse!'

Tish shook her head. 'This isn't a curse, Jules. It's a threat.'

FIVE

The three o'clock break saw Tish sitting in the small meeting room that served as Kitty Flournoy's temporary office, awaiting the arrival of the police.

'It really wasn't necessary to call the authorities,' Tish explained, trying to downplay the hysteria Jules's report had so obviously created. As much as she wanted to get to the bottom of the threatening note that was left in her booth, she saw no reason why this meeting couldn't have waited until the end of the day's baking. She desperately wanted to return to her booth and put the finishing touches on her tarragon chicken. Jules, however, obviously felt that the matter required Kitty's immediate attention and dashed straight from Tish's booth to the bake-off office.

Kitty paced back and forth in front of the folding table that functioned as her desk. 'Oh, no, Ms Tarragon, we're not taking any chances. The minute Mr Davis told me about that note, I saw red—'

Tish glanced up at Jules as he stood silently near the doorway examining his fingernails and avoiding any and all eye contact with his best friend.

'The thought of someone trying to intimidate one of my bakers is unacceptable. Completely unacceptable. Whoever is responsible must be brought to justice.'

As if summoned by the word 'justice,' the rotund, uniformed figure of Sheriff Wade Lightbody stepped through the doorway. 'Oh, no,' Tish murmured as she threw her head back and cursed her luck.

'Miss Flurr-nay, I'm Acting Sheriff Wade Lightbody and this is Officer Clayton.' He introduced the young policeman who'd been on the scene when Tish was shot the previous December. 'We're from the Henrico County—' He stopped talking the moment his eyes focused on Tish. 'You.'

'Hello, Sheriff,' Tish greeted with a tentative smile.

'Ah, you both know each other,' Kitty noted. 'Good. Saves time in introductions. Sheriff, I called you here because Ms Tarragon here has received a threatening note.'

Lightbody chuckled in obvious delight. 'Has she now? I can't imagine why.'

Kitty, clearly confused by the sheriff's reaction, summoned Desmond to hand over the intimidating dispatch. Lightbody reviewed it with a smug smile. 'It would seem to me that you've rubbed someone the wrong way, Mizz Tarragon.'

'Rubbed someone the wrong way?' an indignant Kitty repeated. 'This is a serious matter, Sheriff.'

Lightbody cleared his throat and tried on a somber expression. 'Sorry, ma'am, but this looks like a personal grudge to me. Someone doesn't want Mizz Tarragon to compete, for one reason or another. Though I'm not sure what they meant by "next." You have any idea?'

'Two unrelated contestant deaths have taken place in recent years. Neither occurred at the competition itself, thank goodness, but they've spurred a myth about a curse. That's what the note means by "next" – that Ms Tarragon will be the next to die.'

'A nasty sentiment, but I don't think it's anything to be alarmed about. I doubt they'd actually go through with their threat.'

'How can you be so certain?' Tish challenged.

'Because this is a baking contest, Mizz Tarragon,' Lightbody replied condescendingly. 'This isn't some convention of hardened criminals. I find it difficult to believe that you or anyone else is going to come to harm over something as silly as a baking contest.'

'Silly?' Kitty Flournoy's pallid face was stained bright red. 'So if such a note had been left for a competitor at the antique car show, you'd take it more seriously?'

'No! No, it's just that we're talking about recipes here, not one-hundred-thousand-dollar vehicles . . .' Lightbody blustered.

'Money? That's the criterion? I'll have you know that the Virginia Commonwealth Bake-Off is one of the oldest and most esteemed competitions of its kind in the nation. For eighty-five years, we have set the standard for cookery competitions, and I am not about to stand by and allow my contestants to be threatened and our reputation sullied.'

'Yes, I understand, ma'am, but technically this wasn't a death threat—'

'Not a death threat? What more do we need? For it to be written in blood?'

'No, ma'am. Now if you'd calm down for just a min—'

'I demand you put an officer on patrol here to monitor the situation; otherwise, I will complain to the governor.'

'Now, I'm sure that won't be necessary. If you'd just sit—'

'Desmond! Get Governor Northam's office on the line.' Kitty stormed off behind her desk, leaving Sheriff Lightbody looking utterly defeated.

'All right, ma'am.' He capitulated. 'I'll leave Clayton behind to keep an eye on things.'

'Thank you, Sheriff. You won't regret it.'

Lightbody's face made it clear he already regretted the decision to yield to Kitty's threats.

'I know everyone here at the bake-off will feel much safer with your officer standing guard.' Kitty smugly folded her arms across her chest. 'I haven't told my staff of volunteers about the note yet, but when they hear that some crazy stalker wandered in here and threatened one of the contestants . . . well, they'll be extremely thankful to the sheriff's office.'

'Yes, thank you, Sheriff Lightbody,' Tish seconded. 'I appreciate you allowing us to borrow Officer Clayton. However, I don't think you're looking for a crazy stalker as Kitty described. This was an inside job.'

Kitty became flustered. 'Inside? Don't be ridiculous.'

'I'm not. You closed the exhibition hall to visitors five minutes before everyone broke for lunch and you only opened it up again five minutes after everyone returned.'

'So?'

'So, that note wasn't in my booth when I left for lunch, but it was there when I returned, which was exactly seven minutes prior to the exhibition hall being reopened to the public. That means whoever left that note was already in the building. They're part of the bake-off.'

Jules caught up with Tish as she exited the meeting room and made her way back to the exhibition hall. 'I hope you're not angry with me for going to Kitty with that note.'

'I didn't mind you going to Kitty. I minded you going straight to her without discussing it with me first,' she clarified. 'The next round of cooking had only just begun and you were off like a shot.'

'Sorry.'

'That's OK. I know you only did it out of concern.'

'I did, honey. Watching you cook while knowing someone wants you dead drove me crazy. I couldn't stand it any longer, so I flagged down Kitty and told her what was going on. Once Lightbody arrived on the scene, I realized I might have made a mistake.'

'Yeah, I figured Kitty would call the police and I also figured that if Lightbody saw I was involved, he wouldn't take the case too seriously. Fortunately, he yielded to Kitty's influence and left us Officer Clayton.'

'I feel a lot safer knowing he's around,' Jules sighed in relief.

'Yes,' Tish agreed. 'Officer Clayton might also prove to be a useful source of information.'

'What kind of information?'

'Oh, like the cause of death for Lillian Harwood and Penelope Purdue. Maybe their next of kin. Things that might be difficult to get without a badge or while one is busy decorating a Miss Havisham wedding cake.' She smirked.

'You think that note is linked to the dead women, don't you?'

'Of course. Don't you?'

'No. I thought maybe someone left you the note because they were afraid you might win.'

'It's a little premature for that, don't you think? I haven't even finished baking the first dish. The penalty for threatening another contestant is expulsion. Quite a risk to take to get rid of someone who might not even make it into the top three slots.'

'You do have a reputation at the café. Some of the contestants might be intimidated by that,' Jules suggested.

Tish shook her head. 'I haven't mentioned the café to anyone. The only person who knows is the woman who answered the phone when I called to inquire about stepping in for Celestine. I was concerned I might be banned as a professional, but that classification is reserved for those who've received formal training. Which I haven't.'

'The person you spoke to could have let it slip that you own a café.'

'Possibly,' Tish allowed. 'But I'm pretty sure someone would have mentioned it to me by now.'

'Not everyone spreads gossip like they do in Hobson Glen.'

Tish raised an eyebrow. 'Don't they, Jules?'

He pulled a face. 'Yeah, I guess you're right.'

'Mmm,' she grunted in agreement. 'I think it's far more likely that my questions about the deaths of Lillian Harwood and Penelope Purdue made someone very nervous.'

'Any idea who?'

'No. I had lunch with a few other contestants, but anyone in the hospitality suite might have overheard. Anyone might have wanted Lillian and Penelope dead, too. They were both on target for winning the top prize.'

'They were? No one I spoke with mentioned anything about that.'

'Well, if contestants are putting the whole thing down to some ridiculous curse, they wouldn't see any reason to mention it, would they?'

They had arrived at Tish's booth mere seconds before the next session was about to begin.

'What about the cherry pie? How does that factor into all of this?' Jules questioned as Tish tightened the ties on her apron and prepared herself for more cooking.

'I haven't a clue, Jules. I honestly haven't a clue.'

SIX

I t was half past four in the afternoon when Tish retrieved her piping-hot tarragon chicken from the oven and plated it on a bed of roasted baby new potatoes. Working quickly, she pulled the pot of stewed radishes, peas, asparagus, and lettuce from the rear burner of the stove, gave it a stir, and spooned the vegetables on to the side of the platter, cleaning up any drips with the edge of a white cotton tea towel.

Upon garnishing the chicken with a sprinkle of fresh chopped tarragon, she drew a deep breath, straightened her apron, smoothed her hair, and waved to Willadeane Scott to signal she had completed her entry. After Willadeane logged the time of completion on her clipboard, Tish set off to present her first bake-off dish to the judges.

She arrived at the judges' table at the front of the exhibition hall to discover she was one of the first ten contestants to finish. 'A timely arrival, Ms . . .' Tallulah Sinclair, famed Southern cooking and lifestyle expert, pulled her bifocals down from atop her head of yellowish gray hair and strained her eyes to read Tish's badge. 'Ms Tarragon. It appears you're also bearing the same dish as your name. Clever, clever.'

Tish felt her face blush scarlet. Ms Sinclair had been writing bestselling entertaining books for nearly as long as Tish had been alive – some forty-one years. 'That's simply a coincidence. I'd love the dish even if my name were Smith.'

Ms Sinclair's blue eyes twinkled. 'It *is* quite tasty, isn't it? I remember falling in love with it as a young woman in Paris, but don't tell my readers that I might like it better than fried chicken. They'd never let me live it down.'

The man seated beside Tallulah scowled. 'Oh, please. So what? You'll sell twenty thousand copies of your latest books instead of thirty thousand. You may need to cut your winter getaway in the Caribbean short by a few days. Otherwise, you'd survive.'

'That's not the point and you know it, Vernon. People turn to me to guide them through all things Southern. It simply wouldn't do to endorse a French dish. As delectable as it might be,' Tallulah replied in a soft drawl, but the annoyance on her face belied the sweet tone of her words.

Vernon Staples was a well-respected food critic and had written for the *Richmond Times-Dispatch* for more than fifty years. Although now retired from his weekly column, Vernon was still famous for his heightened sense of taste and his legendary 'feud' with fellow judge Tallulah Sinclair. 'As delectable as it might be,' he mimicked, stroking the gray hairs of his closely trimmed beard.

'Would you two give it a rest?' requested David Biederman. A bagel maker from New York City, Biederman had expanded his business to deliver quality bagels to supermarket bread aisles nationwide. 'This looks and smells absolutely delicious, Ms Tarragon. And your plating is appealing, too. I gotta ask, though, what are these vegetables? Looks like there's lettuce in there.'

'There is. I used lettuce, peas, radishes, and asparagus.'

'Radishes, too? I'd never have thought of cooking those.'

'Lettuce and radishes are often cooked in France and parts of Asia, but the practice isn't as common here in the States,' Tish explained.

'Except for that terrible grilled Romaine salad trend back in the early Noughties,' Vernon complained. 'Horrible stuff – charred lettuce. Didn't you feature a recipe for that in one of your books back then, Tallulah?'

'You know I did, Vernon,' she said through clenched teeth. 'That and my grilled peach dessert. People still write thanking me for those.'

'Charred lettuce *and* charred stone fruit. Who on earth would thank you for those? Cancer doctors?'

'At least I receive thank-you notes and fan mail. When you were a restaurant critic, I heard your mail was filed into four categories: hate, abhorrence, disgust, and death wish,' she quipped.

'Enough,' David nearly shouted before clearing his throat and returning his attention to Tish. 'Thank you for submitting your dish, Ms Tarragon.'

'Yes, thank you, Ms Tarragon,' Tallulah said, following David's lead. 'I look forward to tasting everything, but especially those vegetables. I don't believe anyone's cooked lettuce and radishes for the bake-off before.'

'I don't believe they have,' Vernon Staples agreed. 'Kudos for originality.'

'Wow, you both agreed on something,' David marveled. 'Thank you, again, Ms Tarragon, for bringing our little panel together.'

Tish laughed. 'My pleasure.'

'What do you have in store for us tomorrow?' Vernon asked.

'A pink champagne cake with raspberry mousse filling decorated as Miss Havisham's wedding cake from *Great Expectations*.'

'That's quite a lofty undertaking,' Tallulah said admiringly. 'I look forward to seeing it.'

David was obviously impressed with Tish and her baking skills, for he adjusted his red bow tie and smoothed his dark hair, which was graying slightly. 'I look forward to tasting it. What's your signature bake, Ms Tarragon?'

'Cherry frangipane pie,' she answered and watched their faces.

As expected, the trio fell quiet and their jaws dropped open. Several seconds elapsed before David interrupted the silence. 'You're the contestant who received that threatening note, aren't you?'

'One and the same.'

'What a lousy thing to happen. How are you doing?'

'I'm OK. Wishing someone hadn't told me the last two contestants who planned to bake cherry pies are dead, but otherwise OK.'

Tallulah fidgeted in her seat. 'So you know about those women?'

'Yes, I learned about them and the "curse" at lunch, just before I found the note, although no one seemed to know precisely what happened to Lillian and Penelope. You and Mr Staples are long-time judges. Do you remember what happened?'

'Not exactly. In both cases, we were set to begin the last day of competition when we received word that something had occurred the evening before.' She turned to Vernon Staples. 'In Ms Harwood's case, it was quite unexpected, wasn't it?'

Vernon wrinkled his nose. 'I'm not sure. You were with us that year, weren't you, David? What do you remember?'

Biederman looked surprised. 'Me? Yes . . . yes, I believe it was sudden. If I'm not mistaken, I think the woman died of heart trouble. As women her age often do.'

'And is it true that she was on course to win the competition?' Tish asked.

'I, uh, I believe she did submit two estimable entries, yes.'

'A French–Canadian tourtière for the savory bake,' Vernon recalled. 'And a mountain cake inspired by her grandchildren. Both were excellent.'

'But it's difficult to say whether she might have won,' Tallulah was quick to add. 'These things do come so close to the wire.'

'Of course. And Penelope Purdue last year? What happened to her?' Tish questioned.

'Oh, I wasn't a judge last year,' David said, dismissive.

'No, you weren't.' Vernon frowned. 'Kitty got in some confectioner from Knoxville last year. He'd done a pilot for the Food Network and she thought he'd bolster ticket sales. Terrible judge. Always late for tastings and had a massively sweet tooth which didn't work well for the savory entries.'

Tallulah sighed. 'She didn't ask about the judge, Vernon. She asked about Penelope Purdue.'

'I was getting there before you so rudely interrupted. Ms Purdue made a Moroccan chicken bastilla for her savory bake and her showstopper cake was a peacock. A two-layer cake served as the body of the peacock and she decorated about a dozen cupcakes or so to serve as feathers. It was well executed, if a bit contrived.'

'It was delicious and extremely whimsical.'

'It *was* rather tasty,' Vernon conceded.

'It was more than tasty. The texture was light as a feather.' Tallulah giggled at her pun. 'And her piping was masterful. After years of seven-layer cakes and bulky bakes, it was fun to sample a cupcake. It made me feel like a child again.'

'It took you back *all* that way? Now that was a miraculous cake,' Vernon wisecracked.

Tallulah ignored him. 'You said it made you feel like a kid again, too, David. I remember you tried one.'

'You're mistaken, Tallulah. I wasn't here last year,' David maintained.

'Oh, but you were. Not as a judge, but as a visitor. You were in town introducing your line of bagel products at Ellwood Thompson's and Kitty invited you to come by in the hope your presence would reduce the damage inflicted by her new judge. You swung by at the end of the showstopper bake and then joined us the next day to award the trophy to the winner.'

'That was last year? Really? I thought it was three years ago.' He gave an uneasy laugh. 'Goes to show what the launch of the new grocery line has done to my brain.'

'So what happened to Ms Purdue?' Tish pressed. 'How did she die?'

David flashed a self-assured grin. 'Love to answer that question, but I can't. I don't even recall being here.'

'We didn't see Ms Purdue on that last day,' Vernon explained as he stroked his white beard. 'She'd gone home early.'

'Willadeane Scott presented the peacock cake on Ms Purdue's behalf,' Tallulah continued.

'Willadeane was Ms Purdue's monitor,' Tish mused aloud.

'Yes. Apparently, the woman had become ill and had to leave, so Willadeane took over, as per protocol.'

'Did you know what was wrong with Ms Purdue?'

'No, just that she'd fallen ill.'

'The next day, Kitty announced that Ms Purdue was dead,' Vernon interjected. 'I can't remember the cause exactly, but I think it was an allergy of some sort.'

'Allergy?' Tallulah challenged. 'I thought it was food poisoning.'

'Of course you would.' Vernon shook his head. 'Silly woman.'

'Well, the words Kitty used implied it was. She said Ms Purdue had eaten something that didn't agree with her.' Tallulah looked to David for confirmation.

'Don't look at me,' the bagel baker cautioned. 'I didn't arrive here until lunchtime. And I don't care if you remember differently, Tallulah. I *wasn't* here.'

Having obtained as much information as she could from Tallulah, Vernon, and David, Tish left the judges' table and journeyed back to her booth to dive into the tedious process of cleaning up. As she turned down the first row of booths, she was met, head-on, by a woman rounding the corner in the opposite direction. She was tall and attractive with long, layered caramel-brown hair, a mid-length, light-blue floral dress with billowing, sheer sleeves, and a face that was as expertly made-up as Kitty Flournoy's. In her mitted hands, she held a covered cast-iron Dutch oven.

Tish stepped aside to avoid bumping directly into the woman, but they still managed to brush shoulders. 'I'm sorry. Bit of a blind spot there.'

The tall woman glared at Tish, turned on one dangerously high heel, and went along her way.

Seconds later, Tish heard the cheer of 'Whitney!' emanating from the judges' table.

'Whitney Liddell,' Jules explained as he approached. 'I just tried to get an interview with her, to no avail.'

'I don't think I've disliked someone so much at first sight,' Tish disclosed.

'Probably because she was rude to you just now.'

'Mmm,' she agreed with a grunt.

'And she reminds you of all those mean girls in high school.'

'Possibly.'

'And looks like a Donna-Reed-throwback-Stepford-Wife-hybrid.'

'Umm . . .'

'Like seriously? Who spends the entire day baking in four-inch heels and finishes without their makeup smudged or hair out of place? She can't be human.'

'Are we still talking about me here? Or are you miffed she snubbed your request for an interview?'

'Maybe a little of both.' He folded his arms across his chest.

'Whitney may not be the most approachable person, but the

judges seem to like her.' The sound of laughter and cheering continued at the judges' table.

'Yeah, a little too much.' He dropped his voice. 'If I'd been competing in this bake-off as long as some folks have, I'd be royally ticked at the way Whitney cozies up to the judges.'

'This is my first bake-off and even *I'm* ticked at the way Whitney cozies up to the judges. And yet two women who stood a chance of winning are dead and I've received a threatening note.'

'You'd think Whitney would have received the threat,' Jules realized.

'Exactly.'

'Do you think those two women were murdered to ensure Whitney won?'

'I don't know what to think, but something odd is going on here. One of the judges adamantly denied being here last year, even though he was. And the other two had memorized every detail of the dead women's menus – including the taste and texture of each dish – but neither of them could recall or agree upon what exactly had killed them. Likewise, when I asked if Lillian and Penelope might have won the competition had they lived, the suggestion was played down.'

'Weird,' Jules decreed. 'So what are we going to do?'

'We?' she questioned.

'Of course. You don't think I'm going to let someone send you a threatening note and get away with it, do you? Besides, you have a contest to win. Having an assistant might come in handy.'

Tish pursed her lips. 'You do have a point. Well, then, partner, let's go talk to Officer Clayton. Then I have to beat it back to my booth. I have a ton of dishes to do.'

'I'm not even supposed to be talking to you, Ms Tarragon, let alone helping you,' a uniformed Officer Clayton complained. He was tall, rail-thin, twentyish, and his fair hair had been trimmed into a high-and-tight crewcut.

'My refusal to give him a free coffee really stuck in Lightbody's craw, didn't it?' Tish marveled.

'It's more than that. He's looking to make a big splash by

"cleaning up"' – Clayton added air quotes – 'our district as if it's some crime-infested area or something.'

'Well, there have been a few murders lately,' Jules reminded Tish, prompting her to whack him in the upper arm.

'This isn't about the murders. This is about Lightbody's ego. He wants to be seen as tough on crime so he's planning to enforce a curfew for teens, put more patrol cars in the streets, and impose stricter fines and penalties for first offenders, but so far the interim mayor has shot down his plans, which just makes him lash out at everyone around him.'

'I'm sorry things have been so difficult for you and the department, Clayton,' Tish sympathized. 'And I wouldn't have asked for help except that I honestly believe there's something fishy going on around here. Two seemingly healthy women die suddenly during two consecutive bake-offs and now I'm being threatened. Look, you know I wouldn't ask for help if I didn't think this was serious. You know my track record with Sheriff Reade.'

'I do, but Sheriff Reade isn't here anymore.'

Tish bowed her head. She knew as well as anyone that Reade had left without plans to return, yet it didn't make Clayton's words any less jarring. She had spent the last three months recovering from her wound, getting settled into Schuyler's condo, building her business, and generally feeling thankful for being alive, but the sheriff's hasty departure on Christmas Eve still haunted her. 'I know, Clayton. I don't want you to lose your job, so let's forget this conversation ever happened.'

Clayton exhaled noisily. 'Jim,' he corrected.

'I beg your pardon?'

'My name. It's Jim. Now, what do you want me to find out?'

'You don't have to do this, Jim. I underst—' she started.

'Look, Sheriff Reade wouldn't have turned his back if he thought there was a possibility something was wrong. I'm not going to, either.'

'Are you sure?' Jules asked.

'Positive.' Officer Jim Clayton grinned. 'Lightbody's been hollering at me for almost two weeks now. Might as well give him something to holler about.'

SEVEN

With the dishwasher in her booth making fast work of the day's dishes, a weary Tish left the civic center and made the fifteen-minute drive back to Hobson Glen, pulling her red Toyota Matrix into the driveway of the condo she shared with Schuyler at approximately six o'clock in the evening. As had become the norm since the mayoral campaign switched into high gear, Schuyler wasn't due home until late; however, Tish wasn't to be alone.

Stepping through the coffered oak front door and into the main foyer, Tish switched off the alarm system, threw her keys into her red Coach handbag, and kicked off her shoes, appreciating how the cool hardwood floors had a rejuvenating effect on her sore, tired feet.

Preferring fresh air to that of the condo's HVAC system, Tish switched off the air conditioning and continued straight ahead, into the kitchen. Padding across the ceramic tiles, she unlocked the windows above the farmhouse sink and opened their sashes. A sweet breeze redolent of fresh-cut grass wafted through the kitchen and tickled Tish's nose.

She drew a deep breath and smiled. Between the recent spate of mild weather and the start of Daylight Saving Time, spring was well on its way. With still over an hour of sunshine left in the day, Tish grabbed a rag from the sink, drew open the sliding glass doors of the kitchen, and stepped out on to the paved courtyard that served as the backyard. She leaned over the metal-and-glass patio table and wiped off the layer of fine green dust that had accumulated, then moved on to clean the chairs.

She finished just as the doorbell rang.

Retracing her steps into the foyer, she swung open the front door to allow Mary Jo admittance.

'Hey, honey,' MJ greeted her. Her long dark hair was pinned into a neat bun at the nape of her neck and she was dressed in a white fitted T-shirt and long black skirt.

'Hey, yourself.' Tish gave MJ a hug.

'Sorry I texted you while you were cleaning up.'

'Don't be. All was forgiven the moment you said you were bringing dinner.' She laughed. 'Are the kids out for the night?'

'Yeah, Kayla's working at Chik-fil-A and Gregory's with a friend, studying for a calculus exam.' She followed Tish into the kitchen and placed a brown paper shopping bag on the marble countertop.

'Well, how lucky am I that you're free?'

'We're both lucky. Wait till you see what I have.' MJ reached into the bag and extracted a recyclable foil tray with a cardboard lid. 'Celestine's homemade three-cheese mac and cheese. She dropped it off when she came by to help with some lunch customers.'

'You should keep that for yourself,' Tish directed, knowing how tight things had been for MJ since separating from her husband. 'You and the kids can have it for dinner tomorrow night.'

'I already have a tray of my own. Celestine's stress cooking surpasses even yours. She made enough mac and cheese for her kids, her grandkids, you and me, me and my kids, and my kids' friends.'

'Well, I suppose it's better than being holed up in bed in a darkened room. Apart from the stress cooking, how is she doing?'

'Not bad. She seemed to enjoy being back, but when the lunch crowd left and the café got quiet, it all seemed to hit her again.'

Tish frowned. 'Poor woman.'

'I know. I can't imagine losing a spouse after being married for nearly forty years.'

'I can't imagine being *married* for nearly forty years.'

MJ giggled. 'You and me both.'

'Shall we get the mac and cheese in the oven?' Tish suggested, preheating the Viking appliance to 350 degrees Fahrenheit.

'Absolutely. And while we wait . . .' MJ pulled a bottle of rosé from the bag.

'Ooh. You know you're my bestest friend, right? Jules doesn't even come close.'

'Yeah, you're mine, too. Unless Jules is the bringing the wine.'

The two women laughed. 'Speaking of Jules,' Tish segued as she poured the wine into two stemless glasses, 'I bet he called you to let you know about the note I received today, didn't he?'

'Note? What n—? Oh, what am I doing? I can't lie to you. Yes, he called me right around lunchtime. Knowing that Schuyler's been working late, he was concerned about you being here alone. He would have followed you himself if he didn't have to be back at the studio for his broadcast.'

Tish eyed the foil container suspiciously. 'And the mac and cheese?'

'Oh, I didn't make that up. That's definitely Celestine's. She was going to have her daughter drive it over here and deliver it to you, but since I'd already spoken to Jules, I thought it would make the perfect excuse to drop by.'

'Sneaky.'

'Well, I've learned from the best.' Mary Jo held her glass of wine aloft to toast her friend.

The two sipped their wine and sighed. 'Oh, that hits the spot,' Tish declared and led the way on to the patio where she collapsed into her chair.

Mary Jo sat down at the opposite side of the table. 'How are you?'

'I'm tired and my feet hurt, but otherwise I'm OK.'

'And the note?'

'I'm trying to get to the bottom of that.' Tish brought MJ up to date on everything she'd learned.

'Do you think those women might have been murdered?' MJ asked when Tish had finished.

'It's too soon to say, but I can't help thinking there's something suspicious about their deaths.'

'Each woman died before she had the chance to bake her cherry pie.'

'That reminds me.' Tish excused herself and wandered into the house. She returned several seconds later with two folded sheets of paper. 'You just mentioned how each woman died before preparing her cherry pie recipe, right?'

MJ nodded.

'Lillian and Penelope were supposedly competing with the same cherry pie recipe.' Tish sat down and flattened the pieces of paper on the table.

'What are those?' MJ asked.

'Lillian and Penelope's cherry pie recipes. Each year, the bake-off publishes their contestants' recipes online so that members of the audience can follow or bake along. Jules searched the archives from the past two bake-offs, found these, and printed them off.'

'What are you looking for?'

'First, I want to make sure the recipes were, indeed, the same – and it appears that they are – and then I want to see what was in the recipe. You know, in case there was an ingredient or method that might be proprietary or odd or . . .' Tish threw her hands up into the air.

'Or a reason for murder?' Mary Jo posed.

'Or a reason for *something*. It looks like a standard cherry pie recipe, though. A simple pâte brisée for the crust, sour cherries – not sweet – sugar, cornstarch, lemon, vanilla, kirsch . . . kirsch? Mmm, that sounds yummy.' The mention of cherry brandy reminded Tish of the glass of wine resting on the table beside her. She picked it up and took a sip.

Mary Jo mirrored the action. 'Maybe that standard cherry pie recipe belongs to someone else,' she suggested upon swallowing.

'Now, that's a thought. But then why not raise the issue with the foundation that runs the bake-off?'

'Maybe the person had no proof the recipe was theirs?' MJ took another sip of wine.

'Maybe,' Tish allowed. 'It's just all so strange.'

'What time is Schuyler due home?'

'After eleven or so. Why?'

'Because I have to pick up Kayla from work at nine and I'd feel better if you weren't alone.'

'I'll be fine, MJ. You saw that big honking security system in the foyer, didn't you?'

'Still, I'd feel better if Schuyler was home tonight.'

'I would too, but for other reasons.'

'Well, there's not long until the election. Things will quiet down after that.'

'Not if Schuyler wins. Then he'll be juggling his mayoral duties and the law firm.'

'That's an awful lot for a new relationship to endure,' MJ observed.

'It's difficult at times, but Schuyler stood by me when I was recovering from being shot. I'm not going to abandon him while he's pursuing his dream. This isn't like my marriage to Mitch. At least I know where Schuyler is every night. All I have to do is turn on the news and I'll see him out on the campaign trail.'

'Seeing Schuyler on the news isn't the same as spending time with him. I know from my experience with Glen. I had the kids to keep me company, but it was still lonely.'

'Schuyler and I have discussed how we would handle things if he won. I told him that if we find we don't have enough time together, I would seriously consider closing the café on Sundays.'

'Sundays? But between the late sleepers coming in for brunch and the church crowd looking for a hot lunch after services, Sunday's easily your best day at the café.'

'I know, MJ, but I'm not going to sacrifice my relationship with Schuyler for my business. I often wonder if that was the problem with Mitch.' Tish leaned back in her chair and took another sip of wine.

'You mean, had you been less focused on your banking career, Mitch might not have cheated on you? That's ridiculous. Mitch made the choice to cheat. The responsibility rests on his shoulders and his shoulders alone. That's like me saying that if I hadn't been so focused on being a good mother, Glen wouldn't have run off with a younger woman. Were things perfect in our marriages? No, but our husbands should have expressed their unhappiness to us instead of getting a third party involved.'

Tish smiled warmly at her friend. 'There you go again. Talking sense.'

'Well, between you and Jules, someone has to,' MJ stated with a melodramatic sigh.

'Quite true,' Tish agreed as she rose from her chair. 'I should probably check on that food.'

'I'll come with you.' MJ folded her arms across her chest. 'It's starting to cool down out here.'

'It is, isn't it? Well, at least we got to enjoy a little bit of sun. Grab your glass,' Tish directed as she collected her own glass from the table and stepped through the sliding glass doors. 'We'll have dinner in the kitchen.'

Mary Jo did as she was instructed and followed Tish into the house, sliding the door shut behind her. The smell of mac and cheese permeated the kitchen.

Tish opened the oven door, pulled the square pan from its rack, and placed it atop the range. The cheese sauce was molten and bubbly and the top of the pasta golden brown.

'Mmm, looks good,' MJ remarked as she refilled their glasses with rosé.

'It does. Should I make a quick salad? I've been trying to eat fewer carbs and more vegetables.'

'Nah, the wine is made from grapes. That counts as fruit.'

'I like your thinking.' Tish moved the mac and cheese to a trivet on the table and set about getting plates and utensils. She was interrupted by the sound of her cell phone ringing from its spot in her handbag on the foyer table. 'Just when we're sitting down for dinner. Always.'

'It might be Schuyler,' MJ offered.

Buoyed by MJ's suggestion, Tish dashed into the hallway and answered the phone just before it was about to go to voice-mail. 'Hello?'

'Hi, Ms Tarragon, it's Jim Clayton.'

'Oh, hi, Jim. What's up?'

'I did some digging into the deaths of those two women like you asked.'

'And?' Tish urged.

'Nothing out of the ordinary. Lillian Harwood's death certificate cites cardiac arrest as the cause of death.'

'Which says nothing except that her heart stopped.'

'As for her personal life, she was seventy years old, divorced twice, and had two sons, one of whom is married and has two children. He and his family live in Yorktown. Can't find a trace

of the other son. Penelope Purdue was a thirty-six-year-old
computer programmer, single, no children, and not too much
in the way of family.'

'And her cause of death?'

'Severe anaphylaxis as a result of a nut allergy.'

Tish nearly jumped out of her skin. 'What? That can't be.'

'That's what it says on the death certificate.'

'The death certificate is wrong. Penelope Purdue couldn't
have died from a nut allergy. She made chicken bastilla for
her savory bake.'

Clayton's voice hesitated. 'I–I'm not sure what that means.'

'Chicken bastilla is made with ground almonds. An abundance
of ground almonds. If Penelope had been deadly allergic to
nuts, she never would have made chicken bastilla.'

EIGHT

Officer Clayton, Tish, and Mary Jo were seated around
the condo kitchen table where, following Clayton's
call, they'd agreed to convene to discuss the case.
Jules, minus his suit jacket and tie, joined them immediately
after the evening news broadcast, arriving at approximately a
quarter after seven.

'I got here as quickly as I could,' he announced breathlessly.
'What's going on?'

Officer Clayton, out of uniform and dressed in a blue
checked poplin shirt and a pair of skinny jeans, debriefed Jules
about the dead women.

'So everything sounds on the up-and-up,' Jules replied when
Clayton had finished. 'Right?'

'It isn't,' Tish asserted. 'Vernon Staples told me that Penelope
Purdue made chicken bastilla as her savory bake – a Moroccan
dish laden with nuts.'

'Could Vernon have been, mistaken?'

'That's what I wondered,' MJ concurred.

Tish shook her head. 'Vernon Staples can't be trusted to

remember many things, but he would never forget a menu. When I asked him about Lillian and Penelope, he exhibited more interest in the women's food than the women themselves.'

'I guess that makes sense for a retired food critic,' Jules acknowledged. 'But what does it mean for us?'

'It means Penelope Purdue's anaphylaxis was caused by something other a nut allergy. Whatever caused her reaction, she had no idea she'd been exposed to it.'

'Is that an accurate assumption, though?' Clayton challenged.

'Yes, I think so. People with potentially fatal allergies carry an EpiPen with them at all times. If Penelope knew she'd been in contact with whatever killed her, she would have injected herself. If she didn't have an EpiPen with her at the time, she would have asked for one from the staff at the hospital or even the first-aid crew at the civic center. They're a pretty standard piece of equipment.'

'We carry them in our patrol cars,' Clayton confirmed. 'But what if Ms Purdue didn't know she had this allergy? Or what if she just developed the nut allergy while working with the almonds at the bake-off that afternoon?'

'I'm no doctor,' MJ spoke up, 'but I'm pretty sure it requires more than a few hours' exposure to something to develop an allergy of that magnitude.'

'Oh, hey,' Jules interrupted while eyeing the pan of leftover mac and cheese cooling on the stove. 'Is that Celestine's cheesy mac I spy?'

'Yes,' Tish answered.

'May I have the leftovers? I'm famished.'

'Sure. You know where the plates, forks, and microwave are.'

Jules set about transferring the pasta from the aluminum pan to a plate and reheating it.

'Not to be a jerk, but if Ms Purdue thought her chicken bas . . .' Clayton slid his eyes toward Tish.

'Bastilla,' she inserted.

'Bastilla,' Clayton repeated, 'was a winning dish, she would have practiced making it repeatedly over the past few months. That means she was exposed to those nuts for much longer than just an afternoon.'

'Tish,' Jules interjected again as he snatched his piping-hot food from the microwave, 'do you have any hot sauce?'

'There's some Frank's inside the refrigerator door,' Tish directed. 'I agree, Jim, that Penelope would have been exposed to nuts long before the bake-off, but if she was unaware of the allergy, why is it listed on her death certificate? Was she tested before she died? After she died? Did she tell the hospital staff that her reaction was to the nuts? Or did someone else tell them? Was she alone when she was admitted to the emergency room? Or did she have a friend with her?'

'All valid questions,' Clayton allowed. 'But you're over-looking the fact that if Ms Purdue wasn't aware she had an allergy, then her death was accidental and nothing more.'

'Ow,' Jules exclaimed, pursing his lips. 'I put too much hot sauce on my mac. Do you have some bread, Tish?'

'On the counter, in the box beside the refrigerator,' Tish said, pointing. 'And *you're* overlooking the fact, Jim, that if Ms Purdue's death was, indeed, accidental and nothing more, I shouldn't have received a note warning me that I'm next.'

'Probably just a stupid prank. A fellow contestant using the "curse" to scare you away from competing.'

'Why try to scare me? I've never even competed in the contest before. No one has any reason to think of me as a threat. It makes more sense to scare off Whitney Liddell.'

'Newbie hazing?' Clayton suggested.

MJ clicked her tongue. 'It's a bake-off, not a fraternity initiation.'

'Also, I'm not the only new competitor,' Tish said. 'You questioned other new contestants. No one else received a note.'

'Ooh, you know what would be great right now?' Jules asked excitedly. 'A Dr Pepper to wash down this mac and cheese.'

'Jules, I don't have a Dr Pepper. This is not the café. Now, will you please focus?' Tish sounded like an exasperated mother at the end of summer vacation.

'I'll look into the circumstances surrounding Ms Purdue's hospital visit,' Clayton capitulated. 'And I'll check Lillian Harwood's medical background to see if she had a history of heart trouble.'

'Thank you,' a grateful Tish replied.

'Kayla has a doctor's appointment after the café closes tomorrow. Just a check-up before softball season starts,' MJ explained. 'While I'm there, I'll ask her doctor about life-threatening allergies and how long it would take for someone to die after exposure.'

'Cool. Just explain that you're not planning anything for Glen,' Tish recommended with a wink. 'I'm going to talk to my lunch buddies and see if they can remember anything odd that transpired on the days Lillian and Penelope died. I'm also going to try to find out how close the two women were. We already know they were friends – Penelope chose to bake the cherry pie in tribute to Lillian – but were they close enough to exchange secrets? If so, one of them may have known something that got both of them killed.'

The trio turned to look at Jules, who was standing near the sink, intently eating his pasta and bread.

MJ cleared her throat, spurring Jules to glance up from his plate. 'Hmm? Oh, sorry. I'm going to look into *this*.' He deposited his plate on the center island of the kitchen and placed his phone on the kitchen table for all to see.

Tish, MJ, and Clayton watched as a YouTube video launched, showing Whitney Liddell, dressed in a belted green dress with cap sleeves, a white apron with lace trim, a string of pearls, and pale pink pumps. Her long dark hair blew freely in the wind as she twirled around an expansive car lot, a whisk in one hand and yellow stoneware mixing bowl in the other.

'Who's that?' MJ asked.

'Whitney Liddell,' Tish replied. 'Three-time and current bake-off champion.'

'She looks like the mom from some old black-and-white television show,' Clayton commented.

'Or a demented Julia Child,' Jules countered.

'That's Sheehy Brothers' Auto Sales in Richmond.' MJ identified the car lot. 'They're the largest car dealership in all of Virginia. They have smaller branches throughout the state, too, but the Richmond dealership is their flagship.'

'For all the Sheehy Brothers' money, you'd think they'd have produced a better commercial. This looks like something from the eighties,' Clayton grumbled.

'I think that's the intention,' Tish asserted.

'So they're marketing to old people?'

'Hey, watch who you're calling old there, sparky,' MJ cautioned.

'It's not the look of the commercial that matters,' Jules responded. 'It's the airtime Sheehy Brothers' purchased. This ad premiered during the evening news broadcast and it's scheduled to repeat all through primetime.'

'So?' Clayton prompted, failing to extrapolate the meaning of Jules's statement.

'So it's Tuesday night. That little spot is airing during one of the last episodes of this season's *The Masked Singer*.'

'Yeah, I've been watching it. The ratings are supposed to be huge.'

'That's a lot of publicity for Sheehy Brothers,' MJ remarked.

'Yep, another video for Whitney Liddell's YouTube and TikTok channels,' Tish added. 'It also happens to be a lot of publicity for the bake-off.'

'Mm-hmm,' Jules agreed with a smug smile. 'Publicity Kitty Flournoy would hate to say goodbye to if, for example, another baker were to unseat Whitney Liddell as champ.'

'As Lillian Harwood and Penelope Purdue were slated to do.'

'Exactly.' Jules wandered back to his plate of mac and cheese. 'That's why I arranged to interview both Kitty Flournoy and Whitney Liddell tomorrow.'

'Whitney Liddell? I thought she turned down your interview request.'

'She did. Which is why I contacted her agent.' Jules flashed a self-satisfied grin and took a giant bite of mac and cheese.

'Agent? Why does a bake-off queen need an agent?'

'To manage the myriad of commercials and product endorsements she's racked up over the past three years. She started out by plugging flour and bakeware, but now she's using her name and image to hawk everything from plant seeds and outdoor furniture to cars and a designer line of aprons. Fans call her the Martha Stewart of Midlothian, even though technically she lives in Bon Air.'

'So if Whitney were unseated as champion, she'd lose far more than just a trophy,' Tish mused.

'She'd lose tens of thousands of dollars a year,' Jules stated between chews. 'That might not be an empire, honey, but I'd say it's worth killing for.'

NINE

'I didn't hear you come in last night.' Tish greeted Schuyler as he leaned over the stove, pouring boiling water into a French press. Although it was only six thirty, he was already shaved, showered, and dressed for the day.

'Good morning.' Schuyler wrapped a free arm around Tish's waist and pulled her closer. The smell of his aftershave was invitingly musky. 'I didn't want to wake you. Not only was I later than expected, but you were sound asleep when I came in.'

'Yeah, it was a crazy day.'

'I know you were nervous about competing. Is the bake-off going well?'

Tish untangled herself from Schuyler's embrace and wandered over to the cupboard, where she retrieved two earthenware coffee mugs. 'The bake-off is fine. I submitted what was, quite possibly, the best tarragon chicken I've ever made.'

'Go you,' he cheered. 'So, why do I feel as though there's a "but" coming?'

'Because despite the bake-off going well, there's a lot of weird stuff going on in the background,' she said.

Schuyler took the mugs from Tish and filled them with coffee. 'Weird stuff? What kind of weird stuff?'

Tish, clad in a pair of drawstring pajama pants and a coordinating tank top, ran her hands through her hair and went to the refrigerator to get some milk. 'I received an anonymous note demanding I quit the bake-off,' she stated reluctantly. After having been shot, the last thing she wanted was Schuyler thinking she was in danger. However, she couldn't lie to him either.

'And if you don't comply?'

'I would be next.' She poured some milk into her coffee and took a swig.

'What does "next" mean?' Schuyler asked as he poured some sugar into his coffee and gave it a stir.

'Oh, there's rumor of a curse at the bake-off. The curse of the cherry pie.' She raised her hands and wiggled her fingers for effect. 'Apparently, the last two women slated to bake a cherry pie both died unexpectedly before the bake-off was even over.'

'You don't believe in all that curse nonsense, do you?'

'Of course not. Curses don't leave threatening notes.'

'You should probably call the police.'

'Already done. Kitty Flournoy, the bake-off chair, called Sheriff Lightbody.' Tish took another sip from her mug.

'Good. I met Sheriff Lightbody at a meeting yesterday. He seems like just the man to get to the bottom of that note.'

Tish nearly spat her coffee out of her mouth. 'Did we meet the same person?'

'OK, I know Lightbody's a little rough around the edges—'

'Rough around the edges? He makes porch boy from *Deliverance* look like a *GQ* model who attended Oxford.'

'Funny,' Schuyler replied sarcastically. 'Look, I get that he's not polished, but his resumé is pretty damn impressive. He's the take-no-prisoner kind of law enforcement we need around here.'

'You're right about taking no prisoners. He certainly didn't take any prisoners at the civic center yesterday. In fact, he dismissed my note as a prank and left as quickly as he could. It's only because of Kitty Flournoy's influence that he left Officer Clayton behind to play watchdog.'

'Lightbody has decades of experience. I'm sure if he thought you were in any danger, he'd have his whole crew there in a heartbeat.'

'Yeah, I'm not so sure about that,' Tish disputed under her breath.

'Honey, he's a professional. He might be gruff, but he delivers results.'

'And crashes funerals. That's how I met Lightbody, you know. He crashed the funeral luncheon for Lloyd Rufus and had the audacity to expect a free cup of coffee.'

'So he didn't graduate from charm school. At least I'm not

worried about you getting shot in the back while he's on duty,' Schuyler spat back before taking another sip of coffee.

Tish saw red. 'My being shot was no one's fault but the person who pulled the trigger. No one asked me to get involved in that case. I did it of my own free will.'

'But a better policeman wouldn't have let you do it.'

'That's not fair,' Tish seethed. 'Reade saved my life.'

'After he jeopardized it in the first place.'

Tish slammed her coffee mug on to the kitchen table and plopped on to a nearby chair, her arms folded across her chest. It had been nearly three months since the shooting and Schuyler's anger only seemed to have intensified. At times, it seemed that he was angry at Tish herself for having been shot, for the disruption in their daily lives.

Having been referred to a counselor by the doctor who cared for her in the hospital, Tish suggested that Schuyler join her on some sessions as a means to help him deal with the trauma and his caregiving burdens, but he had declined. Schuyler was already behind at work and on the campaign trail. He had no more time to lose if he were to secure a win.

Schuyler sighed, running his fingers through his sand-colored hair. 'Look, I'm sorry I lashed out. There's a lot of pressure on me these few weeks before the April election. I need to get my polling numbers up.'

'I understand,' Tish murmured.

Several seconds of silence ensued. 'What's your schedule for today?' she asked, in an attempt to salvage the conversation.

'Same as yesterday. I have meetings at the firm first thing, then I'm on the trail. I'll be at the local VFW talking about a new veteran's support bureau in the town hall, then it's off to the senior center for lunch, the Women's League of Voters at two, a childcare center at four, a press conference at five, an American Bar Association dinner on my behalf at seven, and then it's a staff meeting at campaign headquarters to discuss our fundraising dinner a week from this Friday.'

'A fundraising dinner?' This was the first Tish had heard of the event.

'Yeah, the coffers are getting low. Too low to carry us on the last sprint, so we invited my biggest supporters to a complimentary dinner where they can pledge their final contributions.' He took a seat opposite her.

'How many people have you invited?'

'About a hundred.'

Tish took a sip of coffee and briefly pondered the situation. 'Next week is short notice for a crowd that size, but if I get my order in with suppliers by the end of the week, I can do a lovely spring dinner. I'm thinking a starter of stuffed artichokes, then a main of roast wild salmon, baby greens with lemon and mint, and dilled new potatoes and, for the vegan option, a broad bean and pea risotto. Maybe some lemon tarts for the dessert? I'll talk to Celestine. She may even be able to make them gluten-free.'

'Tish, we already hired a caterer,' Schuyler responded matter-of-factly.

Tish couldn't believe her ears. 'You already hired someone?'

'We did. You've been so busy lately and, quite honestly, I don't want you in the kitchen for this event. I want you by my side, as the future first lady of Hobson Glen.' He smiled.

'I could have been at your side and still have catered the dinner. I would have prepared everything in advance and left Mary Jo in charge of the serving staff and Jules in charge of the drinks. I did it before, when you made your mayoral bid public.'

'I know. And it was . . . it was great. Really. But my opponent brings her husband to every event she holds. He doesn't say or do much, but he's there being supportive. You haven't been with me at any of my speaking engagements or my community visits.'

'You haven't asked me.' Tish's blue eyes flashed. 'I told you from the beginning that if you needed me to take a day away from the café, all you had to do was ask and I'd be there like lightning.'

'Well, I'm asking you now. I need you at this donor dinner.'

'But you don't need me at the American Bar Association dinner tonight? Which, just like the fundraising dinner, I knew nothing about until now.'

'The ABA dinner is boring if you're not a lawyer. And you're always so busy with catering jobs and the café. You're in the middle of a bake-off competition right now, for cripes' sake.'

'When did you know about the ABA dinner?' Tish countered.

Schuyler flushed red. 'A month ago.'

'One month ago, the bake-off wasn't even on my radar. And, as for being generally busy, my café closes at four every day and I've yet to have a Wednesday-night catering job since I've opened.'

'OK, I'm sorry I didn't invite you to the dinner tonight. But I do need you at that fundraiser. My staunchest supporters need to see that I have a partner who loves this town as much as they do.'

'If your staunchest supporters know anything about me – and they should, as they frequent my café – they know that I support our local library's literacy campaign, donate food to the inter-faith center soup kitchen, and give discount rates to nonprofits who want to use my café for their meetings. I'm not sure how much more I can do to prove that I love Hobson Glen.'

'I think they have some questions about you and your . . . hobbies.' Schuyler cleared his throat.

'Hobbies?'

'You lead an unconventional life, Tish. Running off chasing crimes while running . . . not just a café but a literary café.'

'My café is popular,' Tish defended. 'And I don't "chase" crimes. They seem to find me. And a good thing too, since I've managed to help solve three murders.'

'Do you hear yourself? This is what I'm talking about. Hobson Glen residents are simple and down-to-earth people. They expect the partner of the mayor to be at his or her side offering support, like Laurie Villanueva's husband does.'

Interim mayor and Schuyler's opponent, Laurie Villanueva, was married to a retired pediatrician. 'Laurie Villanueva's husband doesn't work, Schuyler. He has time to follow his wife around town all day.'

'Maybe we need to free up a bit more of your time,' he suggested. 'Maybe we need to start seriously looking at you closing the café an extra day each week. You know, just so you can be around more during the last few weeks of the campaign.'

'We said we'd think about that if it wound up we weren't spending enough time together,' Tish clarified.

'Well, if I'm saying I need you on the campaign trail, then we're obviously *not* spending enough time together.'

Tish threw her head back and stared at the ceiling as if it might provide an answer. She hadn't anticipated closing on Sundays so soon after making her offer. She had only just introduced her ten-dollar hot Sunday lunch that winter, featuring such home-style favorites as roast chicken, pot roast, and Virginia baked ham, all served up with potatoes, gravy, and seasonal vegetables. For many of the elderly residents of Hobson Glen and its neighboring communities, Sunday lunch at the café – served family-style at long tables – was the only home-cooked meal and socialization they enjoyed after a long week spent living alone. Tish thought she had at least a few weeks before she was faced with the decision to end an event that had brought such joy to so many in such a short period of time. 'I have to give it some thought, Schuyler. It's not as if I can suddenly put a sign on the door saying I'll be closed on Sundays. I'm booked for lunch the next few Sundays, and then there's a group of widows who meets in the morning prior to services.'

'Well, they'll all just have to find somewhere else to go,' he stated.

'Since the Bar and Grill closed, there is nowhere else in town for them to meet, apart from each other's homes.'

'Then they'll have to meet there. Tish, I need you by my side.'

'OK, I'll join you at the fundraiser as a guest and not the caterer,' Tish capitulated. 'But I need to get through the bake-off before I can make any decisions about closing the café on Sundays or any other day of the week. There are too many customers to consider. Understood?'

'Yes, thank you, hon. I knew you'd come around.' He rose from his seat and kissed her on the forehead.

'Out of curiosity, who did you hire to cater the fundraiser?'

'Lemaire.'

'The best restaurant in Richmond,' she noted. 'That's pretty swank.'

'Well, if we're trying to pry a sizable check out of these peoples' hands, we need to give them the absolute best.'

'The absolute best.' She frowned. 'Yes, you're right. I suppose they do deserve that.'

TEN

S chuyler went to the law office shortly after finishing their conversation, leaving Tish to drink coffee and prepare for her day. Schuyler hiring a fancy restaurant to cater his fundraiser, combined with his demand that she close the café on Sundays, had sent her into a tailspin. A mental state she needed to emerge from before competing at the bake-off later that morning. Deciding she'd rather not hang around the condo any longer than necessary, she showered, made the bed, dressed in her standard catering ensemble, and set off for the café.

There she was surprised to find not Mary Jo behind the counter, serving the café breakfast crowd, but Celestine Rufus. She was dressed in her usual combination of bright floral-print blouse, denim capri pants, white sneakers, and pink-framed glasses that coordinated with her cherry-red hair.

'Hey, Celestine,' Tish greeted. 'I didn't expect to see you here. How are you?'

'Oh, hey, honey.' The two women embraced. 'I'm OK. Came down here to try and keep myself busy. I can't stand watchin' those mornin' news shows my daughter has on before work. A far too depressin' way to start the day. Good thing I was here, too. Kayla was running late, so Mary Jo drove her down to school. She should be back in a few minutes.'

'I can help out while I'm here if you need it.'

'Nah, I'm good. It's a quiet mornin'.'

Tish went to the coffee machine and poured herself a cup. 'Want some?'

'Already had two. Drink any more and I'll be in the ladies' room the rest of the mornin'. So, what brings you by?'

'I had some extra time on my hands, so I thought I'd check in before I head to the bake-off.' Tish helped herself to one of Celestine's exquisite lemon and blackberry scones.

'I'm surprised you're not spendin' that extra time at home with Schuyler. He's a lot better-lookin' than I am,' Celestine chuckled.

'Schuyler's been in the office by seven every morning.'

'Campaign stuff?'

Tish broke off a piece of scone and devoured it. 'Normal job stuff. The rest of the day is for the campaign. He got home at midnight last night.'

'I remember those days when Lloyd was first gettin' his business off the ground. To gain new customers, he offered emergency service at no extra charge. People as far as fifteen miles away were callin' him at all hours to find out why their boiler had switched off or why they had no hot water. It was a good move for buildin' a business and a reputation, but it wasn't so good for keepin' a marriage alive.' Celestine sprayed down the empty end of the counter with antibacterial cleanser. 'How are you and Schuyler makin' it through all this?'

Tish wasn't about to complain about her love life to a recent widow. 'We're fine. We make sure we have coffee together in the morning and I try to be awake when he gets home, but I'll be spending more time on the campaign trail the next few weeks, so that will be nice.'

Celestine wiped the counter area she'd just sprayed with a wet cloth. 'You're hittin' the campaign trail?'

'Not exactly hitting the trail, but I'll be participating more than I have been. It all starts next week with a fundraising dinner.' She took another bite of scone and washed it down with a swig of coffee.

'A dinner? How fun! Whatcha gonna make? Do you need me to bake a dessert?'

'Actually, I'm not catering it. Schuyler hired one of the best restaurants in Richmond to do the job.' Tish pasted on a brilliant smile, despite still feeling hurt by Schuyler's actions. 'I'm there as a guest.'

Celestine stopped cleaning and gazed at Tish over the top of her glasses. 'How do you feel about that?'

'I'm great,' Tish lied. 'It will be fun to attend an event where I'm waited on for a change.'

'Well, you're a bigger person than I am. In my family, I'm

the cake lady. That means whether it's a birthday, Christmas, a weddin', anniversary, a shower, or just a plain ol' family supper, I'm the one bringin' the cake. If they were to order one in, I'd be mighty offended.'

'I admit I was surprised at first.' Tish lowered her guard slightly as she ate a few crumbs of scone. 'But now I'm really looking forward to it. I have a bunch of dresses in my closet that I haven't worn in ages. It'll be nice to drag them out of storage and try them on again. Providing they still fit.'

'They'll be fine,' Celestine assured her as she went back to her cleaning. 'Gotta admit, I'm surprised at Schuyler for choosin' such a fancy place to cater his dinner. I was best friends with his mama, and he was raised to be practical. Hirin' a caterer from Richmond when you're lookin' to be the mayor of Hobson Glen ain't sensible. He should have hired someone local.'

'Yeah, but I'm the only local left now that the Hobson Glen Bar and Grill shut down. I mean, there's the place in the center of town that does Thai and Chinese, but it's strictly take-out.'

'That's what I'm sayin'. It doesn't make sense for Schuyler to hire someone other than you. I don't know who's investin' in his campaign, but I do know who he wants to vote for him. They're the folks who come in here for a breakfast of fried eggs and toast and who used go to the Bar and Grill for a burger and a beer on Fridays. They ain't fancy folk.'

'Yes, but Schuyler's law firm is in Richmond. I'm sure he's picked up a few donors there.'

'Maybe,' Celestine allowed. 'But they can't all be from the city. I'm sure some local businesses are donatin' as well. And when they see he isn't supportin' a local business run by his own girlfriend, well, it will make them question if he'll support them and their businesses.'

'You do have a point,' Tish agreed. 'The optics aren't very good, are they?'

Celestine shook her head. 'Besides, people love your food. They'd be grinnin' ear to ear if you served up a Virginia baked ham and some cornbread, or a few of your famous herbed roast chickens with dressin'. That's why we're booked for lunch every Sunday.'

At the mention of Sunday lunch, Tish winced. Thankfully, Celestine didn't appear to notice.

'Hey, everybody,' MJ greeted as she breezed through the front door of the café. She stepped behind the counter, washed her hands, and tied an apron around her waist. 'Sorry about the school run, Celestine. Kayla must have tried on three outfits while getting ready this morning. She would have changed another three times if I hadn't intervened.'

'No problem, honey,' Celestine dismissed. 'I've been there with my two daughters and now I'm witnessin' it with theirs.'

'How'd you sleep last night?' MJ asked Tish.

'Like a log,' Tish answered and ate the final piece of scone. 'I didn't even hear Schuyler come in.'

'Well, that's not safe when you're—' MJ started, before remembering that Celestine hadn't been informed of the note.

'When I'm alone late at night?' Tish quickly inserted. 'That's why we have an alarm system. Well, I'd best be skedaddling. I don't want to be late for the bake-off. It's showstopper bake day.'

'Really?' Celestine became animated. 'What's your showstopper?'

'Miss Havisham's wedding cake, from—'

'*Great Expectations.*' Celestine filled in the blank. 'I remember it from my school days. That should be good and creepy. Send me photos when you're done.'

'I will,' Tish promised.

'And, Tish,' Celestine added before the caterer could head out the door, 'thank you, again, for doin' this.'

'You've already thanked me. Many times, and most recently with mac and cheese, which was delicious, by the way. We're good.' Tish waved a quick goodbye to Celestine and MJ and exited the café through the front door. As she crossed the parking lot to the red Toyota Matrix, Tish bumped headlong into Hobson Glen's library director, Daryl Dufour.

'Tish Tarragon,' Dufour exclaimed as he pushed his bifocals back on to the bridge of his nose. Small in stature and bearing a definitive middle-age paunch, Daryl Dufour was dressed in typical librarian fashion: plaid button-down shirt, tan sports coat with elbow patches, khakis, and loafers. 'Just the person I wanted to see. Do you have a minute or two to spare?'

Tish glanced at her phone. 'Just about. What is it?'

'I want to ask you about Miss Celestine.'

'Oh, well, she's inside, working the counter this morning. You can ask her how she's doing yourself.'

'No, I – I need to speak with you before I see her.' Daryl lifted his hand and nervously smoothed his slicked-back dark-blonde hair, which was graying at the temples.

'OK,' Tish agreed. 'Go ahead.'

'I want to help Miss Celestine through her loss. As you know, she means – well, I care about her a great deal, and . . .'

Tish knew of the torch Daryl still held for Celestine – a remnant of the lengthy courtship they had enjoyed in their youth. 'I know how you feel about Celestine, Daryl. You needn't explain.'

A look of relief passed across Daryl's face. 'Thank you, Tish. Since you know how I feel, you can imagine how awkward it is to try to console Miss Celestine in a manner that's appropriate. I don't want her, or anyone else, to think that I'm eager to take Lloyd's place. At least, not any time in the near future. If there came a day when Miss Celestine found it in her heart to love me, I would be a very happy man, but, until then, I respect her need to grieve. I just want to be there for her, that's all.'

'And you should be there for her. Celestine told me how you loaned her money when Lloyd was out of work due to a back injury. You've always been a good friend to her. Right now, you just need to keep on being that good friend. Ask her what she needs. She'll let you know how you can help, even if that help means you listening and doing nothing more.' Tish smiled. 'I hope that helps.'

'It does. And speaking of good friends, Miss Celestine has a great one in you. So do I.' He gave her arm a friendly squeeze.

'Aw, thanks. You and everyone else in this town have done a great job of making me feel at home in such a short period of time.' She glanced at the time on her phone again. 'Sorry, Daryl, but I had better run. I need to get to the bake-off.'

'Oh, yes. I heard you were competing on Miss Celestine's behalf. Good luck in bringing home that prize money and I'll see you next Friday.'

Tish was about to turn on one heel and head for her car, but Daryl's comment stopped her in her tracks. 'Next Friday?'

'Yes, the planning meeting for the library's summer programs. Remember, you're presenting your ideas for literary-inspired kids' cooking classes.'

'Oh, yes. That's right. I forgot it was next week.' Not just next week, but the same night as Schuyler's fundraiser.

'Yes, we've rescheduled it twice now. First, from two months ago, when Augusta May had just come down with the flu, and then again from last month, when our recording secretary had her baby. Now it's critical that we get moving. There's barely three months until schools close down for the summer.'

Tish was about to mention Schuyler's fundraiser, but she'd already committed to the meeting and the summer programs months ago. With so little time left before summer, how could she not attend? And yet she'd promised Schuyler she'd be by his side at the fundraiser. Perhaps she could arrive at the dinner later, after the meeting – if it didn't run too long.

However, would that count – in Schuyler's eyes – as being by his side? Time would only tell.

'Tish,' Daryl prompted. 'You OK? You are coming to the meeting, aren't you? We need you there.'

'Hmm?' Tish snapped from her reverie. 'Yes, of course I'll be there, Daryl. I promised I would.'

ELEVEN

Tish pulled the Matrix into the civic center parking lot at a quarter past eight in the morning. The first two rows of spaces were already full as contestants, judges, and volunteers arrived for the day's competition.

A yellow Chevrolet Spark pulled into the spot to Tish's right. Its driver appeared to be waving, but the tinted windows of the vehicle made it difficult to ascertain precisely who that driver might be.

The mystery was solved as Riya Patel stepped out from

behind the driver's wheel. She was wearing yet another magnificent sari, this time in red and gold, and a pair of aviator sunglasses. 'Good morning, Tish.'

'Good morning, Riya,' Tish responded as she pressed the Matrix's lock button on her key fob.

'Ready for the showstopper bake?'

'As ready as I'll ever be,' Tish answered as the two women made their way to the civic center's main entrance.

'I'm somewhat surprised to see you here this morning, Tish,' Riya confided. 'What with what happened to you yesterday.'

'Yesterday?' Tish feigned ignorance.

'Yes, I read Kitty's email this morning. You received a threatening note.'

Kitty had issued an announcement stating that a bake-off contestant had been threatened and asking those with any knowledge of the incident to cooperate with the police. However, the announcement did not disclose the identity of the threatened participant.

Tish stopped walking and stared at Riya. 'Kitty's email didn't name names. How did you know it was me?'

Riya stopped and looked Tish in the eye. 'Dolly, Gordon, and I saw you leaving Kitty's office after the break. We saw the sheriff leave her office as well.'

'So much for anonymity,' Tish deadpanned.

'Are you OK?' Riya inquired.

'I'm as well as can be expected.'

'Do the police know anything?'

'Only that the note was left by someone here at the bake-off. And,' she added, even though it was her opinion and not that of the police, 'that it probably has something to do with the deaths of Lillian Harwood and Penelope Purdue.'

'Really?' Riya's brow furrowed and her voice grew anxious. 'Someone from the bake-off. Are you positive?'

'Yes, the note was left while the civic center was closed to the public.'

Riya bit her lip and gazed down at the floor.

'What is it?' Tish prompted.

'Well, I like Dolly. She's been so nice to me since I started competing, but—'

Tish raised a questioning eyebrow.

'She's highly competitive. To the utmost extreme.'

'How so?'

'Everything. She's been a bake-off contestant for years now and feels that she's overdue for a first-place win, but her competitiveness goes beyond that. From being the first to have devised a recipe to having the best baking pans at home – far better than the ones here – to having the best family. She and Lillian actually got into a fight just before the showstopper bake because of Dolly's competitiveness.'

'What happened?'

'Lillian was baking that mountain cake I told you about yesterday. It was inspired by her grandchildren's drawings. It was a labor of love for Lillian and she was extremely proud of her interpretation. She showed us the drawings her grandchildren came up with and photos of the grandchildren themselves. Well, not to be outdone, Dolly pulled out her phone and started showing photos of *her* grandchildren, saying how much better-looking they were than Lillian's grandchildren. And smarter, too.'

'Ouch,' Tish remarked.

'Yeah. Lillian got even, though. She asked Dolly if any of her grandchildren had been bullied at school due to their abnormally large heads.'

'What? Whoa.'

Riya nodded. 'To say that Dolly was livid is an understatement.'

Livid enough to want Lillian dead? Tish wondered to herself. 'What about Penelope Purdue? Did Dolly have any issues with her?'

'She thought Pen was a busybody. She was always asking about our recipes or about Lillian. She talked a lot about Lillian, come to think of it. In a way, I think Lillian had become a mother figure to Pen during their first bake-off. She was hit hard by Lillian's death,' Riya reflected.

'Well, you can hardly hold a grudge against someone for that, can you?'

'Depends on the questions she's asking, I suppose.' Riya grinned and started, once again, for the civic center. 'Dolly also didn't care much for Pen because she was a bake-off newbie.'

'But she died during her second bake-off. She wasn't a newbie,' Tish argued.

'Tell that to Dolly. Unless you've been here five years or more, you're a newbie. And Dolly doesn't much like newbies, especially newbies who earn more points for a dish than she does. I learned that the hard way.'

'I'll keep that in mind.' The pair entered the civic center and, after passing through the metal detectors, approached the board listing the judges' ratings of the previous day's bake. Tish was in second place, just two points behind Whitney Liddell and one-third of a point ahead of Dolly Pritchard.

'Way to go,' Riya congratulated.

'Thanks. Dolly's not going to be happy about this, is she?' Riya shook her head.

'Unhappy enough to leave a threatening letter?' Tish asked.

Riya smiled. 'I would say it is a distinct possibility.'

After Riya departed for the ladies' room, Tish traveled to her booth. On the way, she was intercepted by Gordon Quinn. 'Morning,' he greeted.

'Good morning, Gordon,' she replied.

'How'd you sleep last night?'

Tish thought the question odd and somewhat creepy, given she'd been left a threatening anonymous note. 'OK,' she answered reluctantly.

'You have gumption coming back here this morning.'

'Gumption?'

'Most folks would have dropped out of the bake-off after getting a warning like you did.'

'I guess I'm not like most folks.'

'No, you aren't. I thought you looked familiar when we met yesterday, so I Googled your name when I got home. Seems you fancy yourself a detective.' Quinn's tone was condescending.

'I don't fancy myself anything other than a cook. I just happen to have a knack for uncovering the truth.'

'Well, here's a little truth for you: Riya Patel is the author of your note.' Gordon stuck his hands into the pockets of his dark blue Carhartt duck jacket and swallowed his top lip with the bottom one, in a gesture of self-satisfaction.

'Oh?' Tish prompted.

'Riya has a lot of pent-up anger because folks here at the bake-off don't really understand her food. You heard how her samosas were passed over by the judges? That's just the tip of the iceberg. She's constantly being overlooked. Not out of spite, but ignorance. Judge Riya's creations against other Indian food and you realize how great her skills are. I know, I spent some time in India. But judging her against Western recipes isn't very fair to her.'

'So why would she leave a note telling me to drop out of the contest?'

'Because you're another white woman denying her the trophy.'

Tish didn't quite buy the explanation. 'And the cherry pie?'

'Cherry pie is a quintessential American dessert. George Washington's favorite. And Riya is a foreigner.'

'Really?' Tish sighed and set off for the exhibition hall.

'Wait,' Gordon called after her.

She stopped and turned around. 'If your only reason for accusing Riya is because she wasn't born in this country—'

'No, you got me wrong. I told you I spent time overseas when I was in the Navy. That sort of travel opens a man's eyes and mind. I'm just saying that Riya feels as though she's gotten short shrift from the bake-off judges. And I would agree that she has. She's a very talented baker. She also happens to be here on a mission.'

'A mission?'

'Riya and her husband own a catering business in Richmond. They run it out of their house because they can't afford the overhead of owning an actual restaurant or shop. They've managed to build a decent business serving the Indian community, but she wants to branch out to other neighborhoods. Winning the bake-off would take her far in that endeavor. Not only would the cash prize help fund the marketing campaign, but being the winner of such a time-honored event would cement her reputation statewide. She'd be a critically acclaimed cook and baker instead of someone you call to cater your next Bollywood-themed party. That's why she keeps competing,'

Gordon went on, 'but the closest she's ever gotten in five years is third place.'

'So she's writing threatening notes to scare off the competition?'

'No, it's the pent-up anger I told you about. Riya was hopeful at first that she'd win the bake-off. I've witnessed that hope dissipate each passing year as she realizes that the judges and the committee members will never allow a non-white woman to be the winner, and thereby the "face," of the deeply Southern, deeply conservative Virginia Commonwealth Bake-Off.' Gordon paused and stared off into the distance. 'Any more than they'll allow a man.'

'Gordon Quinn suffers from PTSD from his time in the military,' Dolly Pritchard whispered to Tish as she leaned over the partition that separated the two women's booths.

'PTSD doesn't make people leave other people threatening letters, Dolly,' Tish argued.

'It doesn't make them not write them, either. If his mental state is precarious enough, Lord knows what the man might do.' Dolly pulled the hem of her spring-green cardigan down over her ample hips.

'But what motive would Gordon have for trying to scare me off?' Tish challenged.

'In case you hadn't noticed, Gordon isn't a fan of the fairer sex.'

Tish thought back to his words abut Riya and his condescending attitude toward her detective work, as well as his lament about a man being unable to win the competition. 'I hadn't, but now that you mention it, yes, he can be a bit patronizing.'

'He's been through a bad divorce,' the older woman stated with an authoritative nod.

'Oh? He's told you about it?'

'No, but I asked him once if he was married and he said he didn't want to talk about it. That screams "divorce" to me.' Dolly folded her arms across her chest and nodded.

Tish was about to point out that there might be other reasons Gordon Quinn wouldn't want to discuss his marital status, but she remembered Dolly's alleged competitive streak. 'For a guy who supposedly dislikes women, this is a strange place to spend four days each year.'

'Especially since he didn't take up cooking or baking until just a few years back,' Dolly said, adding fuel to the fire. 'Of course, it's not so strange if he wanted to terrorize the women here with threatening notes.'

'Notes?' Tish remarked upon the use of a plural noun.

'You didn't think you were the only one who was "special," did you?'

Tish felt her nose wrinkle. Receiving a threat made her feel far from special. 'Who else received a note?'

'A couple of contestants in recent years.'

'Would those contestants include Lillian Harwood and Penelope Purdue?'

'I don't know about Lillian – she ate lunch with us every day, but she wouldn't have confided in the likes of me – but I believe Pen got one, yes.'

'What did the note say? Do you remember?' Tish asked.

'Something similar to yours. "Stop baking the cherry pie or you're next." Or something to that effect.'

'Who else received a note, aside from Penelope Purdue?'

Dolly grinned. 'Me.'

Tish raised a skeptical eyebrow. Was Dolly telling the truth or was this an example of the one-upmanship Riya had described. 'You?'

'It was three years ago. I came back to my booth one morning, maybe on the second or third day of the bake-off, and there it was, stuck to my fridge with a magnet.'

The details Dolly recalled made it less likely that Dolly was concocting the story from the top of her head. 'Do you remember what the note said?'

'I'll never forget it. It said, "Change your menu or else."'

'Or else? Or else what?'

'It didn't say.'

'So, what did you do?'

Dolly shrugged. 'I went ahead with my menu.'

'Did you report this note to Kitty or anyone else?'

'No, I didn't see the point. It wasn't much of a threat, was it? "Or else"?'

Tish frowned. Unlike the note she had received, Dolly's wasn't much of a threat at all. 'What was your menu that year?'

Dolly cast her eyes upward in an effort to remember. 'Hmm. I went classic that year, I think. Yes, I did throwback recipes. Let's see . . . I started with Dutch oven Yankee pot roast, then a hummingbird wedding cake, and finally a revamped Tunnel of Fudge cake with salted caramel.'

'No cherry pie?'

'Nope. I'm allergic to cherries. Never touch 'em.'

'No, you wouldn't go near them, would you? Meanwhile, Penelope Purdue was allergic to nuts,' Tish recalled aloud.

'Allergic to nuts?' Dolly guffawed. 'I don't know where you got that information, but it's wrong. Her favorite lunch was sesame noodles with peanut sauce. She ate it every day she competed.'

'Even the day she died?

'Yep. Never knew her to eat anything else.'

Tish finished her conversation with Dolly and busied herself at her countertop while waiting for the judges' signal that the competition would begin. While waiting, she was approached by Jules, who had arrived to cover the day's events. He was wearing a beautifully tailored gray suit, white shirt, and black tie and pocket square. In his left arm, he cradled Biscuit who sported a matching black bow tie. In his right, he balanced a cardboard tray, bearing two cups of coffee.

'Hey,' he greeted as he thrust the tray in Tish's direction.

'Hey. Thanks for this.' She availed herself of the cup closest to her and took a sip. 'Mmm, this is good. Where did you get it?'

'Your café. I missed you by about thirty minutes.'

Tish extricated Jules's cup and watched as he tossed the tray in a nearby trashcan before passing it to him.

'So, what do you think of Walter?' he posed.

'Who's Walter?'

'My potential new middle name. Julian Walter Davis. You know, Walter as in Walter Cronkite, the preeminent journalist of the twentieth century.'

Tish gazed at him and pulled a face. 'You're a little too flamboyant to be a Walter, don't you think?'

Jules appeared to weigh this statement. 'Hmm, you know, I think you're right. Damn. How are you doing this morning?'

'Meh.' Tish was still unsettled by her discussion with Schuyler.

'Want to talk about it?'

'Not right now. My head's still spinning after talking to my bake-off lunch buddies this morning. They sent me in a complete circle. Each of them accuses the other of writing the note. Riya blames Dolly. Dolly blames Gordon. Gordon blames Riya.'

'Did you learn anything new?'

'A few things.' Tish recounted the bakers' stories. 'Oh,' she added when she'd finished, 'and Penelope Purdue ate sesame noodles with peanut sauce the day she died. In fact, she ate it for lunch each day that she competed.'

'So it's not just the bastilla that's incongruous with the allergy story.'

'No, but sesame noodles can also be made with tahini for those with nut allergies, so even though Dolly states they were made with peanuts, unless we know for certain what version Penelope ate, it still doesn't prove anything.'

'But it does, once again, call her supposed nut allergy into question,' Jules asserted.

'Which is why I hope Clayton gets a move on checking into the circumstances surrounding Penelope's hospital visit.' She sighed. 'What I don't get is if Gordon, Riya, and Dolly are so eager to win this contest, why leave a note threatening me? Why not threaten Whitney Liddell?'

'Have you seen Whitney Liddell's booth?'

'No, where is it?'

'Three aisles over, in the corner. And when it's not surrounded by the adoring public, it's under the watchful eye of reporters and security guards. The Flash himself couldn't deposit a note there without being seen.'

Tish's eyes narrowed. 'Security guards?' *Had Whitney Liddell received threatening letters, too?*

'Well, not security guards in uniforms or anything official like that,' Jules clarified. 'But I tried to sneak into enough clubs back in the late nineties to know what a couple of big, bald, no-neck guys dressed in black mean.'

'Why does Whitney Liddell need security guards? She doesn't have that many fans, does she?'

'Not sure, but when you endorse as many products and companies as she does, I imagine plenty of folks will go out of their way to keep you alive.'

'There might also be plenty of folks who wish you dead or, at the very least, out of the competition,' Tish replied.

'You think Whitney may have been threatened?'

'I think it's entirely possible, but there's only one way to find out.' She motioned toward Jules with her left hand and stated in her best television announcer voice, 'We now turn you over to Channel Ten's Julian Jeff— I mean, Julian Davis.'

'You know I'll do my best to get the scoop,' Jules promised.

'I have every confidence you will.' Tish smiled and drank her coffee.

The pair were soon joined by Officer Jim Clayton. He was dressed in a casual ensemble of sneakers, jeans, a white polo shirt, and the jacket he'd worn to Tish's condo the previous evening. He came bearing a cardboard tray holding three recyclable white cups.

'Morning, Jim. Out of uniform, I see,' Tish noted.

'Yeah, I realized if I'm supposed to catch the note-writer in the act, I should probably blend in with the crowd.' He thrust the tray of cups forward. 'Coffee?'

Tish took Clayton up on his offer, even though her right hand still clutched a half-full cup. 'Sure. It's going to be a long day.'

Jules swigged back the contents of his cup, tossed it in the trash bin, and helped himself to the fresh cup offered by Clayton. 'Thanks. Don't mind if I do.'

'If I'm not mistaken,' Tish said after taking a sip and a closer look at the cup, 'this is from my café.'

Clayton colored slightly. 'We're not supposed to visit your café – Lightbody's rules – but since he's not here . . .'

'He'll be none the wiser,' Tish said, completing the thought.

'To call Lightbody "wiser" is to assume he was wise in the first place,' Jules cracked.

'I don't want to diss the guy,' Clayton prefaced, 'but he's not very popular down at headquarters.'

'Gee, I can't imagine why. I'd have thought he'd be the highlight of every party. He already knows how to brighten up a funeral.'

In response to Clayton's puzzled expression, Tish recounted how she first met Sheriff Lightbody while hosting a funeral luncheon at her café.

'I'm not surprised. Miss Enid Kemper called us to her place over the weekend. Langhorne had flown up on to the roof of her house and she couldn't persuade him to come down. Sheriff Lightbody yelled at the poor woman for taking up valuable police time. I secretly texted another officer to swing by and help her after we'd left.' Clayton shook his head. 'Sheriff Reade would have climbed up on to that roof himself, but I don't think Sheriff Lightbody understands the "serve" part of "to protect and serve."'

Clayton's statement about the former sheriff was quite accurate. Tish recalled how Reade had once scaled a tall magnolia tree to retrieve Langhorne, only to have the bird fly off of his own volition, leaving Reade to climb back down on a shaky ladder while Enid administered Langhorne's nightly bath and blow-dry.

'Anyway,' Clayton segued, 'I called Chippenham Hospital first thing this morning to check on the circumstances surrounding Penelope Purdue's visit to the emergency room. The nurse I spoke to emailed me the admitting form and, apparently, Ms Purdue was wearing a medical alert bracelet when she arrived at the ER that night. The bracelet warned that she was allergic to nuts.'

'Well, that would explain why it was listed as the cause of death,' Tish said. 'Did you find out anything else?'

'No. The admitting nurse on duty that night isn't scheduled to work until noon. She's supposed to call me just as soon as she arrives at the hospital, but if she doesn't, I'll call over there again.'

'Thanks for looking into this so quickly,' Tish said appreciatively.

'No worries. Better than standing around here people-watching all day on the off-chance the letter-writer stops by again. If Sheriff Reade were still here—' Clayton stopped himself. 'Well, you know.'

Tish and Jules silently nodded.

'How about you two? Did you find out anything new before I got here?'

'Funny you ask. I was approached by not one, not two, but all three of my lunch buddies this morning. Each of them presented a theory as to who might have written that note,' Tish explained.

'Oh?'

'Yeah, each other.'

A chime sounded and Kitty Flournoy's voice echoed through the exhibition hall.

'That's my cue. We're starting.' Tish drank back her first cup of coffee and passed the empty cup to Jules for disposal. 'Jules, fill Clayton in on this morning's happenings.'

'Sure,' Jules agreed with a nod.

'Without embellishment,' Tish stipulated.

'Embellishment? I'll have you know I'm a professional journalist.'

'Uh-huh.'

Jules clicked his tongue. 'All right, I won't add any of the dramatic flourishes that keep my audience engaged, but if Officer Clayton falls asleep, on your head be it.'

'I'll take my chances.' Tish dashed behind the counter of her booth and tied her apron around her waist. As on the previous morning, the ingredients for the day's baking had been neatly arranged on the work counter. While she awaited the signal to start baking, Tish made a mental check between the ingredients on the counter and those listed in her recipe. Everything appeared to be accounted for, but once given the signal to start, she'd make certain by double-checking against the printed recipe she had folded and placed into the back pocket of her black denim jeans.

Tish shifted her weight from side to side and drew a deep breath. The past sixteen hours, she'd been focused solely upon the note and the mysterious deaths of two bakers. Now, it was time to retrain that focus on the bake-off. With a slight lead over the other contestants and two points separating her from Whitney Lidell, a prize win in Celestine's name was within reach.

Concentrate, Tish told herself. *Just concentrate.*

Fortunately, the day's tasks were to bake the cake, fill it, and apply both the crumb coat and final coat of frosting. The more tedious decorating chores would take place tomorrow, thus giving Tish a chance to ease into the most difficult challenge of the competition.

'Bakers, get baking!' Kitty Flournoy announced as a loud bell chimed, signaling the start of the contest.

Tish pulled the recipe from her pocket and compared ingredients. Satisfied that everything was in order, she plopped the four sticks of softened unsalted butter into the bowl of the professional-grade stand mixer and then sprinkled in three cups of sugar.

Commencing with the first step of the recipe, Tish switched the mixer on to begin creaming the butter and sugar together. To her surprise, nothing happened.

She turned the mixer off and on again before she noticed that the unit was unplugged. Shaking her head and smiling at such an obvious oversight, she retrieved the heavy black power cord from the counter and plugged it into the nearby wall outlet.

Immediately upon contact, the socket made a sizzling sound and began to spark, sending a searing pain rushing from the tips of Tish's fingers, through her hand, and up the length of her arm. She knew she should let go of the offending power cord, but, for the moment, the ability to do so eluded her. After what seemed like a lifetime had elapsed, she loosened her grip and jumped backward with a shriek, allowing the cable to drop to the counter. No sooner had she let go of the cord than there was a loud bang and hers and the other booths in her row went dark.

'Tish!' Jules shouted as he rushed forward. 'Are you OK?'

He was followed closely by Kitty Flournoy and Willadeane Scott.

Tish nodded and embraced her friend. 'I don't know what happened. I plugged in the mixer and I got a shock.'

'That wasn't just a shock,' Dolly Pritchard noted, leaning over the partition of her booth. 'You set the breakers off. Our whole row is out of power.'

'Ms Tarragon, are you sure you're all right?' Kitty asked. 'I've called the first-aid unit. They should be here any second.'

'That's not necessary. I'm just shaken up, that's all,' Tish assured.

'Well, I'd feel better if they take a look at you. We take every precaution to make sure our equipment is safe and functional. Unfortunately, even with our precautions, I'm afraid accidents do happen.'

'This wasn't an accident, Miss Flournoy,' Clayton corrected as he inspected the outlet and mixer. 'The power cord's been tampered with. Whoever did this did it on purpose.'

TWELVE

'Willadeane, get building maintenance in here. Have them fix the power outage and then tell them to inspect every single appliance and electrical outlet in every single booth,' Kitty Flournoy ordered as she paced furiously in front of her desk.

'But how can we do that with the bake-off going on?' Willadeane Scott argued as she pushed her glasses on to the bridge of her nose and rolled the sleeves of her oversized beige cardigan to her elbows.

'Because the bake-off isn't going to go on,' Kitty snapped. She was wearing yet another dark power-suit ensemble, this time with the added feminine touch of a pink, tie-neck blouse. 'Tell everyone that we're done for the day. We'll convene again tomorrow morning and forget this ever happened.'

In the corner of the room, Tish, flanked on either side by Clayton and Jules, was having her vital signs checked by a first-aid responder.

'But that means the bake-off will go through Saturday,' Willadeane argued.

'Yes, that's exactly what it means. I don't imagine you have a date, do you?' Kitty added, snidely.

'No, but some of our contestants are from out of town. They'll need an extra night of hotel accommodation.'

'So? We'll pay for those extra nights. It's cheaper than being sued by the family of an electrocuted baker.'

Willadeane gave a single nod and left the office.

'Desmond,' Kitty shouted. 'Desmond?'

Her young assistant stepped forward from his place near the large picture window. From the expression on his face, it was clear that if he could have disappeared behind the floor-length drapes that edged that window, he would have. 'Yes – yes, Kitty?'

'Call the company that manages the civic center. Tell them our event is running one day longer than anticipated.'

Desmond, wearing a gray suit and bright-purple shirt, gazed at his iPad in wonderment while he poked, tentatively, at some apps. 'Where would – where would I find the number?'

Kitty heaved a heavy sigh. 'Never mind, Desmond. Never mind. I'll make the call. You go out and round up the other volunteers. Tell them to gather up the ingredients and equipment from the bakers' booths and put them in storage for tomorrow morning, just as they would have this afternoon.'

This task was apparently more manageable for Desmond. With a vague smile and a single nod of the head, he departed the office.

'Why do I even keep him around?' Kitty watched him walk away before replying to herself with a cheeky grin, 'Oh, right. That's why.'

The first-aid worker tightened the cuff of a blood pressure monitor around Tish's forearm and instructed her to relax.

Kitty approached, smiling but anxious. 'How's our patient?'

'I feel fine,' Tish replied.

'Her vitals are strong,' the female first-aid responder added. 'I'm just taking a second reading of her blood pressure. The first was a little low, most likely due to shock – of the non-electrical variety.'

'Where is everyone off to? Clayton!' The voice of Sheriff Lightbody bellowed from the hallway outside Kitty's makeshift office.

The first-aid worker glanced at the digital readings on the blood pressure meter. 'Hmm, now you're on the higher side. That's strange.'

'A reaction to stress,' Tish explained.

'Are you experiencing stress right now?'

'No, but I will be in three . . . two . . . one.'

At the count of one, Lightbody appeared in the doorway.

'Sorry,' Clayton apologized to Tish. 'I had to call it in. I hoped he wouldn't show.'

'I understand.'

'Sir,' Clayton greeted his boss as he rose from his chair. 'I told you I had everything under control.'

'Under control? Is that why people are leaving here in droves? You should have locked the site down,' Lightbody criticized.

'I did. The team is scouring the booth for prints and any other evidence that might point to the perpetrator.'

'That's the booths. What about everybody else?'

'Sir, I was on the scene when it happened. I asked contestants and other people in the area if they noticed anyone suspicious entering or leaving Ms Tarragon's booth. Since no one reported seeing anything out of the ordinary, I allowed Miss Flournoy to decide how she wished to proceed. I have the contact information for every contestant and volunteer who was on the floor this morning in case I need to follow up on anything.'

'But what about the general public? In your haste to release everyone, you could have let the fella go.'

'With all due respect, Sheriff, the power cord to the mixer couldn't have been tampered with by a member of the public. I was at Tish's booth at a quarter to nine, just when ticket holders were being allowed to enter the exhibition hall. No one came near Tish's booth – not once.'

'Hardly any wonder why,' Lightbody guffawed.

'Nice to see you, too, Sheriff,' Tish replied sarcastically.

The first-aid worker removed the blood pressure cuff from Tish's arm and gave it a gentle, knowing pat before leaving the room. 'I see what you mean. Your pressure's fine.'

'The tampering must have been done before the start of baking,' Clayton continued, 'and the only people allowed in the exhibition floor before the start of baking are contestants, judges, and volunteers.'

Kitty Flournoy folded her arms across her chest defiantly. 'That's absurd. No one associated with the bake-off could be capable of such a thing.'

'And yet, given the timing of yesterday's letter and this morning's incident, it's the only explanation that makes sense.'

'Sense? None of this makes any sense at all,' Kitty volleyed. 'I asked you for help, Sheriff Lightbody. Help. One-tenth of the exhibition hall is dark, one of my bakers was almost electrocuted, the bake-off has to pay the civic center for an extra day's rent, and now, to top it all off, you're saying someone at the bake-off is responsible.'

'I didn't say that, Miss Flournoy. That's Officer Clayton's theory,' Lightbody said, throwing the junior officer under the proverbial bus. 'Now, personally, I think there's some crazy person tryin' to cause trouble for you folks.'

This response seemed to appease Kitty. 'That does seem more likely, Sheriff. But what will we do? Officer Clayton let everyone go.'

'You told me to let—' Clayton raised his voice, but then adjusted his tone. 'Miss Flournoy, it was your idea to let everyone go home.'

'That doesn't matter now, son,' Lightbody cajoled. 'Let's round 'em up before they get too far.'

'But, Sheriff—' Clayton again began to argue and was again shot down.

'Not now, Clayton. Miss Flurr-nay asked for our help. Let's give it to her.'

As Lightbody and Clayton exited the office and hurried back to the exhibition hall, Tish watched Kitty with intense interest. If the woman had a genuine interest in catching the individual terrorizing the bake-off, she would have realized Clayton's theory was the correct one and stuck by it. Instead, she let Sheriff Lightbody go off on a wild goose chase. Why? To protect the bake-off from negative publicity? Or to protect herself?

Tish was about to ask Kitty a few pointed questions when Whitney Liddell came storming through the office door. 'What the hell do you think you're doing shutting down the bake-off?' she demanded.

'It's only temporary,' Kitty comforted her. 'We'll be back on track tomorrow morning.'

'Yes, but we'll be here all day Friday and Saturday because of the delay.'

'Yeah, sorry about that, but it couldn't be helped.'

'Well, you should have run it past me first, Kitty. I have a victory commercial I'm supposed to film for Sheehy Brothers' Auto Sales this Saturday. What am I supposed to do about it now?'

A victory ad scheduled prior to Whitney actually winning the competition? Tish and Jules exchanged questioning glances. It was clear from the openness with which Whitney spoke that she hadn't noticed the pair seated in the back corner of the room.

'You're just going to have to postpone it, Whitney.' Kitty shrugged. 'I need to shut things down while the maintenance crew checks the electric work in all the booths.'

'*All* the booths? That's going a little overboard, don't you think? Just because some know-nothing newbie switched on her mixer with wet hands, it doesn't mean the rest of the bake-off is in danger,' Whitney scoffed.

Tish could remain silent no longer. Rising from her seat, she introduced herself. 'Hi, Tish Tarragon, owner of Cookin' the Books Café and Catering, aka the know-nothing newbie in question. Oh, and um, for the record, my hands were dry.'

Whitney blanched but was soon back on the attack. 'A professional? Kitty, don't we have rules against professionals competing?'

'That applies to professional chef training, Whitney. *As you know*,' Kitty added through clenched teeth. 'Ms Tarragon here is a self-taught cook.'

Whitney turned to Tish. 'Ah, did you train yourself to plug in electrical appliances, too?'

'That would be funnier if I weren't just two points behind you after the first round of baking,' Tish commented. 'So, tell me. Why does someone schedule to shoot a victory commercial before she's actually won the competition?'

'Simply planning for the inevitable.' Whitney smirked and clutched at the pearl choker that hung around her neck.

'Care to elaborate on that answer?' Jules stepped forward from his spot in the shadows, Biscuit beneath his arm.

Once again, Whitney blanched. 'Who are you?'

'Julian Davis, Channel Ten News.' He extended his hand. In it was a business card, the middle name struck out in black ink.

Whitney took it, a confused expression on her face.

'He's the reporter who was supposed to interview us during the lunch break, remember?' Kitty prompted. It was clear from her tone of voice that she was not entirely pleased with the attitude of the bake-off's biggest star.

'Oh, yes.' Whitney's color returned and she flashed a beatific smile. 'So nice to meet you, Mr Davis. Too bad we're adjourning for the day. I was so looking forward to our interview.'

'Why don't we do it now?' Jules suggested.

'Well, I—' Whitney slid her eyes toward Kitty.

'You were both scheduled to be here all day, so you couldn't possibly have other plans,' he pointed out.

'I'm not sure now's the right time,' Kitty said. 'What with everything going on.'

'Now's the perfect time. An interview gives you an opportunity to tell the public that you have everything under control, and that after a small delay to ensure the safety of your contestants, the bake-off will go ahead as scheduled, just as it has for decades.'

'I suppose you do have a point, but I'm not exactly sure what to say that will instill confidence.'

'Give it some time. Go call the civic center booking folks and do whatever you need to do right now and just let it take root in your brain while I speak with Whitney.'

'Whitney? But I thought this was a joint interview.' Kitty's eyes grew wide.

'No, I'm interviewing you separately to gain two different perspectives on the bake-off – one from a contestant, the other from an organizer. I thought it would be an interesting take.' Jules turned toward Whitney. 'Certainly, folks would want to hear about what's going on here from the star baker herself.'

Whitney nodded. 'I already have a lot of followers with whom I interact on a regular basis. However, it would be good for the bake-off if I could speak directly to my older fans who might not be comfortable on social media. They deserve to see me too.'

Tish felt her eyeballs roll into the back of her head, a reaction mirrored by Kitty Flournoy as she lifted the door handle of her makeshift office and left the room.

'Where's the camera crew?' Whitney asked, smoothing the skirt of her forest-green shirtdress and combing her shoulder-length, roller-set hair with her fingers.

'Couldn't get one on such short notice.' Jules extracted the latest iPhone from his jacket pocket and held it aloft. 'The station lets me use this for candid interviews. The quality of the video is incredibly good on its own, but it's even better with the right tricks from the production team.'

With Whitney's apprehensions eased, Jules arranged three chairs near the plate window and, after settling Biscuit on to one seat, sat down opposite the baker to begin the interview. 'So, where were we earlier? Ah, yes, that commercial.'

Whitney stared over Jules's shoulder. 'Why is *she* still here?'

Jules turned around to see Tish, seated in corner of the room, pretending to examine her phone. He cleared his throat.

'Hmm? What?' Tish looked up, her eyes wide and innocent. 'Oh, sorry. I'm just here resting and recuperating.'

'You can rest and recuperate in the hospitality suite,' he replied. 'They even have coffee there.'

Tish wrinkled her nose. She knew that Jules would get more information from Whitney if he and she were alone for their interview, but it didn't make leaving any easier. Picking her handbag off the floor, she made her way to the door as noisily as possible.

All the while, Whitney smiled triumphantly.

'OK, so that commercial,' Jules said, picking up the conversation thread once Tish had shut the door behind her. 'You must feel quite confident about winning this year's bake-off to have scheduled a celebratory advertisement in advance.'

Whitney bolted upright and looked directly into the camera with the poise of a seasoned actress. 'I'm always confident, but yes, this year I feel that I'm really on a winning trajectory. My menu is comforting, yet inspired. It's the kind of food that makes people feel good, but is just different enough to raise the judges' eyebrows.'

'Terrific. Would you care to share some of your menu with us?'

'I'm afraid I can't share the entire menu. I still have two days of competition left. But I can say that yesterday's savory bake was Cioppino, inspired by the honeymoon to San Francisco I took with my wonderful husband, Michael, eleven years ago. It's a light but hearty dish that's impressive enough to serve to your future mother-in-law or your husband's boss, yet easy enough to throw together for the family on a cold winter night.'

At Whitney's mention of mothers-in-law and dinners with the boss, Jules raised a questioning eyebrow. 'That . . . sounds delicious.'

'It is and very wholesome. The recipe can be found on the bake-off website, VACommwealthBakeOff.com, so everyone at home can give it a try.'

'Great. As you know, the bake-off has been postponed for a day due to an incident involving one of your fellow contestants. Are you at all concerned about your own safety?'

'Not at all. You know, Julian, this is a highly professional operation. One that's been around for eighty-five years now. The organizers of this event have nothing but the safety and wellbeing of their bakers at heart. They're taking the right steps to ensure this doesn't happen to anyone else.'

'And what about the so-called curse of the cherry pie?'

'Once again, any event as old and esteemed as this one is going to have its share of myths and legends.' Whitney smiled, but it was apparent she wasn't comfortable with the current line of questioning.

'What about the two bakers who died in recent years?'

'A tragedy.' She looked appropriately remorseful. 'I didn't have a chance to get know them – things are quite busy over at Whitney HQ, as I call it – but my heart goes out to their families.'

'Do you believe the two women's deaths might have been caused by the curse of the cherry pie?'

'Absolutely not. I believe their deaths were due to what's called coincidence, Julian.'

'Is it also coincidence that those two bakers were on course to win the competition?'

Whitney's mood turned sour. 'I don't know where you got that information, Mr Davis,' she said, relegating him to a last-name basis, 'but it's not true. In fact, it's patently ridiculous. In the past three years, no one's come close to beating me.'

'Actually, I have been told—' Jules started to cite his sources, but Whitney interrupted.

'Before I came along, the bake-off was in the middle of an identity crisis. It had lost sight of its roots and its place in Virginia's history. My win brought a return to the values that made this such a beloved event.'

'What values are those?'

'The values of family, hearth, and home, of course, but also the women who hold them together. Women these days are always out to prove themselves equal to men, but we're not equal. We never were and we never will be. The ability to bear children guarantees that we'll always be different. Being a wife and mother is a privilege no woman should ever diminish. The bake-off was founded to celebrate that privilege and the God-given gifts good women bring to households everywhere.'

Jules was speechless for several seconds. 'So am I correct in assuming that you believe many of the recent bake-off contestants aren't representative of the competition's founding values?'

'You're quite correct,' she answered, the smile returning to her face. 'I understand the bake-off's organizers' need to expand their audience, but in their attempt to be inclusive and accom-modating, they've lost sight of their founding principles. When the bake-off started, it was truly an event. Women from across the state put on their best dresses and presented their best dishes – the dishes they fed to their families and brought to church potlucks. Today, contestants, both male and female, are cooking in jeans and sneakers and making exotic recipes or trendy items such as quinoa and cauliflower rice. Sorry, but that's not what this is about. It's about good old-fashioned American women cooking good old-fashioned American comfort food.'

'And yet you're a social media influencer,' Jules challenged.

'Yes, but an influencer with a conservative outlook on life.'

'Do you think that conservative outlook gives you an advantage in this competition?'

'Definitely,' Whitney purred. 'I think people love seeing a woman who's not afraid to be feminine. A woman who lets her hair grow long and wears high heels and her finest dress and jewelry while taking care of her husband and family is refreshing in our era of yoga pants and ponytails.'

'Do you think that has an appeal with the judges?'

'I know it does. It doesn't hurt that I bring a little extra "something" to the table either.' What that something might have been, Whitney did not say. She merely winked, knowingly, into the camera.

Tish left the temporary bake-off offices and headed down the hall, still slightly miffed at having to leave while Jules conducted his interview of Whitney Liddell. Arriving at the hospitality suite, she grabbed one of the logoed bake-off mugs and placed it beneath the spigot of the single-serve coffee maker. 'There's coffee in the hospitality suite, too, Tish.' She mimicked Jules as she placed a pod in the machine and pressed the start button.

'Penny for your thoughts.' A familiar voice yanked Tish out of her funk and back to the civic center.

She spun around to see David Biederman standing in the doorway of the hospitality suite. He was dressed in a dark blue suit, striped shirt, and a red bow tie. 'Sorry, I didn't mean to startle you,' he apologized.

'That's OK. I must still be a little bit jumpy.'

'That's understandable. I'm sorry to hear what happened to you today. I'm also surprised to find you're still here.' He entered the suite and sat down at one of the round tables at which contestants enjoyed their lunch or coffee.

'Oh, just taking my time before I head back home,' she explained.

'Wise decision. If you're shaky, the last place you want to be is behind the wheel of an automobile. Are you all right otherwise?'

'Yes, clean bill of health.'

'Good. Considering the police have corralled everyone in the exhibition hall, I'm guessing your accident wasn't caused by a faulty wall outlet.'

'You're quite perceptive.' Tish grabbed the full mug of coffee from the Keurig and stirred in a packet of non-dairy creamer before removing the pod from the machine and discarding it.

'I'm not just a pretty face,' he joked.

Tish smiled. With an athletic build and a shock of gray at the front of his thick dark hair, David Biederman wasn't unattractive, but he wasn't what one would describe as classically handsome either.

'Here, sit down,' he instructed as he stood up and pulled a chair out for his guest.

'Thanks,' Tish accepted.

'So what happened today? Do the police know?'

Tish took a sip of coffee and nodded. 'Sabotage. Someone sliced through the rubber insulation and severed the main power wire to the mixer. The police don't know who's responsible.'

David shook his head. 'Kitty Flournoy. That's who's responsible.'

Tish's jaw dropped.

'Not directly,' David amended. 'But in the past ten years, she's done everything she could to turn a quiet, well-respected bake-off into an episode of *Cutthroat Kitchen*.'

'Why?'

'Why else? Money. The more contentious the competition, the more people want to pay to see it. Ticket sales this year are through the roof.'

'Because Whitney Liddell is defending her title once again?' Tish surmised.

'And people are eating it up. Kitty always wanted to find a champion with local appeal and she finally found one. You can't turn on the TV or leaf through a magazine in this state without seeing Whitney's face. Although, personally, I don't get it. Is she attractive? Sure, in a cover-girl-for-*Garden-and-Gun*-magazine kind of way. As a New Yorker, I don't understand the appeal of all that "Bless your heart" baloney. If I want someone to go to hell, I tell them to go to hell.' He shrugged.

Tish chuckled. 'I'm from New York as well. It does take some time to get used to Southern ways.'

'Yeah, I split my time between New York and Richmond, so I'm not sure I'll ever adjust. How long have you been in Virginia? And where in New York are you from?'

'I was born on Long Island and then moved to Westchester as a kid to be closer to my grandparents. After high school, I came to Virginia to attend UVA and I never went back. And if you ask me how long ago that was, you might find some coffee splashed on that suit of yours.'

'I wouldn't dare.' He laughed. 'I haven't survived more than half a century by asking women their age.'

'Wise man.'

'The survival instinct is strong,' he noted. 'Speaking of which, Ms Tarragon, what does your instinct tell you about all of this? Any idea who might be trying to scare you off and why?'

Tish answered honestly. 'No. If I knew, I'd tell the police and put an end to the whole thing.'

'Yet you seemed pretty keen to find out more about those dead women yesterday.' David folded his arms across his chest.

'I thought I should be prepared for what might happen when I bake my cherry pie,' she said flippantly before taking a sip of coffee.

'You don't really believe in the curse, do you?'

'No, but two otherwise healthy bakers dying during consecutive bake-offs is quite a staggering statistic for an event with only one hundred contestants per year. Let's also not forget that the two women in question were expected to unseat Whitney Liddell as champion.'

'Now look who's trying to turn this into *Cutthroat Kitchen*,' David said with a smirk.

'Just stating the facts,' Tish replied.

'You overlooked one fact – you're now a favorite to win,' David remarked. 'Well deserved, too. The tarragon chicken you made was one of the best savory bakes I've ever tasted as a judge.'

'Thank you. I appreciate the compliment. However, I wasn't a favorite when I received the threatening note. I was nothing more than a newbie contestant.'

'Meaning your situation has nothing to do with the two dead women.' David relaxed his arms and placed them in his lap.

'Meaning my situation *seemingly* has nothing to do with the two dead women, but I'm not entirely convinced.'

'You're rather tenacious, aren't you, Ms Tarragon?' David smiled appreciatively.

'Never more so than when my life is in jeopardy, Mr Biederman.' She took a swig of coffee. 'So what else can you tell me about Lillian Harwood and Penelope Purdue?'

'Not much. I've already told you everything I know. Lillian Harwood was an older lady, a grandmother. She made that tasty Canadian meat pie we all loved. I wasn't crazy about her cake, but Tallulah and Vernon loved it. If she had pulled off a great signature cherry pie, she might have won.'

'Did you speak to her when she presented her dishes?'

'There was the typical foodie chit-chat, yeah. The meat pie Ms Harwood made was a recipe from her grandmother in Quebec. She reminisced about growing up in northern Vermont and how her folks would drive over the border once a week to have dinner at her grandma's house. Back then, you didn't need a passport. Her father flashed his driver's license and told the border patrol where they were headed, and they'd be waved through. It's mind-blowing compared with today's high-tech security, isn't it?'

'It is, and yet I'm happy we no longer feel the need to build fallout shelters in our backyards and stockpile canned goods,' Tish observed.

'You're right. I guess not everything was simpler back then.' He pulled a face.

'What's that saying? The good old days are now?'

'Sure doesn't feel that way at times, but you're probably right.'

'Perspective is an interesting thing,' she philosophized. 'So, did Lillian Harwood have anything else to say?'

'Not that day. The stroll down memory lane was time-consuming enough. When she delivered her mountain cake the next afternoon, she was extremely talkative. Showed us the artwork by her granddaughter that inspired the cake and told us all about the rest of her grandkids. We thanked her for her entry and the backstory of the dish and she left the judges' table.'

'Did she appear in good health when she left?'

'Yeah, she was happy and excited about submitting her dish. Giddy even. But you know how heart trouble goes. Fine one minute and gone the next.'

'Mmm,' Tish grunted. Although it was true that cardiac arrest could kill someone instantly, she still doubted whether that was Lillian Harwood's true cause of death. 'What about Penelope Purdue? Did you talk to her at all?'

Once again, David folded his arms across his chest and leaned back in a defensive stance. 'No, I had no reason to speak with her. I wasn't a judge last year.'

'That's true, but you were still here.'

'Just on the last day, to announce the winner and hand out the trophy,' he maintained.

'No, you arrived at the end of the showstopper bake. You joined Tallulah and Vernon in sampling one of Penelope's peacock cupcakes, remember?'

'Oh, yes, that's right. I keep forgetting. But it doesn't really matter if I was there or not, does it? Ms Purdue never made it to the judges' table anyway. Willadeane Scott presented her cake.'

'True. I just thought you might have spoken to her while she was out on the floor. If you can recall speaking to her, that is,' she added slyly.

'I didn't speak to her. Look, it was a crazy time. We were launching my bagel line at Ellwood Thompson's and all the other higher-end Richmond grocery stores. I was visiting five different stores a day, giving the same spiel. And I was meeting with a chef to work on the plans for the new Biederman Bakery Southern lunch menu, which is launching in a few days. Everything from that week was a blur.'

'And yet you still found time to come to the bake-off.'

'Of course.' He dropped his hands to his lap again and broke into a broad smile. 'The bake-off is special to me. Very, very special.'

THIRTEEN

A fidgety Kitty Flournoy sat down in the chair recently vacated by Whitney Liddell. Her eyes scoured the room. 'No camera crew for this?'

'No camera crew needed,' Jules held his phone aloft. 'This is a quiet, intimate interview.'

Kitty nodded. 'What a time to give up smoking,' she remarked as she extracted a wad of gum from her mouth, wrapped it in a tissue, and tossed the lot into a nearby wastepaper basket. 'OK, give me what you've got.'

Jules was unaccustomed to having the subject direct the interview. 'Hold on just a second,' he urged as he switched on his camera and attempted to regain control of the situation. 'All right . . . now then, look into the camera.'

Kitty did as she was instructed, but she was not quite as camera-ready as Whitney.

'Ms Flournoy, as Channel Ten reported earlier, there has been an accident here at the bake-off today. One of your contestants was nearly electrocuted when a mixer began to spark. Can you tell us more about that?'

'Yes, the baker in question was examined by the excellent emergency care workers here at the civic center and, thankfully, it was deemed that she suffered no ill effects from the incident. In fact, I'm told she's already been cleared to return home.'

'And what about reports that this was a case of sabotage?'

'Sadly, it does appear that the shock the baker received came from an appliance with which someone had tampered. The Henrico County Sheriff's Department has been called and is investigating the situation. In the meantime, we here at the Virginia Commonwealth Bake-Off have postponed the competition for the day while we check the electrical outlets and appliances that are being used by our other ninety-nine contestants to ensure they are safe to use.'

'Do you believe you have the situation under control?'

'Yes, I'm confident that with the police on the case and the precautions we're taking, the remainder of the bake-off will go off without incident.' Kitty forced a nervous smile.

'What about the rumors that this is linked to the deaths of two bakers who died during the previous two competitions?'

'You just answered your own question. They're rumors and nothing more,' came her curt reply.

'Even though the deaths of those bakers occurred under unusual circumstances?' Jules challenged.

'We were extremely saddened to learn of the deaths of Lillian Harwood and Penelope Purdue. While it's true that both women died quite suddenly, the circumstances surrounding their deaths were not found to be unusual. I might also note that neither death occurred during the competition, but later, in the evening hours.'

'Many people attribute their deaths to a curse – the curse of the cherry pie – because both women were scheduled to bake a cherry pie on their final day of baking. Do you have any comment?'

Kitty laughed and shook her head. 'I am a rational, educated, Christian woman, Mr Davis. I don't believe in curses. What happened to Ms Harwood and Ms Purdue is an unfortunate coincidence.'

'A coincidence now followed by an incident involving yet another baker – a baker who happens to be a close personal friend of mine,' Jules noted. 'This baker is slated to bake a cherry pie as well.'

Kitty looked away from the camera. 'Yes, she is. Obviously someone decided to pull a prank.'

'A prank?' Jules frowned. 'Did you speak with Ms Harwood and Ms Purdue at all before their deaths?'

'Briefly, yes. In the spirit of Southern hospitality, I make a point to personally welcome each contestant to the bake-off. Beyond that introduction, I have very little interaction with our bakers during the event, as they are very busy.'

'Rumor has it that if Ms Harwood and Ms Purdue had lived, they might have won the competition.' Jules watched the color drain from Kitty's face.

'Every competitor has the chance of winning the top prize.'

Kitty Flournoy fell silent. It was clear that Jules would get no more from her on the subject. 'So, Whitney Liddell is defending her title for the fourth year in a row this year, isn't she?'

Kitty's mood lightened enormously. 'Yes, she's already tied the bake-off record of three consecutive wins set back in 1937. Now she's looking to break it.'

'What do you think Whitney has brought to the bake-off these past three years?'

'Oh, where to begin? Class, style, wonderful home-style recipes, amazing energy, and a dedication to returning family values to the bake-off.'

'Family values? I didn't realize the bake-off had fallen that far off the rails,' Jules partly joked.

'It hadn't. However, with the advent of technology and the internet, we were getting meals that were trendy and full of exotic ingredients instead of dishes that were family-friendly, comforting, and familiar. Whitney brought us back to our roots by proving that tried-and-true recipes can be Instagram-worthy too.'

Kitty's words were eerily similar to Whitney's. Had Kitty coached Whitney on her response? Or vice versa?

'Do you have any parting words for the folks in the audience, Ms Flournoy?'

'I do. I want everyone to know that despite this morning's accident and the postponement of today's events, the bake-off is still going ahead as planned. We guarantee not only that our bakers and our attendees will be absolutely one hundred percent safe, but that everyone involved will have a positively marvelous time. So log on to VACommonwealthBakeOff.com and order your tickets for the next two days. I'm sure they'll be selling out fast!'

'I'm so sorry, Ms Tarragon,' Willadeane Scott apologized, tugging on the sleeves of her oversized beige cardigan. 'I don't know how your mixer could have been tampered with. This is the first time in the almost twenty years I've been volunteering that anything like this has ever happened. Our volunteers and I run a tight ship.'

'You've been here that long?'

'Yes, I started when I was twenty-seven. My mother was a bake-off volunteer for years. When she passed away, I offered to step in for her. I guess I inherited her knack for organizing things. I've been invited back every year since.'

'A chip off the old block, as they say,' Tish said with a smile. Tish got up from the table where she had previously been speaking with David Biederman and grabbed a bottle of water from the refrigerator. Willadeane, meanwhile, moved to an adjacent coffee maker and poured some hot water into a paper cup.

'No one's accusing you or your team of anything,' Tish reassured her. 'Everyone here knows the great job you do.'

Willadeane plopped a tea bag into the cup of water. 'Do me a favor and tell that to Kitty Flournoy.'

'Why? After all this time, she must know how efficient and dedicated you are. She seems to rely on you quite a bit.'

'She does rely on me. That's why she's blaming me for what happened to you.'

Tish narrowed her eyes. Willadeane's words didn't make sense.

'I wasn't here this morning,' Willadeane explained. 'On competition mornings, I'm usually here between seven thirty and eight to check that everything the bakers ordered for the day is in their booths. I'd also greet you and my other bakers at arrival and sign you in.'

'Yes, I was wondering why I had to check in at the lobby,' Tish recalled. 'Yesterday, you said all our comings and goings were to be tracked by you.'

Willadeane nodded.

'So, what happened?' Tish asked.

'Work. I'm responsible for running an office. It's not a big office – I'm the only person there other than my boss – but it's very busy. Lots of people coming in and out all day. I needed to get things set up for the day before coming here. If you think Kitty relies on me, you should meet my boss.' Willadeane smiled proudly. 'He can't do a thing without me.'

'Sounds like you have job security.'

'Oh, yes, but he's never the type to take advantage. He's thankful for all I do.'

'It's always nice to be appreciated,' Tish noted.

'Yes, it should happen *everywhere*,' Willadeane grumbled and took a sip of tea.

'It strikes me as unduly harsh that Kitty should blame you for my mixer incident this morning just because you weren't here.' Tish had been so involved speaking with Willadeane that she attempted to drink her bottle of water without first removing the cap – a situation she quickly rectified. 'Your work here at the bake-off is strictly on a volunteer basis. Job and family should come first. If Kitty was so concerned about you not being here, she should have taken over your duties herself.'

'Yeah, Kitty isn't exactly a "hands-on" sort of person. Unless it's Desmond.' Willadeane drew her hand to her mouth. 'Oh, sorry. I – um – I shouldn't have said that.'

'That's OK. I kind of figured something was going on there.'

'Every single year it's been the same,' Willadeane complained. 'Kitty gets a new boy-toy assistant. Desmond, however, is an exception; Kitty's kept him around for three years now. I wonder how much she's paying him to stay.'

So Desmond *was* working for the bake-off at the time Lillian Harwood and Penelope Purdue died. Had he "assisted" Kitty with their deaths so that Whitney Liddell could continue her winning streak and, in turn, stir up more publicity for the bake-off?

'Well, it still seems unfair that Kitty should blame you,' Tish continued. 'I'm sure the volunteers you left in charge know exactly what they're doing.'

'They do. They've all been with the bake-off for several years now. They'd never do anything to jeopardize the safety of the event.'

'Did any of them see anything or anyone out of the ordinary this morning?'

'No, everyone said it was a normal morning. They're being questioned by police right now.' Willadeane moved her head slowly from side to side. 'I don't see how it could have happened. Unless you purchase a ticket and come through the front door, you need a special pass to get into the civic center. It's not like someone could have found an open door and strolled right in. This place has a state-of-the-art security system.'

Tish took a sip of coffee. She had taken note of the card scanners that had been installed on the entryways throughout the building. They only served to substantiate her theory that the note and the mixer tampering were both inside jobs.

'Do you think this might be related to the curse?' Willadeane asked.

'You believe in the curse?'

'I'm not sure. I didn't at first. I try to take a logical, scientific approach to things, but what with all that's happened . . .' She took a moment to collect her thoughts. 'Two women died just before they had the chance to bake their cherry pies. Two women who were on my watch. And now you, too. You're on my watch and are about to bake a cherry pie and you were almost next.'

'What if it isn't a curse?' Tish posed. 'What if the cherry pie is just a red herring?'

'A red herring for what?'

'I don't know,' Tish confessed. 'You probably spoke with Lillian Harwood and Penelope Purdue more than most people here. What did you know about them?'

Willadeane brought her cup of tea to the table recently occupied by Tish and David Biederman. 'Not much really. Lillian was a retired schoolteacher and divorced – more than once, as I heard her make reference to "ex number one" and "ex number two." She had two sons. Not sure which marriage produced them. And she had two grandchildren. They were the ones who drew the picture that inspired Lillian's showstopper cake.'

'What about her personality?' Tish asked and sat down opposite Willadeane, water bottle in hand.

'She was . . . bold, confident. She bragged a lot about her family, but not in an obnoxious way. She liked to laugh, too – but not at other people's expense, as Kitty does.'

Tish frowned. Kitty's jabs at Willadeane were difficult to stomach. 'What about Penelope Purdue?'

'You mean "Pen." That's what she liked everyone to call her. She was a computer programmer. In her mid-thirties. Lived right here in Richmond. Moved from New England – Vermont or New Hampshire or one of those northern border states. Single, no family. Her wardrobe consisted of various sweatshirts and tees from McGill University. She was an alumna. A proud one.'

'And personality-wise, what was she like?'

'Quiet. Introverted. I only know what I know about her because I overheard her talking to Lillian Harwood at lunch one afternoon. She didn't talk to me very much.'

'So you wouldn't describe her as nosy?' Tish questioned, recalling Dolly's words earlier that morning.

'Not at all. Why?'

'Some of the other bakers said that Pen Purdue asked a lot of questions.'

'Well, she didn't ask me anything,' Willadeane answered, slightly annoyed. 'Except to ask me to check her out when she needed a break. As I said, she was quiet and introverted.'

'Yet she and Lillian seemed to have struck up a close friendship.'

'They did develop a friendship, yes. Although I can't say how close they were.'

'Close enough for Pen to bake Lillian's cherry pie in tribute to her fallen friend,' Tish noted. 'Tell me about the day Lillian died.'

'There's not much to tell.' Willadeane took a sip of tea and wrapped her oversized sweater around her waist as if overcome by a sudden chill. 'It was an ordinary day by bake-off standards. Lillian had finished her showstopper cake. It was a mountain scene. Very ambitious, but she pulled it off. She delivered the cake to the judges, came back, and cleaned up for the day before heading home.'

'And she never complained about feeling sick?'

'No. She seemed in good spirits and genuinely happy with how her cake had turned out.'

'When did you learn that Lillian had died?'

'The next morning. Lillian didn't show up at the beginning of baking, so Kitty called her home and left a message. Just before lunch, her son called to inform us that his mother had passed away the previous evening from a massive heart attack. Desmond took the call and Kitty paused the bake-off to make the announcement.'

'How did Pen Purdue take the news?'

'She was shocked, like the rest of us. She didn't strike me as being unduly upset and she finished the day's baking just fine, but I suppose that's not necessarily a true indication of someone's feelings.'

'And the following year – last year – Pen died before she could bake the cherry pie that Lillian Harwood would have baked. The judges told me Pen went home early.'

'Yes.' Willadeane smoothed the skirt of her earth-toned maxi-dress over her knees. 'She flagged me over to her booth after finishing her showstopper bake to tell me she wasn't well enough to deliver it to the judges' table.'

'So you obliged by taking it to the judges' table for her.'

'I did, but not before asking Pen how she was. She was shaking and her face looked pale. She even leaned on me for support at one point. I asked if I should call for the medical team or an ambulance, but she declined. I was about to call for a taxi so that Pen didn't have to drive home, but Dolly inter-rupted. She had finished her bake and offered to drive Pen home.'

'Did Pen accept the offer?'

'I don't know. I took Pen's cake to the judges' table, reported her illness to Kitty, and then got caught up assisting other bakers. The end of the baking day is busy, as you've seen. By the time I got around to check whether Dolly had given Pen a ride, her booth was clean and she was nowhere to be found.'

'Did you ask Dolly about it the next morning?'

Willadeane shook her head. 'I didn't have the chance. I got the call first thing to say that Pen had died. Pen was wearing her bake-off badge when she was admitted to the hospital, so the police, while trying to identify next of kin, called here first. They thought she might have included an emergency number on her registration form.'

'Had she?'

'Yes – it wound up being her work number. The company she worked for arranged her funeral.'

'Wow,' Tish lamented.

'Yes, it's sad, isn't it?' Willadeane bowed her head.

Given Willadeane's dedication to her job, Tish sensed her familial situation might be similar to Pen's. 'Is it true that, had they both lived, Lillian and Pen might have won the bake-off?'

'They *might* have. Both were within two points of Whitney Liddell.'

'But?' Tish urged. Willadeane was clearly hiding something.

'But Whitney Liddell was still the favorite.'

'With whom? The judges? Oddsmakers?'

'Everyone,' Willadeane answered, although the expression of distaste on her face made it abundantly clear that she was not to be included. 'She's the most popular contestant we've had since I've been volunteering here.'

'Since you've been here as long as you have, can you think of anyone who might not want the bake-off to continue?'

'What do you mean?' Willadeane's eyes narrowed and she took a deep sip of tea.

'I mean that between the mysterious, sudden deaths, the threatening notes, and the faulty mixer, perhaps someone is trying to sabotage the bake-off. Can you think of anyone who might want to do that?'

'Whitney Liddell,' she replied without skipping a beat.

Tish was shocked by both the speed and content of her reply. 'You said Whitney Liddell was the favorite. The most popular contestant in over twenty years.'

'She is, but if she were faced with losing this competition, I can guarantee you she'd burn this whole place down to the ground with everyone in it.'

FOURTEEN

With the departure of Willadeane Scott, Tish rinsed her mug in the sink of the hospitality suite, loaded it in the dishwasher, and headed back to her booth to collect her bag and jacket. Along the way, she heard voices emanating from behind one of the many sets of closed doors that lined both sides of the corridor.

She stopped to listen.

'What are we going to do?' a man's voice whispered.

'We?' a woman's voice replied. 'You got us into this mess.'

'*I* got us into this mess? You act as if I forced you into this.'

'You didn't,' the woman acknowledged. 'But it's gone too far and gone on far too long. We should have come clean years ago.'

'What? And risk everything? You know we couldn't have done that.'

'We're still risking everything. Nothing's changed, except now there's more on the line and there's police everywhere.'

'I know it's unnerving, but we can't let that distract us. So long as we keep calm and hold our course, we'll be fine.'

'I hope you're right,' the woman said with a cry in her voice. 'I very much hope you're right.'

As the couple finished their conversation, Tish hurried along to the exhibition hall to retrieve her belongings.

The voices were too low for Tish to be able to accurately identify to whom they might belong, but there were only two obvious 'pairs' at the bake-off – Kitty Flournoy and her assistant, Desmond and the judges, Tallulah Sinclair and Vernon Staples. Given his ineptitude and ignorance regarding bake-off processes, Tish had assumed that Desmond was new at the job; however, Willadeane had proven Tish's assumption to be false.

Was it Kitty and Desmond behind the closed door? If so, what were they hiding? What should they have come clean about years ago? Not the true nature of their relationship, surely – Kitty had given that away while watching Desmond's finer 'assets' as he walked out the office door. So what secret were they trying to keep hidden? The origin of the threatening notes? Their motive for murder?

Collecting her bag and jacket, she left the exhibition hall, nearly bumping into Jules as he emerged from Kitty's office with Biscuit on his lead.

'Hey, how'd it go?' she asked.

'Honey, I deserve hazard pay for interviewing those two.'

'That bad, huh?'

'Let's just say their views are so old-fashioned they make Binnie Broderick sound like a braless hippie.'

Binnie Broderick, ultra-conservative former library director and victim in the first murder case Tish helped to investigate, had single-handedly purged the Hobson Glen library of all materials she found morally offensive. In the end, nearly five hundred books had disappeared, their final destination unknown.

'Binnie Broderick without a bra. I don't wish to speak ill of the dead, but I might be ill,' Tish quipped.

'You think you're going to be sick? I was stuck listening to Whitney and Kitty all that time. I'm telling you, this place is like the Harper Valley PTA. I can't believe they even bothered to hire judges. It sounds like Whitney Liddell and her June Cleaver family values were the favorite of the bake-off foundation from the start.'

'I wouldn't normally think to put "Kitty Flournoy" and "family values" in the same sentence,' Tish thought aloud as she recalled the woman eyeing Desmond's derriere appreciatively.

'That's the thing about family values. They tend to apply to everyone's family but your own.'

Tish nodded in agreement. 'How about a chilled Chardonnay as a reward for a job well done? We can meet at the condo tonight to discuss our findings. I'll order in some pizza.'

'With pepperoni and mushrooms?'

'You got it. I'm headed to the café, so I'll ask Mary Jo to join us, too.'

'I'll be there just as soon as I finish my evening broadcast,' Jules promised. 'Be careful, will you?'

'Aye aye, Captain.' Tish saluted.

'I'm serious, Tish. You might have been killed today.'

'I know. I'm trying not to think too much about it; otherwise, I'll drive myself crazy.'

The doors to the exhibition hall swung outward, releasing Tallulah Sinclair and Vernon Staples into the civic center lobby.

'Eleven thirty already,' Vernon grumbled, glancing at his watch. 'I thought we'd never get out of there.'

'It's still early enough to salvage the rest of the day,' Tallulah cheerfully countered.

'You're right. I'm going to put on a pair of shorts and smoke a cigar in the backyard.'

'Now, Vernon, you know you're not supposed to smoke. The doctor—'

Tallulah fell silent as she and Vernon noticed Jules and Tish standing just a few yards away. 'Oh,' the older woman exclaimed. 'Ms Tarragon, we didn't see you there. The bake-off is all abuzz, isn't it?'

Vernon scowled. 'The girl already knows the bake-off is abuzz, you silly woman. It's abuzz because her mixer went abuzz and she was nearly turned into Texas toast.'

'Sorry,' Tallulah tittered. 'How *are* you, dear?'

'I'm OK,' Tish replied. 'Just about to head home.'

'We were, too. Another beautiful day out there. You know, the sunshine might do you some good, Ms Tarragon.' Vernon's eyes slid surreptitiously toward Jules and the Bichon Frise at his feet.

'I know who you are,' Tallulah exclaimed. 'You're Julian Jefferson Davis from Channel Ten News. I do love your outtakes.'

Jules opened his mouth to correct Tallulah, but Vernon didn't give him a chance. 'That's right. He's that snowplow fella, isn't he?'

'And, most recently, the man with the burning hat. Oh, I did laugh when I saw that elf hat of yours on fire, Mr Davis, but wasn't that stunt terribly dangerous?' Tallulah asked.

'It wasn't really a st—' Jules started but decided not to bother. 'It was a little dangerous, yes. Um, Ms Sinclair, Mr Staples, do you think I could have a word with you both?'

'You're already having one,' Vernon snapped back.

'I mean for the station,' Jules clarified. 'I'm putting together a piece that will assuage any fears the public might have about attending the bake-off. It will air on the evening broadcast.'

'Well, if it's for the bake-off,' Tallulah reasoned.

'Yes, if it helps the event, we'll do it,' Vernon answered.

'Good.' Jules handed Biscuit's leash to Tish, pulled his phone from his pocket, and began to film. 'I'm here with Ms Tallulah Sinclair and Mr Vernon Staples, two of the Virginia Commonwealth Bake-Off's most beloved judges. Ms Sinclair, Mr Staples, you've been with the bake-off for several years – correct?'

'Yes, I've been a judge for thirteen years and Vernon's been a judge for twelve,' Tallulah answered.

'Eleven,' Vernon corrected.

'It's twelve,' Tallulah maintained. 'I remember the year you started.'

'I skipped what would have been my fourth year,' Vernon explained. 'Food poisoning.'

'Ah, yes. I remember now. Some restaurant gave it to you in retaliation for a terrible review, no doubt.' Tallulah cleared her throat and smiled beatifically.

'Um.' Jules stumbled to regain control of the interview. 'In all your years at the bake-off, have you encountered an accident like the one that occurred this morning?'

'Never,' Vernon answered unequivocally.

'It's rare that Mr Staples and I agree on anything, but upon this we do,' Tallulah added. 'Never in my years at the bake-off has a baker been in jeopardy. The team here always makes certain everyone is safe.'

'So what do you think happened this morning?' Jules prodded.

'An accident, of course. Despite the best efforts of the bake-off's wonderful staff, they are but human after all.'

'There are rumors that today's "accident" might be part of a curse – the curse of the cherry pie. Can you shed any light on this?'

'Only that the notion of a curse is utterly absurd.'

'Again, we agree,' Vernon concurred.

'Is it safe to say that Ms Harwood and Ms Purdue might have won the bake-off had they both survived?' Jules asked.

'My answer to that question is the same as it was when Ms Tarragon asked it earlier: it depends,' Tallulah answered evasively.

'Depends on what?'

'A great many things, my boy,' Vernon replied condescendingly. 'A great many things. The appearance and taste of the baker's final dish, the overall presentation of the dishes, the cohesiveness of the menu, a clear vision of the baker's culinary style . . .'

'And how it all fits with the theme of the bake-off,' Tallulah added.

Jules pursed his lips. 'The theme? I didn't realize there was a theme.'

'Well, there isn't a theme, per se, but since the Virginia

Commonwealth Bake-Off is such a well-respected Southern institution, there is a call for recipes that uphold tradition.'

'By tradition, you mean Southern tradition?'

'Y-e-e-e-s,' she tentatively sang. 'And no. It's more about—'

'Home cooking,' Vernon Staples interrupted. 'Don't dance around it, woman. The bake-off was designed to inspire the home cook. Although poke bowls and acai berry smoothies might be all the rage at your local hipster café, you're not going to find the average person serving them to their families. This is not the place for trends or complicated recipes.'

'It's about good, honest, down-home food,' Tallulah confirmed.

'What about the showstopper bakes?' Jules countered. 'Those aren't exactly "down-home." They're very complicated recipes. Few home bakers could pull off baking a cake that looks like a unicorn.'

'They're not complicated recipes. They're complicated construction and decorating jobs,' Vernon corrected. 'You'd be surprised how many home cooks see those cakes and are inspired to bake smaller, more workable versions for family occasions.'

'That's what we like,' Tallulah commented. 'Recipes that inspire the folks at home. Kitty Flournoy added that very wording to the judging criteria when she took over as head of the committee. Although Mr Staples might disagree, I think it's a lovely concept.'

Vernon Staples rolled his eyes. 'I have no issue with the concept, but I do find the phrasing trite and hackneyed.'

It was Tallulah's turn to roll her eyes and fold her arms across her chest.

Tish, watching from behind Jules, found the gesture overly dramatic. Was she playing up to the camera?

'So, in your professional opinions, did Ms Harwood and Ms Purdue's recipes inspire home cooks?'

'I think both of Ms Harwood's recipes served as inspiration for home cooks,' Vernon declared. 'Both entries were delicious, and I'm sure that alpine showstopper prompted many a camping-themed birthday cake.'

Tallulah pulled a face. 'I agree about the cake, but the tourtière? It was delicious, but I don't see American cooks embracing it.'

'Why not?' Vernon challenged, his face growing red. 'It's a variation of a potpie.'

'No, it isn't. It's not even close. Potpies feature chunks of meat and vegetables in a creamy sauce. Tourtière is pastry filled with ground pork or ground game and nothing else. Now, Ms Purdue's menu—'

'Was flawed. Her cake was tasty and achievable on a small scale, but I can't envision chicken bastilla being embraced by home cooks here in the South.'

'Yet you can envision them whipping up a French-Canadian meat pie?'

'Yes, I can. Tourtière is seasoned with herbs and garlic and onion. Bastilla uses an exotic array of spices Americans would never use in savory meat dishes. Some Southerners won't eat chicken unless it's fried, but here you are expecting them to put cinnamon on it.'

'People are far more broadminded than you give them credit for, Mr Staples,' Tallulah lectured. 'I happen to know many Southerners who take cinnamon for its anti-inflammatory benefits.'

'Anti-inflammatory, eh? Have you tried rubbing some on that big ego of yours?' Vernon Staples grinned.

'Better a big ego than a small—'

'That's a wrap!' Jules intervened. 'Thank you both for your time.'

Tallulah and Vernon shook Jules's hand, waved a farewell to Tish, and departed.

'I don't get those two,' Tish remarked when Vernon and Tallulah were a safe distance away from the civic center.

Jules placed his phone back into the inside pocket of his suit jacket and took Biscuit's lead. 'What do you mean?'

'The way they bicker back and forth.'

'Archenemies. Their feud started back in the late eighties when Vernon said, publicly, that he'd rather eat Hamburger Helper than try one of Tallulah's recipes. Tallulah volleyed by running a full-page ad in all the major Southern papers calling Vernon a hack and demanding that the publishers no longer run his restaurant reviews. Unfortunately, the plan backfired. All the hoopla only made Vernon's column more popular.'

'So why, after all that, are they judging the bake-off together?'

'Years ago, someone hired them to host an event and their back-and-forth repartee was such a hit with the audience that it became their shtick. Tallulah Sinclair and Vernon Staples put in appearances all over the South. People love it.'

'I suppose there's some entertainment value in it.' Tish shrugged. 'Personally, if I wanted to listen to people argue, I would have stayed in my bungalow in Richmond and listened to the neighbors.'

'Oh, I know. Listening to Tallulah and Vernon gives me major anxiety. Still, I do love Tallulah's recipes. My mama used to make her Lane Cake for my birthday every year and it's the absolute best cake ever.'

'Better than my chocolate chip cookies?' Tish teased.

Jules blushed bright red. 'Umm . . .'

'Don't worry.' Tish laughed. 'I don't mind coming second to your mama.'

Behind Jules, Sheriff Lightbody appeared in the doorway to the exhibition hall. 'That's my cue to leave,' she announced with a nod in the policeman's direction.

Jules glanced over his shoulder. 'Mine, too. I'll see you at six.'

Tish nodded and gave Biscuit a parting pat on the head before stepping through the glass double doors of the civic center and on to the pavement. In the heat of the midday sun, the remnants of the cool, overcast morning had dissipated, replaced with what promised to be a bright and breezy seventy-degree afternoon.

Tish drew a deep breath. How good it felt to be out in the world again, away from the fluorescent lights and recycled air of the civic center. Away from the chaos of the competition. Away from whoever wanted her gone. Donning her sunglasses, she removed the hot-pink cardigan she had worn to ward off the morning chill and the civic center air conditioning, tied it around her waist, and made her way across the parking lot to her car.

En route, she noticed two figures moving in the distance. They were on the other side of the chain-link fence that separated the civic center property from the rest of town and strolling side by side along the road that ran behind the parking lot.

Tish ducked behind a nearby car to avoid detection and watched as the pair, chatting amiably, approached a row of parked cars, finally coming to a halt outside a black Jaguar XE with North Carolina plates. After a brief scan of the area, the couple kissed briefly and the man helped the woman into the Jaguar before moving three cars down and getting behind the wheel of a silver Mercedes Benz C-Class sedan with Virginia plates.

Tish remained concealed as the couple drove off in different directions.

When the cars were no longer in sight, she stood up and texted Jules about what she had just seen: *Archenemies, huh? I just saw Talullah Sinclair and Vernon Staples KISSING!*

FIFTEEN

With a free afternoon before her, Tish drove to the café to assist with the lunch crowd. Pulling the Matrix into the parking area at a little past twelve thirty, she entered through the back door, hung her purse on a nearby hook, washed her hands, and donned a clean apron before approaching Mary Jo who, looking cool and comfortable in an ankle-length brown dress and a pair of espadrilles, was serving a group of customers seated at the counter.

'Hey, what are you doing here?' Mary Jo asked at the sight of her best friend.

'Bake-off is closed for the rest of the day. Appliance issues.'

'Yeah, Jules already told me about your "appliance issues."' Mary Jo drew quotes in the air. 'My question is what are you doing here instead of at the condo, resting?'

'I'm here because I was examined by the medical staff at the civic center and given a clean bill of health. Also, I thought if I helped out, you stood a better chance of making Kayla's doctor's appointment on time.'

'Ah, yes, the all-important doctor's appointment. I can't wait to find out what he has to say about that allergy.'

'Me, too. There's also the issue of a medical alert bracelet.' Tish told MJ about Clayton's early morning hospital call.

'Hmmm, interesting. I'll ask Doctor Hobbs about that too,' MJ said.

Tish nodded. 'If you're free afterwards, why don't you swing by the condo so we can discuss our findings? Jules will be there and I'm inviting Clayton. I'm ordering in some pizzas.'

'With spinach and meatballs?' MJ asked.

'Is there any other way to eat a pizza?'

Mary Jo grunted her approval. 'I have to drop Kayla at her PSAT prep class at five thirty. I'll come by after that.'

'Perfect,' Tish deemed as her eyes scanned the full café. 'Where do you want me to start?'

'I've served just about everyone except for table five.'

Tish glanced at table five to see the familiar faces of Daryl Dufour, Celestine Rufus, and Celestine's daughter, Lacey. 'Daryl . . .? What are they all doing together?'

'Daryl stopped by before Celestine left for the day. He had books for the grandkids on how to deal with grief. Celestine thanked him and they got to talking. Lacey checked in from her errands to see where her mom was, and before you know it, Daryl invited both of them to stay for lunch.'

'Nice,' Tish remarked, genuinely pleased to see the trio happily engaged in conversation.

'Yeah, Daryl's sweet to think of the kids that way. I think it's good for both Celestine and Lacey to enjoy some time out of the house and away from the rest of the family for a while.'

'Yes, it is.' Tish stared down at the counter. That Daryl Dufour might actually be Lacey's family – the product of a teenage romance that ended the moment Celestine met Lloyd Rufus – was a secret that remained between Tish, Celestine, and Daryl. 'I'll get their order together if you want to check in on the other tables.'

Mary Jo accepted the offer. 'That would great. I see a few folks out there who might be needing a drink refill.'

'Sure.' Tish nodded and set about fixing the *Zelda Fitzgerald* fried chicken and pimento cheese sandwich, one *Lady*

Cheddarly's Lover grilled cheese, and *The Animal Farm* sandwich, which was listed on the menu as containing five types of meat, all in equal amounts, but, in truth, was simply ham, Dijon, and a salad garnish. All the sandwiches were served with a side of crunchy *George Bernard Slaw* in Irish buttermilk dressing.

Once complete, Tish brought the plates to table five with a warm 'Hello.'

'Tish!' Celestine looked up in surprise. 'What are you doin' here, honey?'

'The bake-off is shut down for the afternoon. Appliance issues. We start up again tomorrow.'

'That's a shame. I know you were eager to get started on your Miss Havisham cake.'

'It's OK. I'll be able to get started soon enough. For now, it feels good to be back.' Tish wasn't exaggerating. After the morning's disagreement with Schuyler and the scare at the civic center, the café felt like the embrace of an old friend – an oasis of calm in the midst of chaos.

As Tish presented the party with their lunches, the phone in the pocket of her apron began to chime. She glanced at it quickly. The call was from Schuyler.

'Sorry, I have to take this.' Tish excused herself from her group of friends who were eagerly diving into their food. 'Hey,' she greeted, placing the phone to ear.

'Tish? Are you all right?' Schuyler's voice was apprehensive.

'I'm fine. Why?' She moved into the kitchen so that Celestine and the other customers couldn't overhear her conversation.

'I heard on the local news there was some sort of emergency down at the civic center and the sheriff's office got called in,' he explained.

'Yeah, I, um, I plugged my mixer in this morning and got a shock. The circuit breakers went off.'

'Wow. Are you OK? You didn't get hurt, did you?'

'No, no, I'm fine. The medics at the civic center checked me out and all is well.'

'Thank goodness. You could have been seriously injured.'

'I know. I was lucky.'

'You were, but why didn't you call me? You should have told me what happened.'

'There wasn't time, hon. All I know is there was a "zap" and a flash of light and then a thud as the power went off. From there, I was whisked away by the medics and Kitty Flournoy. By the time they finished checking me out, the police were on the scene and I had to answer their questions. Then there were the other people on the scene and . . . well, before I knew it, it was going on noon. I would have called you then, but I knew you were busy and I didn't want to worry you. Especially when there was nothing to worry about.'

'I am busy,' he acknowledged. 'But I still would have liked to have known.'

'I understand and I'm sorry. If I'm ever zapped by an electric appliance again, you'll be the first person I call,' she teased.

'That isn't funny, Tish.'

'Sorry,' she apologized again.

'So what's going on? Is the bake-off still going ahead?'

'The civic center's closed for the rest of the day while the police question everyone and the maintenance team check the electric, but we're scheduled to start up again first thing tomorrow morning.'

'Police? Why are they questioning people over an accident?'

'Because it wasn't an accident,' she reluctantly answered. 'Someone tampered with my mixer cord.'

'*Your* mixer cord? But why?'

'To get me out of the competition. To scare me away. Just like the note that was left for me yesterday.'

'Why would someone want to scare you off?'

'I don't know. That's what I'm trying to find out.'

'Well, what does Lightbody say? He's on the case, isn't he?'

'He is, but he was in the middle of questioning the public when I left. Even though it's a waste of time.'

'What do you mean a "waste of time"?'

'Well, it's obvious from the timing of the delivery of the letter and now the tampering with the mixer cord that this is being done by someone involved with the bake-off.'

'Did you tell this to Lightbody?'

'I tried, but Kitty Flournoy, the head of the bake-off, wouldn't hear of it. She's convinced Lightbody that this is the handiwork of some random lunatic.'

'Lightbody's a good cop. He'll figure out who did it. In the meantime, I don't think you should go back there.'

'Where? The civic center?'

'The bake-off. The civic center. Stay away from all of it. Unless Lightbody makes an arrest today, you're still in danger.'

'I'll be fine. Officer Clayton will be there to keep an eye on things.'

'Was he there keeping an eye on things today?'

Tish sighed noisily. 'Yes, but—'

'Then what good is he? I mean it, Tish. I don't want you going back there.'

'Schuyler, I have to go back. With Lloyd's income gone, that bake-off prize money could go a long way to helping Celestine with living expenses.'

'Celestine has a family of her own to help her.'

'She does, but you know none of them can afford to pay both their own bills and Celestine's.'

'OK, but Celestine wouldn't want you to compete if it meant risking your life.'

'This isn't just about me, Schuyler. Two women are dead. Someone needs to get to the bottom of what happened.'

'Not the "cherry pie curse" nonsense again,' he grumbled.

'No, it's not the "cherry pie curse" nonsense again. This menace is entirely human. A human with something to hide.'

'OK, you're probably right. So quit the bake-off and let Sheriff Lightbody find that human.'

'I can't rely on Lightbody, Schuyler. Not only is he as sharp as a bowling ball, but he's completely under Kitty Flournoy's thumb.'

'But him being under her thumb is good. As head of the bake-off, Kitty will want to get to the bottom of this.'

'Unless she *is* the bottom of this,' Tish cautioned.

'Why would Kitty want to harm contestants, Tish? That doesn't make any sense.'

'It does if she was trying desperately to prevent Whitney Liddell, the current champion and the goose that lays the golden eggs, from losing the competition.'

There was a long pause on the other end of the line. 'Look,

let's talk about this later. I have a meeting in a little while, but I can dash home for a couple of minutes if you need me.'

'That's sweet of you, but I'm OK. I'm at the café, actually.'

'At the café? What are you doing there?'

'Since I have the afternoon free, I figured I'd see how things are going and lend Mary Jo a hand. Especially since I might not be around on Saturday.'

'No, I mean, what are you doing there so soon after nearly being electrocuted? You should be resting.'

'I told you, I got a clean bill of health from the medics at the civic center. If the bake-off were still on, I'd be working a lot harder than I am now. At least here, I can take a break whenever I want or go upstairs and lie down if I need too.'

'This isn't just about you resting,' he said, contradicting his previous statement. 'If someone tampered with your mixer on purpose, they could still be after you. I'd feel a lot better if you were home with the door locked and the alarm system on.'

'Schuyler, there are at least thirty people in this café, another five outside, and Mary Jo is here. I'm totally safe.'

'You thought you were safe at the café when you were on the Shackleford case. Instead, you ended up being assaulted in the parking lot,' Schuyler was quick to point out.

'That was different. It was the middle of the night. This is the middle of the lunch crowd.'

'And when the lunch crowd is over?'

'We clean up, and I go home and set the alarm. At least until six o'clock. Jules and Mary Jo are joining me for pizza.'

'Pizza? Don't you think you should relax tonight?'

'It's not like I'm going out for a jog. And I thought you'd be happy I'm not going to be alone.'

'I am,' he answered unconvincingly. 'I am. After the pizza, why don't you guys watch that new mystery series on Netflix? It sounds like the type of thing y'all would like.'

Tish bit her lip. Schuyler would be angry to learn she was running her own investigation into the bake-off, but she couldn't lie to him. 'We're not watching TV tonight. We're getting together to discuss the case. I'm hoping Officer Clayton will join us as well.'

'Tish,' he chided. 'Jeez, why can't you leave things well enough alone?'

'Leaving things "well enough alone" could get me killed,' she said.

'So could getting involved in the case.'

'I'm already involved in the case, Schuyler. I got involved the moment I received that note.'

'Well, it's time to un-involve yourself,' he insisted.

'Un-involve myself?' she scoffed. 'What do you want me to do? Sit around and wait for this person to strike again?'

'I want you to quit the bake-off and let Lightbody do his job.'

'I'd be happy to let Lightbody do his job if I actually believed he'd find the perpetrator, but right now he's at the civic center interviewing ticket-holders on the off-chance one of them is some bake-off-obsessed lunatic when it's quite clear that this is all an inside job.'

'Is that why you helped Reade with his cases? Because you didn't believe he'd be able to catch a killer on his own?'

The mention of Reade's name made Tish see red. 'Don't go there, Schuyler.'

'No, *you* don't go there,' he warned. 'I can't believe you'd do this to me again. And right now, of all times.'

'Do this to *you*?'

'Look, I have to go get ready for my meeting. We'll finish this later.'

'Yes,' she agreed, before disconnecting. 'Yes, we will.'

With the café closed for the day and clean-up and food prep for the following morning complete, Tish bade farewell to Mary Jo and poured herself a cold glass of lemonade before retiring to the swing on the front porch to enjoy the gorgeous weather.

Except for the remarkably low humidity, it might as well have been a late afternoon in July. Children, recently dismissed from school, sped up and down the sidewalk on bikes and scooters. Teenagers drove by in souped-up automobiles, their car windows rolled down and stereos blasting, and seniors, shuffling off the winter chill and embracing the sun before the summer heat set in, strolled through town in wide-brimmed hats.

The scene outside the café stood in marked contrast to the one outside the condo door. With its population of professional couples and second-homeowners, the condominium atmosphere was eerily sterile. Apart from the sound of landscapers' lawn-mowers – scheduled by the homeowners' association to trim residents' front yards at precisely nine o'clock every Monday morning – the only noise Tish encountered on her regular walks was the hum of HVAC systems. With trees in the area having been razed when the units were constructed and backyards paved with cement blocks rather than grass, there was little birdsong. And with high brick walls erected between properties, there was also little socialization.

Tish slipped off her shoes, pulled her legs up on to the swing seat, and stretched them out in front of her in anticipation of a leisurely session of people-watching. No sooner had she gotten comfortable than a small pink nose appeared at the top porch step. Attached to it was a small, long-haired, black-and-white tuxedo cat. He greeted Tish with a whiny meow, just as he had every day since she had returned to work after the shooting.

'Hello,' she answered. 'Let me guess. Tuna?'

The cat climbed on to the porch and mewed.

'OK.' She hopped from the swing and disappeared into the screened front door. She returned, moments later, with a white porcelain dish containing a can of tuna chunks in oil and a bowl of fresh water and placed both at the edge of the porch.

Before Tish could even set the dish of tuna on the porch floor, the cat rushed for it and immediately began lapping up morsels of fish, his tail swishing slowly to and fro in content-ment as he ate.

'Got room for another friend?' Celestine called as she walked across the gravel-lined parking lot of the café.

'So long as you don't want tuna. I'm fresh out.'

'Nah, givin' it up for Lent,' Celestine teased.

'What brings you back so soon?' Tish asked. 'Not that I'm complaining.'

'Was feelin' cooped up back at Lacey's. It's such a beautiful day out, so I decided to go for a walk.'

'You came here from Lacey's? That's quite a walk.'

'Yeah, well, I just kept puttin' one foot in front of the other and before I knew it, I was here in town. But seein' as you're here, I'll sit and stay a spell.'

'Can I get you a lemonade or maybe a sweet tea?' Tish offered.

'A sweet tea would taste mighty good right about now,' Celestine said as she plopped down in one of the white wrought-iron chairs that flanked the swing.

'Coming right up.' Once again, Tish disappeared into the café only to emerge several moments later with a tall glass of sweetened iced tea garnished with a slice of lemon.

'Thank you.' Celestine took a long sip of tea and mopped the perspiration from her forehead with a lace-trimmed hand-kerchief. 'It would appear you have a cat,' she noted as the black-and-white creature lapped up the last morsel of tuna.

'Do I have a cat or does he have me?' Tish posed.

Celestine chuckled. 'He has you, I think. Mary Jo fed him yesterday, by the way. Chicken. He ate it but not like he does that tuna.'

'What I need to do is buy him some cat food.'

'Oh, then you'll really have a cat.' She laughed. 'Once special food comes into the equation, there's no turnin' back.'

'Maybe, but he'll be a café cat only. Schuyler's allergic,' Tish stated. 'Funny, my mother fed one just like him before she got sick. His name was Mr Nibbs. That is until Mr Nibbs gave birth to seven kittens on the chaise lounge on our back patio. Then she was Mrs Nibbs. My mother loved those cats.'

'Strange this little guy should come on the scene when he did, just as you were recoverin'. You think your mama sent that cat there to let you know she's around?' Celestine ventured.

'I admit the thought's crossed my mind more than once.'

'I wish Lloyd would send me a message.' Celestine sighed. 'Let me know what to do. Although this afternoon, for the first time since his passin', it felt like he was nearby.'

'Really?'

'Yeah, when Lacey and me were havin' lunch with Daryl, I could feel Lloyd around me. I never had time for friends and lunches, what with work and the kids and the grandkids. Today,

I could almost hear Lloyd sayin' to me to make time because we just never know. You know?'

Tish nodded.

'Of course, the minute I got back to Lacey's, I felt guilty for enjoyin' myself. Lloyd's only been gone a short while.' Celestine blinked back tears. 'I have no business smilin' and yet . . .'

'You felt Lloyd telling you that life goes on?' Tish assumed.

'Exactly.' Celestine took a sip of tea.

'Well, I think Lloyd would want you to be happy. He loved you. That's what we all want for the people we love: happiness. How are you feeling now?'

'Better. The walk helped and so did being able to talk to a friend. The sweet tea ain't hurtin' either.' The older woman smiled. 'And how are you doin'?'

'Me? I'm fine.'

'Really? I saw on the news there was some trouble down at the bake-off this mornin'. No names were mentioned, but I figured you might be at the center of all that action.'

'You figured right. Someone has been trying to scare me away from the competition. First, it was a threatening note. This morning, it was a shock from a faulty mixer.'

'You OK?'

'Yeah, the emergency medical staff cleared me and I came straight here.'

'Why didn't you say somethin' to me?'

'Because I didn't want to worry you. And I didn't want you to ask me to back out of the competition. I'm in it to win it. I'm also in it to find out what's going on.' Tish told Celestine about the mysterious deaths of Lillian Harwood and Penelope Purdue and the supposed 'curse.'

'You think their deaths are connected with all that's happened to you?'

'I'm willing to bet they are.'

'Well, I have to be honest, I am a little worried about you, Tish. We nearly lost you this December, but I also know you need to get to the bottom of things. You can't help it. It's just your nature.'

'Thanks, Celestine. Officer Clayton has been keeping an eye on me, so I should be fine, but I promise I won't do anything to put myself in jeopardy. Still, I appreciate that you understand my need to investigate. If only others were as understanding.' She frowned.

The small cat lapped up some water and curled up beside his benefactor on the porch swing.

'Seems that little one understands you just fine,' Celestine noted. 'Unless you were talkin' about someone else?'

'Oh . . . it's just . . . well, Schuyler and I had an argument this morning and then again this afternoon. He's demanding I quit the bake-off.'

'Demandin'?'

'He was quite forceful about it. I'm not to return to the competition in the morning. He was also angry to learn I've been investigating the case with Jules, Mary Jo, and Officer Clayton. The four of us are meeting at the condo tonight to discuss our findings.'

'I'm sure Schuyler's just worried about you, honey. Like I said, we almost lost you at Christmas.'

'I understand that and can appreciate it, but he can't expect me to lock myself away the rest of my life for fear I might get injured again. And then there's the whole campaign – I'm trying to be supportive and give him what he needs while simultaneously keeping my business afloat, but it just doesn't seem to be enough.' It was Tish's turn to fight back tears. 'God, now I'm doing what I didn't want to do – burdening you with nonsense. I'm sorry, Celestine.'

'Don't be sorry. You ain't burdenin' me. I'm happy to be listenin' to someone else's problems for a change. Everyone's been tiptoein' around me so much this past couple of weeks, I thought I was a time bomb. Nice to know I'm still useful.'

'As if you'd ever not be.' Tish laughed. 'If anything, you're always in demand.'

'Yep, and that's the way I like it, too.' Celestine took another sip of sweet tea. 'Now, gettin' back to you and Schuyler. Y'all never had a honeymoon period. You went on a few dates, liked each other, and then all of a sudden Mary Jo was movin' into your apartment, you're gettin' shot at, and now Schuyler's runnin' for mayor. You've been together less than a year and you've only been livin' together since Christmas. You've both faced a lot during that short time– more than most couples who have been together for years have faced. With all that pressure, your relationship has been put on the back burner. You know what I think? I think once the bake-off is over, you and Schuyler should plan a night on the town. Get away from Hobson Glen and café menus and detective work and politics. Take some time to be fun-lovin' young people. Remember why you're together in the first place.'

'A night away would be wonderful. I can't remember the last time we went out on a date. It might have been before the shooting, although I can't be sure. Even then we were both busy with the holidays.'

'See? It's time to reconnect.'

'That's a good idea. And until date night?'

'Let him cool down. I'm sure he'll come to his senses and realize he can't hold you back from doin' what you were meant to do. Just as I'm sure you'll do whatever you can to help him to do what he was meant to do.'

SIXTEEN

'Mmph, thanks for the pizza, Ms Tarragon,' Jim Clayton said as he stuffed a sixth slice of pepperoni and mushroom into his mouth.

'You're welcome,' Tish answered graciously, all the while marveling at the empty pizza boxes stacked on the kitchen counter. She had hoped to save some pizza for Schuyler to eat when he got home, but at the rate Clayton was eating, leftovers seemed unlikely.

'Didn't you have lunch today, Clayton?' Jules asked.

'Jules,' Tish chastised. She didn't want the young officer to feel self-conscious.

'Sorry, but the boy's eating that pizza like he's just come home after being stuck on an island with Tom Hanks and that volleyball with a face on it.'

'No, I didn't have time for lunch today,' Clayton replied

between bites. 'I had to call the nurse who admitted Penelope Purdue on my break so Lightbody wouldn't hear me.'

'Oh? What did the nurse say?' Tish asked.

'Mmph, mmshe shaid Penelpsh Poodoo didmn't comms dith anyphody—'

'Jim?' Tish interrupted. 'How about you finish eating and we come back to you later?'

Clayton nodded and gave Tish the thumbs-up.

'I'm ready to report,' Mary Jo announced as she pushed her plate of discarded pizza crusts aside and refilled her glass of Chardonnay.

'Spill it,' Jules urged as he went in for a third slice of pepperoni and mushroom before Clayton finished off the whole pie. 'The news from the doctor, not the wine.'

'So, I asked Kayla's pediatrician about the whole food allergy thing, telling him that a friend of a friend had recently died. I didn't say anything about the bake-off and Penelope Purdue.'

'Wise move,' Tish remarked, refilling her own glass before reaching in for a slice of meatball and spinach.

'First off, Doctor Hobbs made it clear that whatever he said was just his opinion—'

'Because he doesn't want to be sued,' Clayton noted and dove in for yet another slice of pizza.

'Doctor Hobbs is a man of great integrity who has been an excellent doctor to both my children. He wants to make it clear that he's not an expert,' Mary Jo insisted.

Clayton repeated his previous sentiment, this time with his mouth full. 'Sho he dushn't get shued.'

'Jim,' Jules reminded. 'Don't talk with your mouth full.'

'Shorry.' The officer went back to his slice.

'So, when I asked Doctor Hobbs if somebody could have been struck by a sudden allergy, he told me' – Mary Jo pulled out her phone for reference – 'that although new-onset allergies can happen at any time, they are far more common in children than adults.'

'Meaning that if Penelope Purdue had a nut allergy, she most likely would have had it since childhood,' Tish extrapolated.

'Most likely, yes, but Doctor Hobbs warned that we couldn't automatically make that assumption. In his words, things can

go haywire in a person's body at any point their life. However'
– Mary Jo smiled – 'he did make it clear that if someone with
a severe nut allergy was exposed to nuts, their reaction would
be almost immediate.'

'So working with them all day long without a reaction isn't
a possibility.'

Mary Jo shook her head. 'The longest reaction time he's ever
witnessed is a couple of hours, but the majority of reactions
occur within two minutes of contact.'

'Thanks, MJ. This is exactly the information we were looking
for.'

'Wait, there's just one more thing. The medical alert bracelet
Penelope Purdue was wearing isn't something prescribed or
distributed by doctors. You can purchase them online or at drug
stores.'

'So, Penelope Purdue knew she had a nut allergy – an allergy
bad enough to make her go out and buy a bracelet – and yet she
made a recipe with nuts in it?' a confused Clayton questioned.

'She also ate sesame noodles with peanut sauce for lunch
two days in a row before her death,' Tish reminded.

'But why?'

'What I want to know,' Jules added, 'is why there's a medical
alert bracelet for nuts anyway? Allergies to medications like
penicillin, I get, but nuts? If someone finds you lying in the
street, it's not as if they're going to throw peanuts at you. I
mean, unless you're an elephant. Or maybe a circus monkey.'

'Good Lord.' Mary Jo drew her hand to her face.

'Nuts are in many items you wouldn't expect,' Tish patiently
explained.

'Like?' Jules prompted.

'Not now, Jules,' she warned.

'OK, so back to the bracelet,' Clayton urged. 'Why wear
something warning of her allergy and then expose herself to
the very thing she warned everyone about?'

'Simple,' Tish replied. 'It wasn't her bracelet.'

'It wasn't her bracelet?' Mary Jo cried.

'Doctor Hobbs said they can be purchased in drug stores by
anyone, without a prescription and regardless of whether they
have an allergy or not.'

'He did.'

'That leaves us with two possible scenarios. One, that Penelope lived or stayed with someone who also wears a medical alert bracelet and their bracelets got switched when left on a bedside table or a bathroom sink.'

Mary Jo wrinkled her nose. 'You'd think they would have checked before leaving the house.'

'Not if Penelope or the other party was in a hurry that morning. It was the second day of the showstopper bake.'

'Possible,' Clayton allowed. 'However, Ms Purdue lived alone and had no friends. Her work number was listed as her next of kin. What's the second scenario?'

'The bracelet was purchased by or belonged to someone else and was put on Penelope's arm so that doctors would believe she died of a nut allergy.'

'But why?' Jules asked, reaching for the bottle of Chardonnay and finding the ladies had polished it off. With a roll of his eyes, he trudged off to the refrigerator to retrieve a second bottle.

'Why? To cover up what really killed Penelope. Jim,' Tish addressed Clayton, 'can you take a break from your pizza and tell us what you found out from the hospital?'

Clayton swallowed his mouthful of pizza and washed it down with some beer, straight from the bottle, before speaking. 'Ms Purdue was taken to the hospital by taxi. She was admitted to the hospital at five thirteen p.m. She was unconscious and alone.'

'So Pen did go by cab,' Tish interrupted. 'And the time of arrival suggests she took the cab directly from the civic center.'

'Yeah, she was picked up there. The cab driver said so. Why is that important?'

'Because, according to Willadeane Scott, Dolly offered Pen a ride home. Willadeane wasn't certain if Pen had accepted the offer or not.'

'Apparently, she didn't if she wound up in a taxi,' Jules stated.

'Who called for the cab, Jim?'

'The number the dispatch office recorded was from Penelope's cell phone,' Clayton replied.

'That doesn't help much, does it? Anyone could have used her phone to place the call. I'll talk to Dolly tomorrow. Apart from the cabbie, she may have been the last person to see Penelope Purdue alive. Go on, Jim,' Tish urged.

'The cabbie reported that Ms Purdue was groggy when he picked her up, but by the time they made it to the hospital, she was unconscious. The cabbie went into the ER and explained to the admitting nurse what had happened. Orderlies went out to the cab, retrieved her from the backseat, and brought her in by stretcher. Doctors administered epinephrine and CPR but it was too late. She died shortly after being admitted.'

'And the nut allergy? Did she say why they settled upon that as the cause?'

'Doctors are positive Ms Purdue died of anaphylactic shock. Between the contents of the victim's stomach and the medical alert bracelet, doctors assumed the nuts were the cause.'

'Whatever caused the allergy, Penelope had to have been in contact with it no more than two hours before her death,' Mary Jo said. 'Most likely even less than that.'

'Yet she was at the bake-off the entire time,' Jules mused aloud.

'Putting the finishing touches on her showstopper bake,' Tish said, completing the thought. 'Jim, are you able to track down her regular doctor? He or she should have a record of Penelope's allergies.'

'Already on it,' Clayton replied. 'I sent out a request to a Doctor Jonathan Sherman on Main Street in Richmond. I'm just waiting to hear back. But there's something else you need to know about Penelope Purdue.'

'Oh?'

'Penelope Purdue wasn't always Penelope Purdue.'

Tish looked a question at Clayton.

'When doctors did an autopsy on Ms Purdue, they noted that she had undergone gender reassignment surgery.'

'Wow. One thing's for certain, after surgery that extensive, Penelope's doctor would most certainly be aware of any allergies she might have had.'

'Penelope Purdue assigned male at birth,' Jules stated aloud. 'Interesting.'

'How so?' Tish asked.

'When I interviewed Kitty and Whitney today, they both stressed the importance of "family values" in the bake-off.'

'Ugh, I hate that term,' Mary Jo complained.

'You and me both. My sister uses it all the time to defend her stance on my "lifestyle," as she refers to it, but it's just an excuse to shun people who are different. That's why we haven't spoken in months.'

Several seconds of silence elapsed before Jules spoke again. 'So, could anyone at the bake-off have found out about Penelope's surgery?'

Clayton pulled a face. 'Those records are sealed pretty tight, for obvious reasons. Only way someone might have found out is if Penelope herself told them.'

'Hmm, I wonder . . .'

'We can't read your mind, Jules,' Mary Jo reminded him.

'Well, as a trans woman, Penelope Purdue wasn't the kind of champion the bake-off wanted. Far from it. The fact she was within breathing distance of winning the championship and defeating the pinup girl for the *Leave It to Beaver* set would have been unthinkable. If you wanted a motive for someone to bump her off, I can't think of a better one.'

'And what about Lillian Harwood?' Mary Jo challenged. 'How does she fit in?'

'Lillian Harwood was twice divorced,' Jules explained. 'That might be enough to ruffle the feathers of the family-values crowd, especially when Lillian was poised to strip their queen of her throne, but maybe Lillian had some other skeletons in her closet.'

'I'll see what else I can dig up,' Clayton offered.

'Everyone I spoke with today said that Penelope and Lillian were very close,' Tish said. 'Penelope apparently looked at Lillian as a mother figure. Probably because she had no contact with her own family.'

'Sadly, not unusual given her circumstances,' Jules lamented as he fed a scrap of pizza crust to Biscuit, who was seated on the ceramic-tiled floor beside his chair. 'All my life, my mama's been nothing but supportive of me. Even after coming out to her. I remember after I told her I was gay, she took me on a road trip to Nashville to celebrate finding my true self. We went to the Grand Ole Opry and drank champagne. It was incredible. But I'm one of the lucky ones.'

Again, the group fell silent.

'I don't know about this whole family-values killing theory,' Mary Jo said with a frown. 'Maybe it's because I'm in the midst of one, but divorce doesn't seem that scandalous to me.'

'You didn't hear how Whitney Liddell and Kitty Flournoy spoke,' Jules argued. 'They were full-tilt anti-modern woman, talking about cooking dinner for your husband's boss and wearing dresses and high heels in the kitchen. Whitney Liddell said she was the champion the bake-off had been searching for.'

'If she referred to herself as the chosen one, I'm going to need more wine,' Tish remarked.

'I think I cut her off before she could go there.'

Tish grunted in disgust. 'If you don't like Kitty and Whitney for the crime, MJ, rest assured there are plenty of other suspects to choose from. I spoke to the members of my lunch group and every single one of them had a motive. Dolly had an argument with Lillian just before she died, and she thought Penelope was a busybody who asked too many questions about Lillian. Riya needs to win the competition to save her and her husband's business. And Gordon is supposedly angry because the bake-off favors women. Oh, and he's only taken up cooking and baking in the past few years – whatever that means.'

MJ spoke up. 'If all these people are so competitive, then why not threaten Whitney Liddell?'

'Can't get near her,' Jules replied. 'Her booth is surrounded by security guards.'

'Also, Lillian and Penelope were both in second place. They were what stood between the other competitors and Whitney Liddell. Knock them out and then you're head-to-head with the champ,' Tish explained. 'Then there are the judges. The more I talk to David Biederman, the more I'm convinced he's hiding something. He wasn't a judge at the time of Penelope Purdue's death, but he did put in an appearance. Still, he claims to remember very little about that day.'

'Oh! Don't forget Tallulah Sinclair and Vernon Staples,' Jules said excitedly, nearly spewing wine from his mouth. 'They were kissing this afternoon.'

'The judges? No,' Clayton was incredulous.

'It's true. I saw them behind the civic center as I was leaving earlier,' Tish explained.

'No way! They hate each other.'

'Yes way,' Tish maintained. 'I know what I saw.'

'I read up on the bake-off and they've worked together for some time, haven't they?' MJ said. 'What you probably saw was a kiss on the cheek between colleagues.'

'This wasn't a kiss on the cheek. It was a warm embrace followed by a sustained, passionate kiss on the lips.'

'Ew,' Clayton exclaimed. 'They're old.'

'Old*er*,' Mary Jo corrected. 'You know the saying: just because there's snow on the roof doesn't mean there isn't a fire in the furnace.'

'What does that even mean?'

'That desire and physical love aren't exclusive to young people.'

'Ew,' Clayton repeated, much to Mary Jo's obvious displeasure.

'So,' Jules interrupted, 'how do you think Talullah and Vernon's romance fits in with everything?'

'I haven't a clue,' Tish admitted. 'But I doubt they'd want word to spread that they get along. They've built an entire career around hating each other.'

'Do you think either of the dead women might have caught them in the act?'

'Well, if I saw them, I suppose anyone might have. There's also the matter of a conversation I overheard.' Tish described the whispered exchange she listened to in the civic center lobby.

'"It's gone too far and gone on far too long,"' Jules quoted. 'Sounds kinda sinister.'

'Depends on what they're talking about,' Clayton replied. 'Tish, are you sure you can't identify who was talking?'

'Positive. I've been tossing it around in my mind all day and I've come up blank. All I know is that it sounded like a man and a woman, but they were both whispering. It might have been Kitty and Desmond or Tallulah and Vernon or even Gordon Quinn and one of the female contestants. I just don't know.'

'Everyone seems to have a motive for wanting you, Lillian, and Pen out of the competition,' MJ noted.

'I know. I actually drew up a chart showing all the motives

and relationships between everyone.' Tish retrieved an over-sized sheet of graph paper from the front entryway and placed it in the center of the kitchen table for all to see.

'I've seen these on cop shows,' Clayton mentioned. 'They're usually on whiteboards. I haven't seen anyone down at the station use one.'

'And with Lightbody in charge, you probably won't. It would require him to learn how to read.' Jules chuckled. 'This is very thorough, Tish, except you left out the link between Lillian and Penelope.'

'Oops,' Tish exclaimed before grabbing a pen from the kitchen junk drawer and returning to the table. 'Friends,' she said aloud as she wrote the connection on the chart.

'But were they really friends?' Mary Jo challenged.

'I don't know what you mean.'

'Well, the two women met at the bake-off the year Lillian Harwood died, right? That's not a lot of time to get to know each other.'

'Supposedly, Lillian was a maternal figure.'

'Yeah, I get that – but why? I mean, maybe she was kind to Penelope who was there on her first bake-off, but for Penelope to pay tribute to Lillian by baking a cherry pie denotes a great amount of affection and respect. They had less than three days to get to know each other, so what bonded them?'

'MJ has a point,' Jules agreed. 'The three of us are best of friends, but that's because we all liked the same music and clothes—'

'And boys—' MJ interjected.

'And we spent a lot of time together at UVA. Y'all were room-mates' – Jules pointed between Tish and MJ – 'and the three of us worked in the campus bookstore in addition to having some classes together.'

'Then there were the marathon movie nights,' MJ added.

'Which you didn't always make because you were dating Glen.' Jules growled. 'You should have listened to me then.'

'Yeah, yeah, I know. At least I got two great kids out of the deal.'

'That you did.'

As Jules and Mary Jo reminisced, Tish thought about what

Lillian Harwood and Penelope Purdue might have had in common. The answer came to her, seemingly out of the blue. 'Canada.'

'What?' Clayton asked.

'Canada. Lillian Harwood grew up in northern Vermont, just a stone's throw from the Canadian border. She and her parents would drive to visit her grandmother every weekend. And Penelope Purdue came from up north as well and graduated from McGill University.'

'So?'

'So, New England borders Quebec. If Lillian Harwood's family traveled there for a weekend visit, her grandmother most likely lived in the southern part of the province. McGill University is located in Montreal, which is also located in the southern part of the province. The two women both spent time in Quebec – that's the connection!'

'I'll look into it,' Clayton promised. 'Are we meeting again tomorrow night? Because this has been cool.'

'I'm game if everyone else is. Only tomorrow, I suggest we order Thai.' Jules cast a dirty look at the policeman as he stuffed the last slice of pepperoni and mushroom pizza in his mouth. 'And this time Jim's buying.'

SEVENTEEN

Tish waited up past midnight in anticipation of Schuyler's return. When he texted at twenty minutes past to say he wouldn't be home until one, a weary, heavy-lidded Tish could wait no longer. Trudging off to the bedroom, she crawled beneath the covers and promptly fell asleep.

What felt like hours later, she awoke to the restless movement of a warm body lying beside her. 'Hey,' she greeted groggily while glancing at her bedside clock. It was a quarter to two.

'Sorry,' Schuyler whispered, rolling on to his back. 'I didn't mean to wake you.'

'It's fine. I tried to stay awake until you got home but I just couldn't.'

'It's just as well. I'm totally shot.'

'Well, you're home now. Get some good rest.'

'Mmph,' Schuyler grunted.

Tish leaned her head towards his and kissed him on the lips. 'I'm sorry about this afternoon.'

He didn't return the kiss. He just lay on his back, lips together. 'We'll discuss it another time.'

'OK. Goodnight.'

Schuyler didn't answer.

As Tish flopped back against her pillow and pulled the covers up to her chin, Schuyler rolled on to his right side, his back to her.

Lying awake in the dark, listening as his breathing slowed into a soft, steady rhythm, a single tear rolled silently down her cheek.

She hadn't felt so alone in years.

The alarm rang at six thirty and, just like every other morning that week, Tish awoke to find Schuyler's side of the bed unoccupied. Rubbing the sleep from her eyes, she staggered off toward the kitchen, where she found Schuyler, fully dressed in a navy-blue suit, white shirt, and tie, packing his briefcase for the day ahead.

He nodded toward the coffee maker. 'I put that on for you.'

'Thanks.' Tish collected her favorite mug from the cabinet closest to the refrigerator and filled it with the steaming-hot elixir. 'You're earlier than usual this morning.'

'I have to get the team ready for three house closings and a will reading before heading off on the campaign trail.'

'Busy day,' she noted, diluting her coffee with the milk Schuyler had left on the counter.

'Yes, it is. I'd ask you what you have lined up for the day, but I'm fairly certain I already know.'

'I'm sorry, Schuyler, but I have to go.'

'Even though I begged you not to.' He glared at her.

'You didn't beg, you commanded. How did you expect me to react to that?' she challenged.

'By respecting my feelings.'

'The same way you've respected mine?'

'I've tried to respect your feelings, Tish, but I just can't comprehend why you have to be the damn hero all the time.'

Tish shook her head. 'That's not true.'

'Yes, it is. Whenever something like this happens, you jump right in there, looking for answers, putting yourself at risk. For once, just let the police handle this without you.'

'But they're not handling it, Schuyler. The very fact my mixer was sabotaged proves that they aren't.'

'OK, so maybe they're not doing the best job. You can still remove yourself from danger. Leave the bake-off. Just leave, and the notes and the near-miss electrocutions, and God-knows-what-else will stop. It will all stop. It's as simple as that.'

'It isn't that simple and there's more at stake here than your disapproval.' She put her mug down on the counter and folded her arms across her chest.

'You're right, there is. I can't go through all this again. I just can't.'

Tish's jaw dropped. 'What do you mean?'

'I mean that after years of hard work, the firm is finally taking off and making some serious money, and I'm *that*' – he held his thumb and forefinger in the air, approximately one inch apart – 'close to becoming the youngest mayor of Hobson Glen, and my plans for this town have the attention of the town council. I can't take time off to nurse you back to health again, Tish, just because you keep rushing into burning buildings. You can't ask that of me. You can't expect it.'

As Tish's recovery took place while Schuyler's law firm was closed for a two-week Christmas break, he had, in truth, taken just one week off from work, but Tish wasn't about to escalate the argument. Schuyler had already landed a soul-crushing blow.

'I won't expect it, then,' she replied in a near-whisper.

'I have to go,' he announced, fastening the last buckle on his briefcase and turning toward the foyer.

'I hope you get everything done that you need to,' she said in farewell.

'Yeah, me, too,' he grumbled before disarming the house alarm and making his way out of the front door. He slammed it closed behind him, leaving Tish alone in the kitchen with her coffee, her thoughts, and her fears.

Tish finished her coffee, showered, dressed in her customary uniform, donned a denim jacket to protect her from the chill of the civic center air conditioning, and, as she had done the day prior, drove off for the café to check in on the morning crowd.

She arrived at the cafe to find Mary Jo moving between four occupied tables offering refills of coffee and decaf. When she had finished, she joined Tish behind the counter. 'Hey,' Mary Jo greeted, placing the carafes back on their hot plates. 'I didn't expect to see you here this morning.'

'Change in plans. Need some help?'

'No, I've got it. Thursdays are mellow.' She gestured at the mostly empty café. She looked well rested and relaxed in a red blouse and dark capri pants. 'Tomorrow's the rough one. Seems like the whole town comes in here on payday.'

'Well, I can pop in a little earlier tomorrow if you'd like,' she offered, fixing herself a piece of avocado toast.

'No, Celestine will be here tomorrow. She took this morning off to gear up.' Mary Jo adjusted her apron and flashed her friend a quizzical look. 'How come you have so much time all of a sudden?'

'Hmm?' Tish looked up despondently from her breakfast, prompting MJ to frown.

'OK, what's wrong?'

'Nothing. Just a little tired.' Tish took a bite of toast and, deeming it needed a bit more heat, sprinkled it with more dried chili.

MJ folded her arms across her chest and raised a skeptical eyebrow.

'Stop it,' Tish said. 'You're doing that "mom" thing you always do.'

'That's because, just like my kids, I can always tell when you're lying.'

Tish put her toast back on to her plate. 'I had a disagreement with Schuyler this morning.'

'Another one?'

'Technically, a continuation of yesterday's disagreement. Schuyler still hasn't forgiven me.'

'You mean he's still angry?'

'He wouldn't even kiss me goodnight.'

'What time did he get in?'

'After one.'

'Well, he was probably tired.'

'He was, but it wasn't that. He was still upset with me this morning. No "hello," no kiss goodbye, just disapproval over me continuing to compete in the bake-off.' Tish picked up the avocado toast and took a large bite.

Mary Jo fetched a mug from beneath the counter and poured her friend a cup of coffee. 'He's worried about you, Tish.'

'Yes, I know, and I can understand that, but there are times when it sounds as if he's more worried about his career. He told me this morning that the firm is doing better than ever and he could become the youngest mayor Hobson Glen has ever elected and he doesn't want my actions to compromise anything.'

'I don't see how you could possibly compromise anything.' MJ scooped her hair up, twisted it into a bun at the back of her neck, and secured it with a ballpoint pen.

'Apparently, I'll compromise Schuyler's career by risking my life at the bake-off, by not spending enough time on the campaign trail, by not being on his arm at speaking engagements, by wanting to cater the fundraiser dinner next Friday, by not immediately limiting my Sunday café hours so that I can work on campaign stuff . . . the list is seemingly endless.' Tish frowned. 'Sorry for whining. I'm just frustrated with the whole situation. It's like he's putting up this wall between us.'

'You're not whining. Although it sounds like he might be,' Mary Jo asserted.

Tish looked up from her breakfast.

'Sorry,' Mary Jo apologized, albeit insincerely. 'But the thought of you doing anything to ruin his prospects is completely absurd. He announced he was running for mayor on Christmas Eve – the day you were released from the hospital – without telling you first, and despite that, you've been with him every step of the way. You've never complained about the late nights and early mornings. You've offered to close your café on Sundays so you can spend more time with him. You've brought food down to headquarters for him and his staff. You've offered to hold functions at your café—'

'Which he's declined. Next week's dinner is being catered by Lemaire.'

'Why is a restaurant in Richmond doing the catering? He is running for mayor, right? Not Virginia state senator?'

Tish shrugged. 'He wants the food to be the very best.'

'And the price tag, too. Why he'd want to waste upscale food on the crew at town hall is beyond me.' Mary Jo shook her head. 'Still, it must have bothered you that he asked someone else to do the catering.'

'It did. It does. I mean, cooking and catering are what I do. If I can't do it for him – someone I love – at a time when he needs that service, what does it say? What does it mean? Other than maybe I don't know Schuyler the way I thought I did.'

'Solving crimes is also what you do,' Mary Jo reminded.

'Yes, although I'm wondering if I should give it all up.'

'Because of Schuyler?'

'Partly. I've already been shot while trying to solve a case and here I am involved in yet another one. I must be crazy.' She washed a bite of avocado toast down with a swig of coffee.

'I don't think you're crazy at all.' Mary Jo poured some coffee into her own cup and added a splash of milk. 'It's not as if you go out of your way to look for crimes to investigate. They find you.'

'Yes, but why?'

'Because you're good at what you do and it's as if something in the universe knows that. It knows that you're the one who will restore balance.'

'You honestly believe that?'

'I do. If my marriage to Glen has taught me anything, it's that the things you chase after and struggle to hold on to are the things that you've either outgrown or were never intended for you in the first place. That's not to say that you shouldn't work for your dreams. What I'm saying is when you need to sacrifice your own happiness to attain something or hold on to someone, then that thing isn't for you. The people and things that wander into our lives when we least expect them and provide us with what we both want and need – those are the things to grab on to.'

'I've never seen this side of you before, Mary Jo. You're very . . .'

'Hippie-ish?' Mary Jo offered with a giggle.

'No, philosophical.'

'Well, you can thank my therapist. But I do think it's a valid viewpoint.'

'It is and far different from the one Schuyler was espousing this morning. He said I solve crimes because I always want to play the hero.' She broke off a corner of toast and nibbled it pensively.

'I don't view it that way at all. I see your detective work the same way I view your cooking. You have a talent and skill that benefits others, and not only do you put it to good use, but you put your heart into it. Look, I don't want to see you get injured again any more than Schuyler does, but I also know that what you're doing is helping people. Just look what you did for the theater group last Christmas. One couple's married, another is patching things up, and yet another is embarking on a new romance. That's all because of your sleuthing. You do way more than catch killers, Tish. You listen to people and help bring them together. If that's playing the hero, then more people need to do it.'

Tish smiled. 'You're good for a girl's self-esteem – you know that, don't you?'

'I'm just pointing out the truth,' Mary Jo said. 'You're a kick-ass hero.'

'Takes one to know one. Working for Augusta Mae and at the café while raising two teenagers? That's Wonder-Woman-level greatness.'

'Aww, thanks, honey. I get a lot of help from you and Jules.'

'Well, it takes a village, as they say,' Tish stated as she took a final bite of avocado toast.

'And coffee,' Mary Jo added, holding her mug aloft. 'Lots and lots of coffee. Oh, and wine. Don't forget the wine.'

EIGHTEEN

Feeling better than she had in hours, Tish arrived at the civic center parking lot at quarter past eight and parked in a far corner of the contestant lot, beneath a shady tree. Before she could step out from behind the steering wheel of the Matrix, she was met by Officer Clayton. He was dressed casually in a logo T-shirt, jeans, and sneakers.

'Morning,' he greeted.

'Morning. Have you gone rogue?' she asked, remarking upon his wardrobe.

'Kinda. Lightbody's in meetings all day, so he won't be stopping by here.'

'Tragic.' She stepped on to the asphalt and, finding the outdoor temperature had risen considerably since getting dressed that morning, removed her jacket and flung it on to the driver's seat before shutting the door and locking it.

'You'll be glad you did that. The civic center air conditioning is only functioning at half capacity. Something to do with yesterday's power surge.'

'Seriously? I'm alive but the AC is dead?'

'Yep. Ms Flournoy's been freaking out trying to find someone to repair it. It's supposed to get up to eighty-five this afternoon.'

'Add the one hundred ovens that will no doubt be operating right after lunch and it promises to be downright toasty in there. You're here bright and early, by the way,' she noted as they made their way to the civic center entrance.

'Sticking close by, just in case something else happens.'

'Did Lightbody suggest you do this?'

'Yeah, no.' He laughed. 'I took a page out of the WWRD playbook.'

Tish's face was a question.

'What Would Reade Do? The answer is he'd keep an eye on you to, A, make sure you were safe and, B, smoke out the suspect when they come after you again. Because' – Clayton paused as if searching for the correct turn of phrase – 'I think there's a good chance he or she might come after you again.'

'I do, too,' Tish agreed.

'Damn, I wish Reade was working this case with us right now.'

Tish remained silent. She too wished Reade were there. Her makeshift detective squad was loyal and effective, but she missed how she and Reade could practically know what the other was thinking. She missed how easily she could express herself to him and how readily he would respond, even if her ideas were sometimes farfetched or obtuse. But, most of all, she missed having a partner who completely trusted her judgment.

'I did some digging into Ms Harwood and Ms Purdue,' Clayton said.

'What did you find?'

'Not much. Lillian Harwood was born Lillian Jean Atkinson in St Albans, Vermont. Her mother was Québécois, born in Saint-Jean-sur-Richelieu, just an hour's drive from St Albans.'

'The grandmother she visited,' Tish interjected.

'Yep. As we know, Lillian Harwood was a teacher. Got her degree from Middlebury College in 1973. She married twice – first to a man by the name of Pelletier, also from Quebec. She had two sons with him, Guy Junior, born in 1977, and Paul, born in 1985. She and Guy Senior divorced in 1987. Lillian moved back to Vermont where she worked as an elementary school teacher. She remarried in 1989, this time to Mr Harwood. That marriage lasted just seven years. They divorced in 1996. Lillian retired from teaching in 2010 and moved to Poquoson, just outside Yorktown, presumably to be closer to Guy Junior and his family. There's nothing else on her until her death in 2019.'

'Pretty basic,' Tish noted.

'Yeah – as I said, it wasn't much.' He held the main door of the civic center open to allow Tish admittance.

'Thanks. Anything on Penelope Purdue?'

'Even less than Lillian. Most of what I found comes from her employer, Shockhoe Bottom Development. They're a software development firm and a subsidiary of Milton Technologies in Montreal. Penelope worked for Milton for four years before applying for a position with Shockhoe.'

'So Penelope pulled up stakes and moved to Richmond? She must have been a valuable company asset for Milton to pay for both her moving expenses and her visa.'

'No visa necessary. Penelope Purdue had dual citizenship. According to her employment paperwork, she was born in Quebec in 1985 to an American-born mother and Canadian-born father.'

Tish stopped walking. '*When* was she born?'

'1985.'

'Same year as Paul Pelletier.'

'Yeah, I guess so.'

'Huh. So, Lillian's older son, Guy—' Tish pronounced the name as Ghee.

'Who?'

She repeated the name with the same pronunciation. 'It's how you pronounce the name Guy in French.'

'Um . . . OK.'

'So we know Guy is married and living in Yorktown. Do we know anything about Lillian's younger son, Paul?'

'I didn't do much digging, but I didn't find anything. But there was nothing in Lillian's files to suggest either son was in trouble with the law at any time, either, if that's what you're thinking.'

'That wasn't what I was thinking, but hmm,' Tish wondered aloud.

'What's "Hmm"?'

'Well, both Penelope Purdue and Paul Pelletier were born in Quebec in 1985.'

'Yeah, so? You think Penelope might have been Paul's girlfriend?'

'It's possible,' she allowed. 'But there's also another possibility.'

'Which is?'

'Penelope Purdue was born in Quebec in 1985, and she had an American-born mother and a Canadian-born father. Just like Paul Pelletier. She had the same initials, too.'

Clayton's eyes grew wide. 'You're not saying . . . no, get out.'

'It's a long shot, sure, but we can't just write it off. After all, who was Penelope Purdue before she was Penelope Purdue?'

'Don't know yet. When she underwent gender reassignment,

she changed all her essential documents. Even her Canadian birth certificate lists her as female. I've issued some inquiries regarding Penelope's life before transitioning, but I haven't heard back yet. Nor can I be sure I'll even get any info back. The Canadian government is very protective of the privacy of its LBGQT citizens.'

'Rightly so. There's a lot of hate and misinformation out there,' she commented as she led the way to the exhibition hall and her booth.

'Oh, I inspected your booth this morning. Your mixer, ovens, range, and refrigerator all seem to be working properly,' Clayton informed. 'So do the sink tap and drain.'

Tish was surprised by Clayton's efficiency. 'That's . . . very thorough of you.'

He placed his hands on his hips in something akin to a superhero pose. 'WWRD, Tish. WWRD.'

After the standard check-in with Willadeane, the rest of the morning unfolded as anticipated. Tish was grateful. Between her argument with Schuyler and the pressure to bake and then unmold a perfect pink champagne cake, she might have buckled had anything else occurred before she'd had a chance to break for lunch. Instead, she found herself enjoying the familiar rhythm of sifting and weighing flour and sugar and whipping egg whites until they formed billowing peaks.

By the time the noon buzzer rang, she was feeling much more relaxed. She was, however, quite ravenous, having only eaten a slice of avocado toast that morning. Rapidly untying her apron, she reached down for her handbag and started to make her way to the hospitality suite.

She was right outside the door when an ebullient David Biederman blocked her path. 'Tish, how are you?'

'Oh, hi, David. I'm fine. And you?'

'I'm great. I have a surprise for you.' He held a large brown paper bag aloft.

'For me?'

'Since you mentioned you were from New York, I called my Richmond bakery crew and had them send over some of Biederman's Bagels' famous bagel sandwiches. I've got shrimp salad, egg and cheese, pastrami with mustard, hummus with sundried tomato and spinach, the classic lox with a schmear of cream cheese, and a product we're launching as part of our new lunch menu this weekend: hot chicken and sweet pickle. As I told you before, the new menu was devised by a Southern chef and was years in the making. Let's have lunch together. You can have first pick.'

'That's a lot of sandwiches. Who else are you inviting?'

'Just you. There's a park nearby; I thought we could sit outside and get out of this stuffy environment.' He loosened his gray silk necktie as if to emphasize the increasing temperature inside the civic center.

'That's most kind of you, but I'm afraid I'm going to have to give it a miss.'

'But why? It's not a date if that's what you're thinking.'

That David Biederman felt it necessary to classify their potential luncheon as something other than a date confirmed, in Tish's mind, that he had more in mind than bringing a taste of home to a native New Yorker. 'That's good to know, as I am in a relationship. However, my reason for refusing is that I don't believe it's ethical for a contestant to strike up a friendship with a judge. I'm certain there's something about it in the bake-off regulations.'

'This is a casual event, Tish. We don't put too much stock in rule books. Besides, Kitty's too busy screaming at Willadeane and the civic center people to get the air conditioning repaired to notice that we've gone. So, what do you say?'

Tish opened her mouth to utter a second, sterner, refusal, but she didn't need to.

'Tish,' Dolly exclaimed, placing a beefy, navy-blue cardigan-sleeved arm around the caterer's shoulders, 'there you are. We've been waiting for you before we start eating.'

'As I was going to say, I already have a lunch date,' Tish informed David with a broad smile.

'Bad luck for me, then,' he remarked with a sideways glance at Dolly. 'But you can't escape me tomorrow.'

The tone of David Biederman's voice was slightly menacing, sending a chill down Tish's spine. 'Enjoy your lunch, ladies,' he purred before taking off down the main lobby.

'Thanks, Dolly,' Tish said appreciatively. 'I could have handled it myself, but I'm glad you were here.'

Dolly removed her arm and placed her hands on her denim-clad hips. 'I'm sure you could have handled it, but it would have taken up half your lunch break to disentangle yourself from him and his slimy little tentacles. Trust me, I've seen it before. But why don't you go fetch yourself something to eat and we'll talk more at the table.'

A hungry Tish heeded Dolly's advice and helped herself to the buffet, grabbing a plate of salad topped with a scoop of tuna and a glass of chilled hibiscus tea. Juggling the two items, she joined Dolly, Riya, and Gordon at their table, settling into the seat that had been reserved for her.

'That David Biederman has always been a masher,' Dolly stated, before sinking her teeth into one of several varieties of sandwich halves stacked upon her plate.

'A masher?' Tish asked, confused.

Gordon, his unshaven face making him look more unkempt than it had the day before, uttered a cry of pain. 'No one uses that word anymore, Dolls. What year do you think this is? 1956?'

'All right, quiet down,' Dolly ordered. 'Masher is the term my mother used to describe a man who thinks he's more attractive to women than he actually is. You know – a sex pest, an octopus, a letch.'

'Ah.' Tish dove into her salad. 'So, Mr Biederman's asked contestants to lunch before?'

'Oh, yeah.'

'More than that even.' Riya looked up from her vegetarian wrap. She was resplendent in a bright yellow sari and gold accessories. 'He goes out of his way to give the winners of the competition an extra hug or kiss on the cheek.'

'You mean "on the cheek" if you turn your head away fast enough.' Dolly laughed.

'Did anyone ever file a complaint about David Biederman?' Tish asked.

'Not that I am aware of,' Riya replied. 'He's one of the judges. No one here wants to be on his bad side.'

'Yeah, I don't think Kitty Flournoy would do much to

discipline him anyway,' Gordon added to the conversation. 'The bake-off audience likes him. They like how he tries to make peace between Vernon and Tallulah and how he adds a Yankee spin to the judging. They even like how he seems to have no idea what Southerners actually like to eat.'

'Have you had some incidents with him, Riya?' Tish questioned.

'Yes, I have. Twice he's been by my booth to say "hello" and he's let his hands linger on my back just a little too long.'

'I haven't had any run-ins with him,' Dolly said proudly. 'He doesn't go after the old ones.'

'I don't think age has anything to do with it, Dolly,' Riya argued. 'He tried to charm Lillian Harwood, remember? She was about your age.'

Tish paused, fork in the air. 'How did Lillian react to that?'

'She told him she was too old to have to put up with men smooth-talking her and other such horse poop. Only, she didn't use the word "poop."' Riya's face colored. 'Mr Biederman wasn't happy.'

'Because Lillian overreacted,' Dolly stated. 'Boys will be boys. She was old enough to know that. All the man did was compliment her on whatever monstrosity of an oversized top she was wearing.'

'It was a tunic,' Riya corrected. 'She wore it over slim-fitting pants. It was a very attractive look for her.'

Tish ate her salad and listened eagerly.

'Regardless, Lillian should have accepted David Biederman's comment with a polite "thank you" and gone about her business. She knew that he treats everyone that way.'

'Everyone?' Tish quizzed.

'Not me,' Gordon said with a smile before biting off a hunk of tuna sandwich.

Dolly made a face at him. 'Everyone who was female. Come to think of it, I do believe he may have thrown a flattering remark my way once or twice, but I honestly can't remember what he said.' Dolly shook her head. 'Anyways, it wasn't important. No one ever gave David any fuss, other than when Penelope Purdue slapped him.'

'She slapped him?' Tish repeated.

'Yeah. It was the first day of her second year of competition and David moved in for a kiss to welcome her back. Poor thing had gone for emergency dental work just the day before which made her lips swell like . . . well, I don't know how to describe it.'

'It looked like she'd gotten lip fillers,' Riya explained. 'Bad lip fillers that had settled in all the wrong places.'

'Yeah, that's what it looked like,' Dolly agreed. 'Well, David went in for a kiss anyway. I don't know if she was still under the influence of laughing gas or Novocaine or if she'd just lost her mind, but she slapped him, right across the face. Caught him completely by surprise.'

'Once again, Mr Biederman was not happy,' Riya noted.

Tish munched on her salad, lost in thought. Could David Biederman have murdered Lillian Harwood and Penelope Purdue because they had humiliated him in front of other contestants? 'What about Whitney Liddell?' she asked. 'Surely he hasn't tried anything with her.'

'Ho, ho, don't let Mr Biederman fool you,' Dolly advised, moving on to her second sandwich. 'He might say that he doesn't understand Whitney's Southern charms, but he's enraptured by them nonetheless.'

'And she?'

'Oh, that woman knows exactly where her bread is buttered. He's a judge – a judge who's voted in her favor the past three years. She's not about to tell him "no" to anything.'

'Anything?' Tish prodded.

'Anything,' Dolly emphasized and raised her eyebrows.

NINETEEN

The lunch group broke up at around twelve forty-five, leaving the foursome ample time to strategize the next round of baking. Riya set off for the ladies' room while Tish requested a few words with Dolly, alone.

'What is it, Tish?' Dolly asked.

'On the day Penelope Purdue died, you offered her a ride, didn't you?'

'How did you—? Oh, Willadeane told you, didn't she?'

Tish nodded. 'But you didn't take Penelope Purdue to the hospital. She was taken there by taxi. What happened?'

'You tell me,' she retorted. 'If you know how she got to the hospital, then you know a helluva lot more than I do.'

'Just tell me what happened,' Tish urged.

'I finished my showstopper cake at around four o'clock that afternoon, so I flagged down Willadeane to let her know I was ready to take it to the judges. Willadeane came over to my booth, but she was distracted. Pen wasn't feeling well and Willadeane was about to call a taxi to take her home. Since I'd been cleaning as I went along – as I usually do – all I had to do was turn on my dishwasher before I left for the day, so I offered to take Pen home. She lived right in town, so it was no bother, and I felt kinda weird about her being in a cab with some strange driver when she was sick. It's the mother in me, I guess. Well, Pen wouldn't hear of it. She didn't want to inconvenience anyone. She wanted to drive home herself, in her own car, get some rest, and start the contest fresh the next morning. But as she was talking, I could see she was getting worse, you know? Willadeane had left to attend to some other bakers, so I took matters into my own hands. I found a chair and had Pen sit down in her booth while I went to retrieve the first-aid team. When I got back, Pen was gone.'

'Gone?'

'Without a trace. I asked the bakers in the vicinity if they'd seen Pen leave, but they were so focused on their cakes they hadn't noticed anything. I asked other volunteers, but they were so busy they hadn't noticed anything either. You know how it is during that last hour of the day. It's organized chaos.'

Tish acknowledged that the final sprint to the judges' table was, indeed, stressful for everyone. 'What did you do next?'

'I went home. I assumed – wrongly, as we now know – that Pen had started to feel better and drove herself home as she wanted. I was going to wait around to ask Willadeane if she knew whether Pen was feeling any better, but she was running around like a chicken without a head, so I left for the day. I had every intention of talking with Pen and Willadeane the next morning to find out what happened, but I was late – car trouble – so I checked in and went directly to my booth. The booth next door – Pen's booth – was empty. It was just before lunch rolled around that Kitty announced Pen was dead.'

'Pen took a cab to the hospital that evening. It picked her up here. Were you aware of that?'

'Nope, but it's not surprising. She was determined to drive herself. Poor thing probably got as far as the parking lot, found out she wasn't well enough to drive after all and called the cab herself. Makes the most sense, doesn't it?'

'Yes,' Tish replied, although she wasn't convinced. 'Yes, I suppose it does.'

Tish followed Dolly back to the exhibition hall to catch up with Clayton and check in with Jules, who was slated to start his bake-off coverage at one. As she hurried along the civic center's main lobby, she heard Gordon's voice calling to her. 'Tish. Tish?'

Tish turned around to find he had trailed her from the hospitality suite. 'Sorry, Gordon. I didn't know you were behind me.'

'No worries. I didn't say anything because I didn't want Dolly to see me. I need to talk to you.'

'Sure. We have a few minutes before the competition starts again.'

'Not now. There are too many people around.' Gordon glanced nervously over his shoulder.

'How about we talk at the end of today's contest, when Dolly and Riya have left for the day?' she suggested.

Gordon agreed. 'The hospitality suite is usually empty at that time since all that's left in there is the coffee machine.'

'Good, I'll meet you there after the crowds have dispersed.'

'Deal – but lose the bodyguard.' He nodded to a location over her right shoulder.

Tish turned her head to see Jim Clayton standing approximately ten yards behind her. 'Sorry, but he stays. Depending upon what you have to say, Officer Clayton doesn't have to be privy to our conversation, but after the mixer incident, I'm keeping him nearby.'

'All right,' Gordon capitulated. 'I'll see you later.'

'What was that about?' Clayton asked when Gordon had gone.

'He wants to talk to me at the end of the day. In private.'

'I hope you said no.'

'I said yes, but that I'd meet him in the hospitality suite and that you'd be nearby.'

'Good. I heard from Ms Purdue's doctor. No nut allergy, but she did have a severe allergy to penicillin. She took it once for an upper respiratory infection and her throat nearly closed in from the swelling.'

'*Pen* Purdue was allergic to *pen*icillin. Why do I feel as though we should have seen that coming?'

'Because it's like a really bad dad joke,' Clayton replied. 'The doctor also told me that Ms Purdue underwent gender reassignment surgery in Canada ten years ago. He has no idea as to her identity before she transitioned. He only had access to her medical records and, of course, her current ID.'

'Did you find out anything else?'

'That's it for now, but I'm still digging.'

'Well, I learned some interesting things at lunch.'

'Like?'

Tish gestured toward the civic center doors, through which Jules, dressed in a dark suit, bright-green tie, and Wayfarer sunglasses, had just entered. He held a green-bowed Biscuit in his arms as he made his way through the metal detector. 'Let's wait until he's here so I don't have to repeat the story.'

The pair watched Jules as he made it through the security checkpoint, collected his phone, wallet, leash, and keys, and approached. 'Hey, y'all. What do you think of Fabulous for a middle name?'

'What?' Tish was incredulous.

'Middle name for whom?' a confused Clayton asked.

'For me. I'm ditching the Jefferson. It's insensitive.'

'That's pretty woke,' Clayton acknowledged.

'Is that good or bad?'

'It's good.'

'Cool. So, what do you guys think? Julian Fabulous Davis. Walter wasn't flamboyant enough, but Fabulous is . . . simply fabulous.'

'Is it legal to use a superlative as a name?' Clayton asked Tish.

'It's not a superlative. It's an adjective. An "extra" adjective, as you would put it, but an adjective, nonetheless. As for the legality, if it isn't illegal, it probably should be,' Tish answered, aside. 'Um, Jules, don't you think that might be a little over the top?'

'Yes,' he allowed, 'but it's a middle name. It can be over the top. You have the classy, businesslike, respectable Julian up front. And then, behind it, the fun, party-like Fabulous,' he explained.

'Business in the front. Party in the back. Are you looking for name or a mullet?'

Jules removed his glasses. 'I take it that's a "no," then?'

'It's a "no" with an extra side of "seriously?"'

'Choosing a name is hard, Tish,' Jules whined. 'Biscuit and I have been up all night thinking about it.'

'Don't worry. You'll eventually come up with something that suits you and yet doesn't make DMV employees laugh every time you renew your driver's license.'

'I guess so.' Sulking, Jules put his glasses in his suit pocket. 'So, did we miss anything this morning?'

Clayton filled him in about Penelope's allergy and his conversation with the doctor.

'And I just found out that Penelope had a dentist appointment the day before last year's bake-off began,' Tish informed.

Jules's eyes narrowed. 'What do you think it means?'

'Given the fact that Pen's lips were swollen after her appointment, it means the dentist might have prescribed her with the penicillin that killed her.'

'But that would mean her death had nothing to do with the bake-off,' Clayton surmised with disappointment.

'It would,' Tish agreed, 'but we need to look into it. WWRD, remember?'

Jules was puzzled. 'WWRD?'

'What would Reade do,' Tish explained.

'He'd explore every lead,' Clayton said.

'And, therefore, so do we.'

'I'll see if I can track down who her dentist was.'

'Thanks. While you're at it, you may want to delve into David Biederman's past and see if he has any record of violence toward women.'

'Violence?'

'Yes, he approached me right before lunch with a bag of bagel sandwiches and—'

'Oh, did you try one? How was it?' Jules asked, agog. 'I've been dying to get over to one of his bakeries and try one of their onion bagels, but I haven't had a chance.'

'I didn't eat the sandwiches, Jules. His invitation to lunch was a thinly veiled attempt to hit on me.'

'Hit on you?' Jules's excitement dissolved into shock. He pulled Biscuit closer to his chest.

'Yes, Jules. You might be surprised to learn that some men aren't put off by the two-foot-wide hump on my back and my chronic halitosis,' she deadpanned.

'Huh? What?'

'Well, you needn't have sounded so surprised, Jules.'

'Oh, no, I didn't mean it that way. I was surprised because David Biederman is a judge. Honest!'

'I was a bit taken aback, too, but then Dolly told me David puts the moves on all the women at the bake-off.'

'All?' Jules and Clayton cried in unison.

'All,' she confirmed. 'He compliments the older women on their hair or wardrobe. The younger ones he tries to kiss on the lips, among other things.'

'By all, are you including Ms Harwood and Ms Purdue?' Clayton asked.

'I am. However, both women shunned his advances, which is a rare occurrence because no one wants to tick off a judge. Lillian Harwood swore at him when he praised her outfit and Penelope Purdue actually slapped David across the face when he tried to plant a kiss on her lips.'

'You think he might have retaliated against the two women for rejecting him,' Clayton guessed. 'Is that why you want me to check his background for violence?'

'It is. Violence is a common reaction for guys like him. Especially when that guy is accustomed to using his power as a judge and a CEO to get his way.'

'What about Whitney Liddell?' Jules ventured. 'I'm sure he didn't get his way with her.'

Tish bit her bottom lip and cocked her head to one side.

'Get out! You mean the Ice Queen didn't have her security guards escort him back to the judges' table?'

'According to Dolly, Whitney has always been very accommodating to Mr Biederman.'

'Accommodating how?'

'Do we really need to know the details?' Clayton questioned, his face growing red.

'In every possible way,' Tish told Jules, much to Clayton's chagrin.

'So much for family values!' Jules whooped.

'Not so fast. We've yet to prove what Dolly told me. It could be a case of sour grapes. Although Riya and Gordon didn't dispute the tale.'

'Oh, boy! I can see our channel's teaser now. "From Red Velvet Cake to Scarlett Letter: Bake-Off Queen and Bagel King Caught in Torrid Affair."'

'I'm investigating old-person sex again,' Clayton remarked. 'Terrific.'

'WWRD, Officer,' Jules reminded. 'WWRD.'

TWENTY

Just like the morning, Tish's afternoon passed without incident, enabling her to assemble the layers of the pink champagne cake, fill them with raspberry mousse, and apply a crumb coat – a thin layer of icing that would help give the finished product a smooth surface – as well as a final coat of icing.

Pleased with her work, she tidied her workstation, ran the dishwasher, and reviewed her decorating sketches until the buzzer rang at five o'clock sharp.

Bidding a good evening to Dolly and Riya, she watched the two women leave the exhibition hall before meeting with Willadeane to sign out for the day. With Clayton at her heels, she then made her way to the hospitality suite, where she flopped into a cushioned chair and waited for Gordon Quinn to arrive.

The Navy retiree stepped foot in the suite at seven minutes past the hour and sank into the upholstered chair opposite Tish. 'Thank you for agreeing to see me.'

'Not a problem. Officer Clayton is waiting just outside the door, should I need him, but I requested that he stay far enough away that he won't overhear our conversation. Now, what was it you wanted to talk to me about?'

'I don't know how else to say this except to just say it. I wrote the note.'

Tish was dumbfounded. 'You? Why?'

'It's . . . complicated.'

'Did you also write the threatening notes that were left for Lillian Harwood and Penelope Purdue?'

'Yes,' Gordon confessed.

'And Dolly Pritchard?'

'Dolly never received a note. Nor has anyone else. That was Dolly trying to take center stage again.'

'What about the mixer? Was that you as well?'

Gordon leaned forward in his chair. 'I had nothing to do with your mixer sparking like that. I swear I didn't. That's why I'm here. To tell you about the notes before the police find out about them and accuse me of rigging your mixer.'

Tish narrowed her eyes. She was uncertain whether she could trust Gordon Quinn, but she wanted to hear more of his story. 'So, why the notes? The only things I have in common with Lillian and Penelope are landing in second place after the first day of baking – which is a doubtful motive since you left me the note before the judging took place – and cherry pie.'

Gordon's otherwise stony face melted into grief. 'Cherry pie was supposed to be *her* dish. It was supposed to win her the trophy.'

'Who? Who was supposed to win the trophy, Gordon?'

'My wife, Anh. Winning the bake-off meant everything to her. Everything.'

Tish reached into her handbag and presented Gordon with a tissue.

'Thanks.' He took it and blew his nose. 'I met Anh at the

end of April 1975, in the days before the fall of Saigon. She and her family were refugees fleeing the city – our ship was the one used to transport them to a new life. I was supposed to ensure that she and her family were safely deposited at the naval base in Guam where they'd be processed and transferred to a tent city to await transport to the United States. I wasn't supposed to fall in love, but when I saw Anh, it was like the world stood still. Cliché, I guess, but looking at her face, that's exactly how I felt.

'The next few weeks, I spent every minute I could with Anh. I communicated with her in broken French in the very early days. Soon, Anh had taught me how to speak some Vietnamese and I'd taught her how to speak some English, but when you're that young, you don't need a lot of words to communicate.' He chuckled. 'Weeks passed and Anh and I grew closer. So did the time that she and her family were to leave for America. A few days before they were set to be transferred, I told Anh that I wanted to keep in touch and visit the next time I was back home on leave. That was when she gave me the news: her family wasn't settling in the States; they were using it as a stop on their journey to Canada where other family members were already living.

'I already knew I wanted to marry Anh, but the idea of her moving to another country made me take action. I proposed to her then and there. With her family's permission, we married in Guam one week later. I was twenty. Anh was eighteen. My family thought I was crazy, but I didn't care. Still don't. Marrying Anh was the best thing I've ever done.

'Over the years, we found ourselves stationed all around the world. Anh was always excited at the chance to see a new corner of the universe. She took classes in bookkeeping and English as a second language when we were first married, so she'd find a part-time administrative job at whatever base we were stationed at, but what she most enjoyed was learning about the culture and people of the country we were living in. She'd take out books from the base library and brush up on the local language and try cooking the regional foods. She loved it.

'Still, she missed having a stable home. So, ten years into our marriage, when I had the opportunity, I accepted a full-time position as an engineman in Norfolk. Anh was thrilled. We got ourselves a sweet little house and she had a great time decorating it and being in the kitchen cooking my favorite American foods. She still worked as an admin for the base radio station, but she really enjoyed being a typical American housewife. Except, to others, she wasn't. Most people were cool and welcomed her to the base, but there were always those who'd call her a "gook" or spit at her as she walked down the sidewalk.

'Anh was such a sweet, generous soul. The attacks brought her down, like they would anyone, but she'd always remain positive and upbeat. When I'd lose my temper and want to take on everyone who treated her that way, she'd remind me that they'd probably lost friends and family during the war. I doubt she was correct in every instance, but it goes to show how much she was willing to give others the benefit of the doubt.

'As time moved on and we grew farther from the memories of the Vietnam War, things got better, but there was always someone who'd pass a comment about immigrants and how they should go elsewhere, even though Anh was a naturalized American citizen. It weighed on her through the years. I never realized how heavily until . . . for her forty-fifth birthday, Anh made a request. She wanted to compete in the Virginia Commonwealth Bake-Off. She'd become a truly phenomenal cook, with a catalog of recipes that spanned the globe, but Anh wanted to compete with an American menu.'

'She wanted to prove herself,' Tish presumed.

'Yes. As if winning the competition might make her more accepted.' His eyes welled with tears again. 'More American.'

Tish handed Gordon another tissue and got up to retrieve a glass of water, which he readily accepted. 'Anh made a Colonial American oyster pie for her savory bake, a bald eagle cake with strawberry and blueberry fillings for the showstopper, and, for the signature bake, cherry pie. What could be more American than that?

'By the end of the second day, she was in third place. She was so confident she was going to win, but at the end of the final day, she was told that her cherry pie wasn't creative enough and that she probably should have stuck with a dish from her own country that she might have known and executed better.'

Tish cringed. 'Poor Anh.'

'She took it hard. Real hard.'

'The judges who told her that, are they . . .?'

'Still here today? Nah. Long gone. For a while there, I wanted to hunt them down and strangle each and every one of them, but Anh talked me out of it, of course. She was never the same after that bake-off. That September, she was diagnosed with ovarian cancer. She'd always had trouble with pregnancies. That's why we never had any children. Anh had miscarried several times, and with me being a glorified mechanic, adoption was too costly.' Gordon's voice tapered off. 'Anh passed away in January of the following year.'

'I'm sorry, Gordon. It must have been difficult for you,' Tish sympathized.

'It has been. She shouldn't have gone. Not that young. At first, I had my work to distract me, but after I retired, I needed a hobby, so I took up cooking and baking. That's when the idea came to me: why not enter the bake-off? For her. In her memory. She didn't win, but maybe I could. But when I entered and saw Kitty Flournoy and Whitney Liddell in action – well, it seemed pointless. Still, every year, I try, mostly because I don't know what else to do with my time. I still miss her so.'

'And the notes?' Tish gently prompted.

'I wrote them to scare you and the other women off from baking a cherry pie. That pie belonged to Anh. It was supposed to be her winning dish. Her triumph. I couldn't bear to see someone else win with it. I couldn't.' He sobbed. 'But I wouldn't have hurt any of you. I wouldn't.'

Tish stood up and placed a comforting hand on Gordon's shoulder. 'I believe you,' she whispered.

After debriefing Clayton about her meeting with Gordon Quinn and inviting him to another brainstorming supper that evening, Tish gathered her belongings and headed for the contestant parking area.

Although the air conditioning had been repaired just after lunch and the high ceiling of the civic center helped to trap the heat, the exhibition hall floor was still quite stuffy – stuffy enough that stepping outside into the breezy, eighty-degree weather felt akin to stepping into an air-conditioned room.

Tish donned her sunglasses and breathed in the fresh air. Despite a bumpy start and an attempted seduction-by-sandwich by David Biederman, the day had gone smoothly. She felt good about her showstopper bake and even better about having gotten to the bottom of those threatening notes. Now, all she had to do was to get back home, kick off her shoes, order up some food, and meet with her 'squad' to find out who tampered with her mixer and why.

She walked past the section of the parking lot reserved for volunteers. It was still packed with cars as helpers worked through the evening to prepare for the next day of baking. Meanwhile, in an adjacent area of the lot, the contestant's parking section was completely empty, save for the presence of Tish's red Toyota Matrix.

Tish approached the vehicle with a bounce in her step. How she longed to leave the fast-paced environment of the bake-off and relax on the condo patio for a few quiet minutes of sunshine before dinner. As Tish drew closer to the vehicle her pace slowed.

There, on the windshield, scrawled in bright red icing were the words: QUIT NOW, and to emphasize the seriousness of the warning, what appeared to be a dead rat had been left beneath the message, on the Matrix's hood.

Tish felt the handle of the bag she'd been carrying slip from her fingers as she frantically scanned the parking lot for a trace of someone – anyone – who might have perpetrated such an offense, but there was no one in sight.

'I don't understand it. Why isn't Gordon Quinn in jail right now?' Jules plunged a pair of chopsticks into the white cardboard container of pad see ew and lifted a tangle of noodles to his lips.

'Because Tish isn't pressing charges,' explained Clayton, a double portion of pineapple fried rice with prawns spread out before him. 'And Lillian Harwood and Penelope Purdue – the other note recipients – can't.'

'What about the rat and the message on her windshield this evening?'

'Despite his confession, there's no evidence Gordon Quinn is responsible for the message on Tish's car. Not only is this an entirely different MO, but Tish was parked in a quiet corner of the contestants' parking area with no other cars parked near hers, which means anyone could have slipped out there, hastily scrawled the message, and left unseen.'

'Anyone?' Mary Jo challenged. 'You mean any baker. That red icing proves this was done by another contestant.'

'Not necessarily,' Tish argued. 'That icing is the kind sold in supermarkets. It wasn't homemade and it didn't require any skill whatsoever to pipe it.'

'But Gordon Quinn left just before you did,' Jules maintained.

'It doesn't matter. In addition to the scheduled lunch and afternoon breaks, everyone affiliated with the bake-off – baker, staff, or volunteer – is entitled to a ten-minute break during the day. That break can be taken at any time. That means anyone could have excused themselves, gone to their car, retrieved the rat, deposited it on my car, scrawled the message, and still have plenty of time to get back to their booth or station.'

'By "retrieve the rat", what precisely do you mean?'

'We think the rat was kept in a cooler in someone's car until use,' Clayton explained as he sipped his cup of green tea. 'The perpetrator couldn't have kept the rat with them – all bags entering the civic center are subject to search – and they couldn't have kept it in their car on a hot day without it smelling, so the cooler is the only explanation. We sent the rat out to the lab to see where it might have lived before it died. They can identify its environment by what it ate.'

'I'm sorry I asked,' Jules said, picking at his food with his fork.

'We were hoping to have caught someone on the parking area surveillance cameras,' Clayton continued, 'but the power surge from Tish's mixer fried them. They won't be repaired until early next week.'

'What about that mixer? Can't you charge Quinn for that?' Mary Jo asked as she slurped her tom yum goong.

'According to surveillance footage, Gordon Quinn was nowhere near Tish's booth the morning of the incident. After talking to Tish, he went back to his booth, on the next row, and waited there the entire time. And there's no trace of him in the footage from the storage room where the mixers were kept, either,' Clayton further elaborated.

'That's because his recipes haven't required any specialized equipment,' Tish elucidated as she munched on a spicy green chicken curry with brown basmati rice. 'Apart from a Dutch oven for the savory bake, which was left in his booth at the start of the bake-off, everything he's needed is standard equipment. He bragged about it at lunch today – how he won't be wasting valuable baking time rummaging around the storage racks.'

'Only problem is, according to our surveillance tapes, nobody tampered with Tish's mixer.' Clayton washed down his fried rice and frustration with another sip of green tea.

'How can that be?' Mary Jo questioned.

'Except for a volunteer who performed an inventory with an iPad, the footage didn't show anyone lingering at Tish's booth long enough to sever the mixer cable. Then there's the storage room. We checked the footage against one of Willadeane Scott's gazillion spreadsheets and no one entered that room who shouldn't have. Everyone who checked in with Willadeane went to an area away from where the mixers were stored, got their piece of equipment, and left. The only people who did go near the mixers were the volunteers who distributed them to the bakers' booths the night before the showstopper segment. Although it was something of a free-for-all, I didn't see any of them hanging around long enough to cut the wire. Then again, there is a section of hallway between the storage room and the exhibition hall where there is no camera. However, someone would have had to have been super quick to avoid being seen.'

'Why would a volunteer tamper with Tish's mixer anyway?' Jules challenged.

'Unless they were directed to do it by someone in charge, I can't think of a valid reason,' Clayton conceded. 'Even then, the volunteer would most likely have questioned the request.'

'Which volunteer took my mixer from the storage room to the exhibition hall?' Tish asked.

'Myrna Lucas. Seventy-five years old and a bake-off winner from back in the seventies. She lives over at Coleton Creek. You solved a case there a little while ago, didn't you?'

'Yes, while catering for the garden club luncheon.'

'Uh-oh, maybe that Coronation chicken salad you made was a little too spicy for good ol' Myrna's liking and she decided to bump you off. Revenge for her heartburn,' Jules teased.

'Myrna was tasked with delivering mixers to all the booths in your row, Tish,' Clayton continued. 'But since it was the end of a very long day, other volunteers pitched in so they all could get home quicker. I spoke to everyone on mixer duty that night and no one remembers who, precisely, delivered the mixer to your booth. The surveillance camera in that area cycled to another part of the exhibition hall just as the volunteers reached your row, so there's no visual record of it either. In addition, none of the volunteers recall anything unusual happening to any of the mixers during the distribution process.'

'What is the process?' Tish asked.

'Each bake-off mixer is given a serial number at the time of purchase. That serial number is recorded on a spreadsheet, alongside the baker's name, just before distribution takes place.'

'Which means that if someone had access to that spreadsheet, they would have known which mixer was mine and therefore could have tampered with it,' Tish concluded.

'Yeah, but only in the hours immediately prior to the distribution of the mixers,' Clayton pointed out. 'In the storeroom footage from that time, no one appears to do so. Like I said, no one could have done it, and yet they did.'

'There has to be something we're missing,' Mary Jo stated the obvious.

'A tech guy back at the station is looking at footage from the rest of the cameras in the civic center to see if they captured something the others didn't, but I'm not sure what else to do.'

'I can take another crack at some of those volunteers tomorrow,' Jules offered. 'They might reveal more to their trusted local newsman than they would to a police officer. They see me in their living rooms on a daily basis.'

'Getting wiped out by a snowplow or smothered with a fire blanket,' Mary Jo quipped.

'My vulnerabilities make me that much more approachable. Not to mention lovable.' Jules smiled and sipped at his green tea.

'And we do love you, Jules,' Tish answered.

'Hear, hear,' MJ echoed. 'Although it's way too tempting – and satisfying – to poke fun at you.'

'Aww, thanks, y'all,' Jules said, beaming. He glanced at Clayton.

'You're, um, you're pretty cool,' the police officer stated awkwardly. 'My mom enjoys your weather segments.'

'She does? How sweet.'

'Yeah, she likes you a lot better than the weather person on Channel Twelve, even though their forecasts are more accurate.'

Jules wrinkled his nose. 'Don't you have anything else to tell us about the case?'

'Hmm? Oh, yeah, I checked out David Biederman's record and he's had two complaints of sexual harassment filed against him. Both complaints were made from former employees and were settled out of court.'

Mary Jo nearly choked on her soup. 'David Biederman? The bagel baker David Biederman?'

'Yeah,' Tish confirmed. 'It was pretty creepy. He brought a bunch of bagel sandwiches from his bakery and asked me to have lunch with him.'

'Oh! How were the sandwiches? I've heard so many great things about them.'

'I didn't eat the sandwiches, MJ.'

'Really? A mom at Kayla's school said they're terrific.'

'I've heard that, too,' Jules rejoined. 'Folks at the station are raving about them. You should have tried them, Tish.'

'I didn't eat the sandwiches because David Biederman, who might be a murderer, was trying to hit on me and lure me away from the civic center,' Tish reminded her friends. 'What's wrong with you two? No sandwich is worth getting killed over.'

'Sorry,' the pair murmured and went back to their food.

'You really think David Biederman might be the murderer?' MJ asked after a reasonable amount of time had elapsed.

'It's possible. The two dead women both rebuffed his advances,' Tish said.

'If Biederman is a predator, it would be in keeping with his personality to become angered when rejected,' Clayton confirmed.

'It might also explain why he was so adamant about not being at the bake-off last year,' Tish theorized. 'He wouldn't want to be remembered being around when Pen Purdue became ill.'

'It might, but Biederman being a judge means it would have been difficult for him to have committed the crimes without being seen, wouldn't it?'

'That's true,' Jules agreed. 'Everyone at that bake-off knew who David Biederman was. If he had stopped at Penelope's booth at any point that afternoon, someone would have remembered it.'

'I'll try and track Biederman's movements for both days,' Clayton said.

'And I'll ask my lunch buddies,' Tish added.

'The last item I have might be the most interesting. That dentist you told me about, Tish – the one who saw Penelope Purdue the day before the bake-off opened – was Lillian Harwood's dentist, too.'

'Really?'

'Uh-huh. Lillian Harwood was a patient of Doctor Joel Reasoner for years. She first became a patient back when Joel's father, Theodore, owned the practice and carried on after the old man retired and passed the practice to his son. Penelope Purdue was a patient for a little less than a year, from April the year before she died.'

'That timeline is interesting. Did Lillian recommend the dentist to Penelope?'

'I asked the woman who answered the phone if that was the case, but she didn't know. She was filling in for the regular secretary. I asked for both Lillian's and Penelope's files. I should get them tomorrow.'

'Yet another connection,' Tish pondered aloud. 'Did Lillian Harwood happen to have an appointment prior to her death, as well?'

'I didn't ask, since the receptionist on duty didn't seem too knowledgeable. It sounded really busy there, too. I figured we'd get a list of each women's appointments when we got their medical records.'

'Of course,' Tish agreed, thoughtfully tucking into her green curry. 'Do you think the woman on the phone was telling the truth about being a temp? Or was she trying to get rid of you?'

Clayton bit his lip. 'Tough to say. She sounded nervous. I assumed it was because she was overwhelmed at her job and couldn't answer my questions, but it might have been because she was hiding something.'

'It might be interesting to send someone over to the office and see if the regular secretary is back or if she was even gone at all. It might be helpful to get a feel for the place, too.'

'I don't have the authority to dispatch someone to Reasoner's office. I've been assigned to be at the civic center each morning to patrol the premises and investigate any unusual activity, but no one else is supposed to get involved. I only have a tech guy looking at the additional camera footage because that tech guy is getting married to my sister this summer. My family's being all extra about the wedding plans,' Clayton mentioned to Tish, aside.

'You want me to check out the dentist?' Jules proposed in between bites of pad see ew. 'I can stop by there tomorrow under the guise of seeking an appointment.'

'Yeah, because that won't look weird at all,' MJ scoffed. 'Your friendly local newsman, the dude who shows up in your living room every day, stopping by the office the day after the police have called asking for the records of two dead women.'

'It's not like I'd tell them I was there in an investigative capacity.'

'It doesn't matter. One look at you and they'd clam up worse than they did while on the phone with Clayton.'

Clayton gestured his agreement. 'She's right. Sending you in won't work.'

'That's why I think I should go,' MJ stated.

'You?' Jules gasped. 'You have two children. You can't be doing detective work. It's not safe.'

'This isn't detective work, Jules. It's a reconnaissance mission.'

'Jules isn't alone. I'm not too crazy about the idea of you going over there, either,' Tish rejoined.

'I'm going to a dentist's office in the middle of the business day to schedule an appointment for my child. I'm not searching through or stealing secret files,' MJ argued. 'Where's the office located, Clayton?'

'Richmond City Center.'

'Not a problem. Opal and Celestine are helping out tomorrow. Since it's a workday, the bulk of the breakfast crowd is gone by nine thirty. That gives me plenty of time to drive in, get a feel for the dentist's place, and drive back before the lunch rush.'

'I don't care about the café,' Tish said. 'You could shut it down for the day if you needed to. What I care about is you and your safety.'

'I'll be super careful, Tish. If I drive there and don't feel safe leaving my car, I'll turn around and come back home. If I don't like the look of the office, I won't go in. If I'm there and get a whiff of anything strange, I'll leave and call the police.' MJ's brow furrowed. 'Wait one minute. I sound like—'

'Me.' Tish laughed. 'You sound like me.'

'We've switched places.'

'No, you haven't. You've just given me another person to worry about,' Jules exclaimed.

'I'll be fine,' Tish and Mary Jo each replied in unison.

'Maybe, but until Biscuit and I *know* you're both fine,' he asserted while feeding the little white dog a treat, 'we're going to be a mess!'

TWENTY-ONE

After another pot of green tea, Jules, Mary Jo, and Clayton wrapped up their leftovers, loaded their plates, cups, bowls, and utensils into the dishwasher, and bade each other a good night. Shutting the door behind them and setting the alarm, Tish stretched, yawned, and headed to the bedroom. Although the civic center hadn't been as hot as it might have been, Tish had still done her fair share of perspiring that morning and eagerly anticipated a cool, relaxing shower, followed by a change into cotton pajamas and a good night's sleep.

As she walked down the entry hall and into the kitchen, her cell phone, which she'd left on the counter, chimed to denote a new message. Tish paused and considered her next move. As much as she desperately wanted to ignore the text completely and get on with washing away the cares of the day, she was fearful that if the message was sent from Clayton, her friends, or Schuyler, not answering might cause concern.

Exhaling noisily, she retrieved the offending device from its spot near the refrigerator and switched on the display. There, in the notifications tab, was an announcement that she had received a new text message.

According to the number displayed, the text message had been sent from her own phone. Puzzled, but expecting it was some sort of technical glitch, Tish pressed the notification to open the message. What she saw made her catch her breath: *QUIT THE BAKE-OFF BEFORE IT'S TOO LATE.*

With shaking hands, she dialed Clayton's number and described the message she had received. He was still driving home from the condo when he took the call. 'Do you want me to turn around and come back?'

'No.' Tish declined. What she wanted to do was bolt all the doors, forget the message, go to bed, and stay there for a week. 'I don't think that's necessary.'

'I'm going to need to see that text message. Forward it to me now and then I'll check the original message on your phone in the morning. As soon as I hang up with you, I'll call my future brother-in-law and see what he has to say, but I'm pretty sure I'll need to have someone run your phone down to head-quarters first thing so he can trace the message.'

'Yeah, that's fine. I can't have it on during competition anyway.'

'How are you doing? Are you OK?'

'Mostly. I'm just trying to make sense of everything. If Gordon Quinn is our letter-writer, then who sent this text?'

'No idea. I doubt it's Gordon, though. He confessed to the notes and was relieved to get off with a slap on the wrist. Why would he re-incriminate himself by threatening you again?'

'He wouldn't,' Tish maintained. 'Someone who doesn't know he confessed is emulating him because I'm getting too close for comfort. The real perpetrator has been hiding behind the notes and the legend of a curse to obscure their real motives.'

'And now the real perpetrator has your number.'

'Yeah, I'm not too happy about that, although it wouldn't have been too difficult to obtain. If someone knew about the café, all they'd have to do is check out the website. The restaurant landline and my cell phone are both there.'

'Does anyone at the bake-off know you own a café?'

'Kitty and Whitney know. I told them after the mixer incident.'

'And Kitty and Whitney probably blabbed to the rest of the foundation board and maybe the judges, but that's just conjecture. Can you think of anyone else who had direct knowledge of your café?'

Tish felt the blood drain her face. 'Gordon Quinn.'

'Gordon Quinn, the note writer. First the windshield message and now this. Sounds as if I'm going to have to ask Mr Quinn a few questions,' Clayton determined. 'I'll send a patrol car to your neighborhood tonight. Just to be safe.'

'Thanks.' Tish thought about Schuyler and his possible reaction to the need for police surveillance. 'Um, Jim, is there a way you could send an unmarked car? My boyfriend is running for mayor and I'm pretty sure he'd like to keep all of this quiet.'

'Yeah, sure. I'll have our officer stop by your house to introduce himself so you know who he is and what car he's driving. Don't open the door until he identifies himself and presents his badge.'

'I won't. Thanks, Jim. Goodnight.' Tish disconnected the call and immediately rechecked the windows, door locks, and security system. Forgoing her shower, she quickly slipped into her pajamas and robe and watched through the slats of the living-room Venetian blinds for a sign of the officer on sentry.

Standing alone in the dark, she thought back to a night not that long ago, when she awaited the arrival of Sheriff Clemson Reade. It had been sticky and hot that night, and her body had ached from being struck down in the parking lot of her café while trying to apprehend the person vandalizing her car. Reade arrived within minutes, bandaged her wounds, and then stuck around while she went back to bed feeling safe and reassured.

Tish neither wanted nor needed rescuing – indeed, she had rushed after the vandal that night with a cast-iron skillet – and she was pleased with the manner in which Jim Clayton had handled her current situation, but she missed having Sheriff Reade on the case. She missed his strong and steady presence. She missed his calm demeanor and his sense of reason and justice. And although she loved having her "squad" with her to solve this case, she missed how easily she and Reade connected, each filling in the missing blanks until the mystery was solved.

This case had her feeling adrift. She was confident that Gordon Quinn did nothing more than write the notes, and yet how else to explain the text message on her phone? Yes, she had attributed the act to another suspect in the case, but was that a correct assumption? Or had Gordon Quinn used his wife's death to sucker them into believing he was innocent of the mixer tampering?

Then there was the matter of the mixer itself. Who could have severed the main wire? And how and when? If the video footage was accurate, no one had either the time or opportunity, and yet the sabotage had been performed.

Tish cradled her phone in her hands and lost herself in its ambient blue glow. There was something about this case that she was missing. Something that she could see glimmering at the surface but that still remained frustratingly out of reach.

Tish gazed at the phone and its list of contacts, her eyes coming to rest on Reade's name. She wondered where he was and what he was doing. She wondered, as she often did these past three months, what had driven him away from Hobson Glen so abruptly. She wondered if he would ever return.

Tish let her thumb hover over Reade's listing in her phone's contacts folder, as if about to dial, and then paused. Was it still Reade's number or had he changed it when he changed his address? If it was still his number, would he answer the phone and speak to her if she called? And, if she heard his voice, what would she even say? That she needed his help on a case? That she appreciated him saving her life? That Hobson Glen still needed him? That she still needed him?

That she missed him?

Tish's reverie was interrupted by the ring of the doorbell. She looked up from her phone to see a dark Ford sedan idling at the curb just outside the front door of the condo. Placing the phone in the pocket of her robe, she peered through the peephole. On the other side of the door, a tall, clean-shaven man in his late thirties to early forties held a badge aloft. He was dressed in a casual ensemble of button-down shirt and chinos. 'Ms Tarragon? Police.'

She entered the code into the security system and unlatched the door.

'Sergeant Klinger,' he introduced himself, stepping over the threshold, his badge still aloft. 'Henrico County Sheriff's Department.'

'Hello, Sergeant. Yes, Sheriff Reade – er, I mean Officer Clayton – told me you were coming.'

'Yes, Clayton told me about the threatening text message you received. No one's been by here since you called him, have they?'

'No. It's been quiet.'

'Good. Funny you mentioned Sheriff Reade. Have you heard from him lately?'

'No. No, I haven't, unfortunately.'

'Shame. I know you two were tight. You closed some pretty tough cases together.'

Tish cast her eyes downward. 'Yes, we did.'

'Well, I know you've been under watch before, but I'll give you a quick refresher just the same. I'll be in the area until six a.m. and doing drive-bys every twenty minutes or so. However, if you have any trouble at all, you call nine-one-one. Even though I'll be in the area, there might be another officer who's even closer than I am. The nine-one-one dispatcher will send whoever can get to you the fastest.'

Tish nodded. 'I've got it. Thank you.'

'No worries. Just stay safe, huh, and if you happen to hear from Reade, say "hi" for me. Tell him it ain't the same without him,' Klinger instructed as he stepped away from the front door and headed to his car.

Tish shut the door behind him. 'No, it's not the same, is it?' she said to herself before resetting the alarm system and fixing herself a cup of tea.

It wasn't the same at all.

Schuyler returned home just as Tish was filling a tall glass with water to keep on her bedside table as she slept. 'Hi,' she greeted, refraining from presenting him with a kiss until he made it clear he wanted one.

'Hey.' He plopped his briefcase down on the floor near the kitchen table and draped his dark-blue suit jacket across the back of one of the chairs. 'You're up late.'

'I was just about to turn in. Couldn't sleep.'

Schuyler bypassed the kiss and went straight for the fridge.

'There's some leftover Thai green chicken curry if you'd like it,' she suggested.

'I might take you up on that. It's been a long day.'

'Everything OK?'

'Yeah, the usual campaign stuff plus preparing for next week's dinner.'

Tish drew a deep breath and held it. *The dinner.* With everything going on, she'd forgotten to tell Schuyler she was going to be late. 'How are the plans coming along?'

Schuyler placed the container of curry and rice in the microwave and set the timer for three minutes. 'They're complex. We wanted the event to start at seven, but most of our attendees can't make it until later, so we might have to push it off until eight.'

Tish exhaled. She felt as though she'd been granted a stay of execution. 'That should be fine. It's the start of the weekend. No need to wrap things up by ten.'

'Yeah, I guess so,' Schuyler allowed. 'I'd ask how your day was, but I'm not sure I want to know.'

Tish drank her water in silence and thought about the unmarked patrol car making the rounds. *No, he probably didn't.*

'How's your cake coming along?' he asked in a clear effort to open communication.

'Good. I'm really pleased with it. Tomorrow's the tough part: decorating. I'll have to make extra sugar cobwebs to cover any mistakes in my piping.'

Schuyler extracted his food from the microwave and, finding it too hot to eat, let it rest on the kitchen counter while he approached Tish. 'I'm sure you'll do a terrific job.' He wrapped his arms around her waist and pulled her to him.

Tish buried her face in his chest. It felt good to be close to him again.

'How's everything else going?' he asked.

She held her breath again. 'We, um, we found the writer of the notes.'

Schuyler kissed her on the forehead and moved to the counter to eat his late-night supper. 'That's wonderful news. You must be relieved.'

'Y–y–es,' she answered, her voice halting.

'Oh, come on, Tish. Be happy the culprit is behind bars.' He carefully stirred together the still steaming curry and rice. 'Now you can focus on winning the contest and getting on the campaign trail. We've narrowed the gap to four points this past week.'

'The note-writer isn't in jail,' she blurted out, as if by saying what she needed to say quickly, Schuyler wouldn't have time to comprehend what was being said.

'Why not?' He helped himself to a heaping forkful of the curry and rice mixture. 'Did Lightbody make that decision? If he did, I can call and put some pressure on him.'

'No, I, um, I decided not to press charges.' She braced herself for Schuyler's reaction.

'What?' He threw his fork down on the counter. 'Tish, you can't give people like that any quarter. If you do, they'll just do it again. He nearly killed you with that mixer stunt of his. Do you want him to do that to someone else?'

'I don't think he will. I don't think he's the one who sabotaged the mixer. He wrote the notes, yes, but someone else is behind the electrocution attempt and the deaths of the previous contestants.'

'Why can't you just let the case be done? You found your guy.'

'Because I don't think I have found "my guy"' Tish replied,

the deeper meaning of that statement not lost lost upon her. 'I found someone who was lost and grieving, but I'm almost one hundred percent certain he's not a killer.'

'Almost? Almost doesn't warrant you letting the creep get off scot-free. Nor is it enough to warrant you pursuing it further. You need to stop it, Tish. The case is closed.'

'It's not closed. Not yet.' She was about to tell Schuyler about the text message she had received, but he didn't give her a chance, for he launched into a tirade.

'I just don't get it,' he cried, throwing his head back and gazing at the ceiling. 'I really don't. We're on the verge of something great here – the law firm, my becoming mayor. Most women would be thrilled to be part of it.'

'I am thrilled,' she insisted, 'for *you*. But I'm not really part of it, am I?'

'You're not a part of it because you choose not to be. You'd rather be at the café or the bake-off or out chasing criminals.'

'I'm not a part of it because you don't include me. Look at the ABA dinner this week. Look at the fundraiser dinner next week. I could have supported you by coming through with a killer dinner, one that would have pleased the local business people far more than some fancy spread. Instead, you hired some glitzy Richmond restaurant to do the job, without even consulting me.'

'Is that what this is all about?' he jeered. 'Me hiring someone else for the catering?'

'It's part of it, but not everything.'

'I hired someone else because you're busy, Tish. You'd have had no time to be with me and organize the dinner.'

'I've done it in the past. I've catered larger parties than your fundraiser while simultaneously hunting down a murderer, cementing a relationship with you, helping Mary Jo and her kids, caring for Biscuit, and talking Jules out of moving in with an eighty-year-old woman, so don't use that as your excuse. You never gave me the opportunity to cater your dinner. You simply told me when and where to show up.'

'I really don't see why it matters,' he stammered.

'You don't? Well, then, next time I or someone else needs a legal opinion or advice, we'll just consult Charles Bruckner up in Ashland, seeing as how busy you are with the campaign and the firm.' With that, she topped her glass up at the kitchen sink and stormed off toward the bedroom. 'Goodnight.'

TWENTY-TWO

Tish awoke on Friday morning at the customary hour, but instead of getting up and wandering into the kitchen for a cup of coffee, she lingered in bed, waiting until Schuyler had left for the day before emerging from her darkened cocoon. She felt like a coward for avoiding him, and perhaps she was. She knew she should have told him about the text message straight away, but she'd held back for fear that doing so would cause the evening to end in yet another showdown, with Schuyler insisting she quit the bake-off and join him on the campaign trail, and with Tish determined to win the trophy and solve the case.

After a sleepless night and faced with a challenging day of decorating and the knowledge that a potential murderer was still at the bake-off, Tish simply couldn't stomach the thought of starting yet another day by quarreling with Schuyler. The endless bickering was beginning to take its toll.

At the sound of Schuyler's key in the front door, Tish crawled from her bed and, opting to avoid café small talk, made herself some coffee and toast to be eaten in silence at the kitchen table.

Leaving both only partially consumed, Tish showered, dressed in a comfortable red cotton-jersey dress, sandals, and a denim jacket, and set off for the bake-off. She arrived at eight o'clock, just as unarmed security guards were opening the front doors to contestants. Once her badge was scanned and handbag examined, she stepped through the metal detectors and into the civic center lobby. As he had been the day before, Clayton was waiting for her, coffee in hand; however, today he was back in his business casual attire of trousers, button-down shirt, and suede chukkas.

'Keep this up and you'll be my best customer,' she smiled, feeling somewhat better now that she was outside the confines of the condo.

'Nah, Sergeant Klinger's fierce. Right after Lightbody told us we were banned from your café, Klinger went out and bought everyone at the station coffee and breakfast sandwiches.'

'Yet another reason to thank him.'

'How did it go with the watch last night? Did you get any sleep?' Clayton took a swig of coffee.

'A little. I was glad to know Klinger was around. Thanks for setting it up.'

'Hey, WW—'

'—RD,' Tish completed and took a sip of coffee. 'I'm going to check in with Willadeane and make sure my booth is outfitted with everything I need for the day. Unless, of course, you need to inspect it first.'

'Already did. I'm going to check some emails while I wait here for Gordon Quinn to arrive. I got a warrant for his phone. A uniformed officer will be here at nine to take his phone and yours to headquarters.'

'Sure.' Tish pulled her phone from her handbag and passed it to Clayton.

'If it was his phone that sent that text message, I'll bring him in and then link him to what happened to your car.'

She nodded. 'I'll see you later.'

She set off for the exhibition hall only to find that Willadeane Scott was nowhere to be found on the floor. Searching for another volunteer, she ran across a gray-haired woman with a slight hunch. She was dressed in a pink sweatshirt bearing an embroidered cat emblazoned on the chest and a lanyard ID tag that hung around her neck. It was Myrna Lucas.

'Good morning, ma'am,' Tish greeted. 'I'm supposed to check in with Willadeane this morning as she's my row monitor, but I haven't seen her around.'

'Detained by work. Again,' Myrna summarized. 'That girl really needs to learn to say no to her boss. Though I don't see that happening anytime soon.'

'Oh?' Tish presented her badge so that Myrna could check her name off the list of contestants.

'No, Willadeane's got the hots for him. Puts in overtime without being properly compensated. Talks about him all the time. I blame it on her mother. She never brought Willadeane up to have confidence in herself. Not to say Willadeane is a beauty, but she has a good head on her shoulders, she's organized and efficient, and obviously loyal. A good man would appreciate those traits.'

'Maybe Willadeane's boss does,' Tish suggested.

Myrna snorted with skepticism. 'Tish Tarragon,' she read aloud. 'You're that poor thing who had the mixer trouble the other day, aren't you?'

Myrna's description of Tish's near electrocution made it sound like a minor household mishap.

'I am,' Tish confirmed.

Myrna looked as though she might cry. 'I'm so sorry about what happened to you, Miss Tarragon. I hope you know none of us had anything to do with it. We all take pride in our bake-off work. It's a serious business for us. Very serious.'

'I know how dedicated you and the volunteers are, Myrna. I just don't know who could have accessed the mixer.'

'It is a pickle, isn't it?'

'It is,' Tish agreed.

'All I can say is that no one had a chance to do anything to your mixer that night, Ms Tarragon. We were really hustlin' to get everything done. Larry, my husband, was loading the mixers on the carts in the storeroom, then we volunteers would push the carts out on the floor and everyone would take turns grabbing them off the carts, checking them against the list, and putting them in the booths.'

'And this list? When do you receive it?' Tish asked, although Clayton had already provided the answer.

'Oh, the list is given to us a little while before the mixers go out on the floor.'

Tish bit her bottom lip. There was nothing new to be learned from Myrna . . . or was there? She was struck by a sudden idea. 'Myrna, who creates that list?'

'Oh, Miss Flournoy does, but I reckon she has that young fella of hers do it for her. Why?'

*   *   *

Tish hastened back to her booth, eager to share what she had learned with Officer Clayton, but he had not yet returned from questioning Gordon Quinn and securing his phone. Making the most of her time before the start of competition, Tish extracted her notes for the day's baking from her purse and leaned over the counter to review them.

She had been hunkered over the counter for several minutes when she was stirred from her studies by a warm breath on her neck followed by a whisper in her left ear: 'What are we going to do, Ms Tarragon? You know you can't avoid me forever.'

The voice. The words. *What are we going to do?* Both were identical to what Tish had overheard in the hallway. She whirled around, her face devoid of color.

'Sorry. Looks like I startled you again.' David Biederman leered, clearly enjoying Tish's discomfort.

Tish stepped away from him 'What do you want?'

Biederman moved forward, closing the distance between them. 'To reschedule yesterday's lunch. I thought if I got to you before your dorm mother arrived,' he remarked, gesturing toward Dolly's booth, 'I might stand a chance.'

'You thought wrong.' She took another step back.

Biederman again stepped forward. 'Come on. Don't be that way. Let's be friends.'

'I already have a boyfriend. We're very happy together.' At this particular moment in time, Tish may have been frustrated with Schuyler and his behavior, but she certainly wasn't about to reveal that to Biederman.

'Stop being so pedestrian, Tish. Us having lunch together won't preclude you from going back home to your boyfriend tonight. It will be two New Yorkers getting together, reminiscing, and celebrating the launch of Biederman's new chef-devised lunch menu this Saturday . . . er, Sunday. What do you say?'

'I say you might want to extend your invitation to someone else.'

'I don't want to extend the invitation to anyone else. I want to have lunch with you.' He grabbed her by the wrist. The gesture was a demonstration of dominance rather than a means to inflict harm.

'I'm sure you could find someone at this bake-off who'd be

more than delighted to have lunch with you today.' She extricated her wrist from his grip. 'Someone no one knows about. Someone you probably meet in secret.'

'Jealous?' he joked in a bid to divert her line of questioning, but it was apparent from the expression on his face that her words had hit too close to home.

'Suspicious.' Tish folded her arms across her chest and stared defiantly at Biederman. 'Nearly being electrocuted can do that to a person.'

He was quiet for several seconds before barking in annoyance. 'You know what? Forget it. Forget I ever invited you.'

As Biederman sulked off toward the judges' table, Jules, dressed in a pinstripe suit and a purple silk tie, arrived on the scene carrying an equally well-groomed Biscuit. 'The sandwich seduction continues, I see,' he teased.

Tish rushed forward and caught her friend in a bearlike embrace.

The move caught him by surprise. 'Hey. Hey, what's wrong, honey?' he asked as he wrapped his free arm around her torso.

Blinking back tears, she told him about the text message and the seemingly never-ending arguments with Schuyler.

'No wonder you're upset,' Jules said. 'You're plain ol' stressed and tuckered out.'

Tish relinquished Jules and reached for her coffee cup, which was resting on the counter in her booth. 'I am, but there's still more.'

'More? Good Lord, it's not even eight thirty in the morning.'

Having observed Officer Clayton entering the exhibition hall, she waited until he had joined them before launching into her findings. 'While looking for Willadeane Scott so that I could check in this morning, I ran into Myrna Lucas. I asked Myrna about the list the volunteers check against while distributing mixers. Get this – that list is given to them by Kitty Flournoy.'

'So Kitty would have known which mixer was yours,' Clayton deduced.

'So would Desmond. According to Myrna, he's the one who drafted the document.'

'Meaning the voices you overheard Wednesday afternoon probably belonged to Kitty and Desmond,' Jules added.

'No, they didn't. At least, the man's voice I heard didn't belong to Desmond. It belonged to David Biederman.'

'Biederman?' Clayton cried out in surprise. 'Are you sure?'

'Positive. Just a few minutes ago, he whispered the same words in my ear that were whispered that day: "What are we going to do?" I can't believe I didn't make the connection earlier, but then again, I've never heard David Biederman whisper before.'

'On top of everything you've already been through these past few hours, you had to deal with Bagel Boy whispering in your ear. You poor thing.' Jules draped a sympathetic arm around her shoulders.

'But who's the woman?' Clayton asked.

Tish exhaled noisily. 'I honestly don't . . .' She suddenly remembered Biederman's comment about his lunch menu launch. 'Wait one minute.'

Jules beamed. 'Atta girl, Tish. I knew you'd figure it out. You always do.'

'Don't congratulate me yet,' she warned. 'Jules, do you happen to have your phone on you?'

'Sure. Don't you have yours?'

'No, Jim has it. He's taking it back to headquarters so the tech guy can trace the source of that text message I received. Can you retrieve that commercial Whitney Liddell made for Sheehy Brothers?'

'Sure.' Jules complied and opened the video from his browser history. 'You can't hear it very well. Let me raise the sound.'

'No.' Tish slapped his hand back from adjusting the on-screen volume control. 'Please, I want to hear it as it is.'

'Sixty years of great service and competitive prices,' Whitney Liddell proclaimed at the end of the commercial. 'Sheehy Brothers', where nothing's changed but the cars.'

'Nothing's changed,' Tish repeated, her voice a whisper. *'Nothing's changed, except now there's more on the line and there's police everywhere.'*

'Do you think the woman you overheard talking to David Biederman was Whitney Liddell?' Clayton asked.

'I do,' Tish asserted, playing back the end of the commercial. 'Whitney has a very distinct accent. It's not Southern and yet it is. Listen to how she nearly drops the 'g' in the word nothing. The woman I heard did the very same thing.'

'Are you positive? I still have footage of my interview with her, if you'd like to see that,' Jules proposed.

'No, that won't be necessary. I wanted to watch that commercial for more than just Whitney's voice.'

'What do you mean?' Clayton asked.

'The cars on the Sheehy Brothers' lot – they were all this year's models,' she noted.

'The majority of them, yes.'

'And although the commercial was filmed on a sunny day and Whitney's dressed as if it's the middle of spring, the trees in the background are bare. Trees here don't lose all their leaves until the end of November at the earliest, meaning that this commercial was filmed sometime this winter.'

'I didn't notice those trees last time we watched, but yeah, most likely,' Clayton concurred.

'And all of us agree that this advertisement isn't of the highest quality, correct?'

Jules and Clayton both indicated agreement.

'What are you getting at, honey?' Jules quizzed.

'When the bake-off was extended into the weekend, Whitney Liddell became quite angry. She was angry because she claimed to be shooting a victory commercial for Sheehy Brothers' this Saturday.'

'That's right. I was with you in Kitty's office when she made a big scene over it. We both thought it was odd at the time.'

'Because it *is* odd. Think about it. Sheehy Brothers' only filmed this ad this winter – just two months ago.'

'How do you know it was that recent? It could have been earlier,' Clayton argued. 'It might have been filmed in December, which puts it at three months.'

'It wasn't filmed in December. There were no Christmas decorations in the car showroom windows,' Tish detailed. 'Those decorations would have been put up Thanksgiving weekend and have stayed up until after the New Year. The earliest this might have been filmed is the second week of January.'

'OK, but I still don't see why that's important.'

'It's important because why would Sheehy Brothers' be

filming a new commercial so soon? I know they're the largest auto dealership in the state, but even they have a limited marketing budget. Why would they pay to shoot two poor-quality ads featuring Whitney Liddell – whom I'm certain didn't come cheaply – when, for the same price, they could have shot one ad of excellent or, at the very least, above-average quality to broadcast during the finale of *The Masked Singer*? Wouldn't they have wanted to look their best during primetime?'

'They would.' Jules pursed his lips, meditatively. 'More importantly, if Sheehy Brothers' did plan to make two commercials, those commercials would have been filmed back to back instead of over two days. We've had to hire freelance film crews at the station from time to time and even the cheapest ones receive a per diem in addition to their hourly rate. Add in the set-up and tear-down time and the travel expenses, and a two-day shoot still winds up being far more costly than a one-day with overtime.'

'That's very useful information, Jules,' Tish thanked him.

Jules attached a lead on to Biscuit's collar and lowered him to the ground before running a hand through his perfectly coifed chestnut hair. 'Well, you know. It's the biz.'

'It strikes me,' Tish continued, 'that the Sheehy Brothers' marketing team weighed their options and decided to make a lesser-quality ad so they could put the majority of their budget into purchasing primetime airspace.'

'Is it possible the first ad did so well that Sheehy Brothers' made enough money to shoot another one?' Clayton suggested.

'I doubt they could have recouped their money that quickly. We're talking Whitney Liddell dressed as a fifties housewife, Jim, not the "Where's the beef?" lady.'

'Who's the "Where's the beef?" lady? What are you even talking about?' a bewildered Clayton asked.

'What?' Jules gasped. 'You don't remember those commercials? I knew you were young, but exactly how young are you, anyway?'

'Twenty-four.'

'Sweet baby Jesus, I own shoes that are older than you.'

'The "Where's the beef?" lady was this little elderly . . .'

Tish was about to describe the fast-food commercial to Clayton but decided she had more important things to communicate. 'Never mind. What I was getting at is that Sheehy Brothers' sells cars, not hamburgers. It's not as if people seeing the ad are going to dash out and impulse-buy a new Range Rover. Also, if Sheehy Brothers' had, in fact, used most of their marketing budget for this quarter, I hardly think they would take a risk by booking Whitney Liddell to do a second commercial before she actually won this year's competition.'

'And before their initial primetime ad had time to produce results,' Jules inserted.

'So if Whitney wasn't planning to go to Sheehy Brothers', where was she going?' Clayton asked.

'The party to celebrate Biederman's Bagels new lunch menu,' Tish stated.

'I guess it would make sense for them to meet up there,' Jules said, 'if they were, as everyone has said, having an affair.'

'Given Biederman's track record and Whitney's ambitions, I have no doubt the pair started a sexual relationship. I mean, how else to shore up a win than by sleeping with one of the judges? And Biederman sure as hell wouldn't have said "no." Kitty probably got wind of it and that's why, despite his popularity, he wasn't invited to judge last year's competition. Kitty couldn't risk her golden girl's reputation being tarnished.'

'But Biederman *was* at last year's competition.'

'Yeah, even though he tried to deny it,' Clayton added.

'He tried to deny it because I believe there's another side to his and Whitney's relationship that they've taken great pains to keep hidden. I believe they're business partners.'

'Business partners?' Jules and Clayton exclaimed in unison.

'Biederman told me that his new lunch menu took years to create and that it was developed by a Southern chef,' Tish said, smiling.

'You think Whitney developed the menu,' Clayton guessed.

'It would certainly explain Biederman's secretiveness about his comings and goings. He claims he was in town last year to unveil his bagel line at Elwood Thompson's, but what if his primary reason for being in town was to connect with Whitney? She's married and has a family. He lives in New York part-time. I doubt the two get a chance to meet in person very often.'

'It's against the rules for a contestant to be in a business partnership with a judge, isn't it?'

'Whitney would be disqualified from competing,' Tish confirmed.

'I see only one flaw in your theory,' Jules opposed. 'Whitney Liddell isn't a chef.'

'Well, either David Biederman is exaggerating her prowess for the sake of selling sandwiches, or . . .' She broke into a wide smile.

Jules's mouth formed the shape of an 'O.' 'Whitney Liddell would be more than disqualified for that. She could be sued. So could he.'

'All the more reason to keep things quiet.'

'All the more reason for David and Whitney to be panicked over police presence. Those are grounds for fraud.'

'But wouldn't the bake-off committee know if Whitney had professional training?' Clayton quizzed. 'They do vet their contestants, don't they?'

'They run a basic background check, yes. But that doesn't mean anything. Back in 2008, Food Network had a chef named Robert Irvine who hosted a very popular show on their channel. Among other things, Mr Irvine claimed to have been a chef at the White House and to have baked Charles and Diana's wedding cake. Turns out Mr Irvine did neither of those two things. He lied about his resumé.'

Clayton opened his mouth as if to ask a question.

'If you're about to ask who Charles and Diana are, so help me, I'm going to scream,' Jules warned.

'No, I know who they are – I think. I'll look into Whitney Liddell's background and see what I can dig up. I'll also check out Biederman's lunch menu and see if I can find out the name of the chef who worked with him.'

'Sounds good,' Tish approved. 'Did you find out anything?'

'Nothing that gets us closer to a solution. I received an encrypted email from the surgeon who performed Penelope Purdue's surgery. She wasn't Paul Pelletier.'

Tish and Jules groaned in disappointment.

'Well, it was a longshot, I suppose,' Tish acknowledged. 'And Gordon Quinn?'

'Um, yeah, I'm pretty sure he's not our guy.'

'Why not?'

'That text you received is what's known as a spoof message. When something's spoofed, it means the identity of the sender has been changed to match the identity of the recipient. People get them in email form all the time.'

'Oh, yeah, I get them at work,' Jules said. 'The first time it happened, I thought my account had been hacked. Now they're just super-annoying.'

'Spoofed emails are common,' Clayton resumed. 'Spoofed text messages are a bit more unusual because service providers make it difficult to change the number from which a message has been sent. But there is software out there that can work around it. According to our tech guy, there are several apps you can purchase that will, at first glance, replicate the recipient's phone number, but they do leave traceable information behind. That's what we're hoping to find on your phone, Tish.'

Tish felt elated. 'So it can be traced. That's good news. But why does that mean Gordon Quinn is no longer a suspect?'

'His phone.' Clayton reached into the front pocket of his shirt and retrieved a small plastic bag containing a dilapidated flip-top cellphone. 'No internet. No apps.'

'Do you charge it by pedaling a stationary bike?' Jules teased.

'I don't think so.' The officer examined the phone through its plastic sheath. 'Looks like a standard firewire.'

'It was a joke, Clayton. I was comparing the phone to one of the gadgets on *Gilligan's* – oh, never mind.'

TWENTY-THREE

With the breakfast crowd dwindling, Mary Jo Okensholt pulled her black SUV out of the Cookin' the Books parking lot a few minutes past nine a.m. and drove south on Route One until she reached the Richmond city limits. There, she followed the road as it turned southeast toward downtown, ultimately parking in a pay garage on East Broad Street a few blocks northwest of the convention center.

She placed her ticket on the dashboard, locked the SUV and, crossing East Broad, walked south one block on North Adams Street before turning right on to West Grace Street. Dr Reasoner's office was located at number 320, in an early twentieth-century three-story brown-brick walkup.

As Mary Jo approached the entrance of number 320, she noticed a parking area to the left of the building. *Damn*, she thought to herself, thinking of the four dollars she would have saved by parking there instead of the garage. That was before she noticed a group of men congregated at the rear of the lot, huddled near the fence that separated 320's parking area from that of the building behind it. They were unshaven, dressed in dirty jeans, T-shirts, jackets, and sneakers, and judging from the plastic grocery bags, empty food containers, and sleeping bags in their environs, it appeared that the parking lot was their campground.

Mary Jo walked up the cement steps of the building and opened the brown paneled door that led to the small, stuffy main vestibule of the building. There, on the wall to the left of the door, was posted a directory of businesses. Dr Joel Reasoner, DDS, could be found in Suite B on the second floor.

Mary Jo hiked the hem of her long, paisley-printed sundress to her knees and trudged upstairs to the second floor. The journey was not a long one, but the staircase was narrow and steep and, with the unseasonable heat of the past week, had become stiflingly hot.

Arriving on the second-floor landing, Mary Jo lowered her skirt and smoothed any resulting wrinkles, located Suite B, and opened the heavy, fireproof metal door. She was met with a welcome blast of cool air, courtesy of the air conditioner balanced upon the sill of the room's only window.

Mary Jo closed the door behind her and surveyed her surroundings. With its dark wood paneling, Formica-topped coffee table, and extruded plastic chairs in a brilliant shade of orange, the waiting area was a throwback to the 1970s. The dated interior design didn't seem to deter the people gathered there, for all but two seats were occupied and there was a lengthy line of patients outside the receptionist's glass-walled cubicle.

Mary Jo joined the end of the seven-person queue and waited her turn to speak with the attractive blonde receptionist, happy to have an opportunity to quietly assess her surroundings. The people in line ahead of her, however, were rather impatient, twitching, sighing, anxiously shuffling their feet, clearing their throats, and shifting their weight from one side to another.

Those seated also appeared to be in various stages of aggravation. There was a mother – young, thin, with bleached hair – and the cranky, shoeless infant she was bouncing on her lap, an elderly woman with a walker seated beside a middle-aged woman Mary Jo assumed was her daughter, a man in painters' whites perched on the edge of his seat with his elbows on his knees, a couple in their late thirties – gaunt and pale and sickly-looking – and a fortyish woman in a business suit. No one glanced at their phones or perused the array of magazines artfully arranged on the coffee table. They all sat, staring straight ahead or at their hands, waiting to be called.

The line Mary Jo stood in was moving more rapidly than she had anticipated. No one said more than a word or two to the woman behind the glass, and soon after they did, they turned around and left, each with a slip of paper in hand.

Mary Jo watched carefully. The slips of paper were prescriptions.

Soon, it was Mary Jo's turn. A queue of five people had formed behind her.

'Good morning,' Mary Jo greeted through the window. 'Um, I'm here to make an appointment with Doctor Reasoner.'

The receptionist was pretty, fortyish, and well turned-out, but beneath her expertly applied makeup she looked haggard. 'Are you a current patient?'

'No, I'm not. This appointment is for my daughter. She's been in pain for over a week.'

'Is your daughter a current patient?'

'No, she isn't.'

'We're not accepting new patients unless they're referrals. Have you been referred to us by a current patient?'

'Yes, my aunt.' Mary Jo searched her memory for the first dead woman's name. *Hawthorne? Hayworth? Haywood?*

'Harwood. Lillian Harwood. She's no longer with us, but she was a patient of this clinic for years. Going back to when old Doctor Reasoner ran it.'

At the sound of Lillian Harwood's name, the receptionist halted. 'I – I, um, I'm not the regular receptionist. I'm just – let me get my husband.'

The woman pressed a button on the nearby telephone and, lifting the receiver to her mouth, said quietly, 'A niece of Lillian Harwood is here . . . OK . . . I'll tell her.' Replacing the receiver in its cradle, she directed Mary Jo to step aside until the doctor could meet with her.

Under the watchful gaze of the other patients in the waiting room, Mary Jo left the queue to allow Mrs Reasoner to attend to the other persons who had lined up, single file, behind her. Several seconds elapsed before the door to the left of the receptionist's cubicle opened.

A man in his twenties emerged first. He had fair hair and a pallid, almost grayish complexion. He was overdressed for the weather in a plaid flannel shirt, down vest, and corduroy pants that looked to be the only clothes he might own. He was nervous to the point of jumpiness. 'Thanks, man,' he said to the professional-looking man in a white coat who held the door open behind him. 'I really appreciate this. Like, you don't know how much I appreciate this. I drove all night from North Carolina.'

'I know,' shushed the other man as he escorted him out of the office.

'I'll get this filled right away. There's a drug store off route sixty-four—'

'No, you need to take this to Lafayette Value-Rite, remember? They're just down the road.'

'Oh, right. Lafayette. Sorry. I'll go there right now. Before I leave town.'

'Good. Lafayette Value-Rite will get you set up in no time.' The professional-looking man gave the younger man a brief wave before shutting the office door behind him.

Turning on one heel, he then approached Mary Jo. 'Joel Reasoner,' he introduced himself. 'And you are?'

'Mary Jo,' she started, then, deeming it unsafe to use her

actual last name, added, 'Harwood. My aunt was Lillian Harwood. Your patient and your father's.'

Joel nodded his head. He was in his mid to late forties and of average height and build, but his posture and bearing made him appear taller. He was clean-shaven with neatly cropped auburn hair and glasses. 'Yes, she was a nice lady, your aunt. She passed away a couple of years back, didn't she?'

'Yes. Heart failure. It happened suddenly.'

'Shame.' Reasoner clicked his tongue. 'How may I help you today?'

'I need to make an appointment for my daughter. She's had a toothache all week and our regular dentist is booked. I remembered how highly my aunt thought of your practice so I thought I'd try here.'

'I'm very sorry you made the trip, but we're not accepting new patients at this time.'

'Oh, had your wife told me you weren't accepting any new patients, I wouldn't have bothered you.'

'Sorry, my wife is overwhelmed at the moment. Our usual office person is out of town for a few days, and she's filling in.'

'I don't blame her for being overwhelmed. It's awfully busy, isn't it? Perhaps you should try hiring a temp, just to help her out,' Mary Jo suggested.

'No, we tried that once a couple of years back. It was awful. I can't remember the name of the person the agency sent – David, Donald . . . perhaps Derek? – but he was awful. He was a student. Couldn't file or find records on the computer. But this really isn't the sort of office suited for a temp anyway, is it?'

'True, it would be difficult to train someone like that in an office this busy. I don't think I've ever seen a dentist office with this many patients zipping in and out,' she observed.

The smile that had graced Reasoner's face quickly evaporated. 'Fridays are free clinic days. We do what we can for the less fortunate.'

Mary Jo was doubtful that a free clinic day would involve so many prescriptions, but she played along. 'How lovely. No wonder that young man drove all night to get here. If I had a toothache and no insurance, I would, too. So, there's no way I could bring my daughter by later today, is there? I'd pay, of course. I have insurance. And from what I can see, these people don't have appointments.'

'Sorry, but it's much too busy today. I'd want to give her X-rays and a new patient exam before addressing her pain issues.'

'Of course. That makes sense.' She put on a disappointed face. 'Can you recommend any other dentists in the neighborhood?'

'Erm, no, not really. We're so busy here that we don't have a chance to mingle much.' Reasoner eyed her suspiciously. 'But you know what? Since you're Lillian Harwood's niece, why don't you leave me your number? If something opens up next week, I'll give you a call.'

'Oh, no. I couldn't—' she protested.

'Please, it's the least I can do for the relative of such a dear lifelong patient.'

'I don't think my daughter can wait that long.'

'Oh, but if you can't find anyone else. I do hate to think of your daughter being in such pain. I hate to think of anyone in such pain.'

The tone of Reasoner's voice sent a shiver down Mary Jo's spine. Not wanting to share her own number, she gave the first one that came to mind. He wrote it down on the back of a business card he'd had stored in the front pocket of his smock.

'I'd better let you get back to work,' she said, trying to extricate herself from the office.

'Yes, I need to get back. There are a lot of people waiting for me. Sorry I couldn't help you, Ms Harwood.'

'Oh, no, I understand. Have a good day.' She smiled and made her way to the door.

'You, too. I hope, someday, we here at Reasoner Dentistry will be able to be of service.'

TWENTY-FOUR

I t was just going on ten in the morning when Tish finished her double batch of spun-sugar cobwebs, placing the delicate tendrils of super-heated corn syrup and sugar to one side of the counter to cool. Moving on to the icing for the piped cake decorations, Tish put the pot of sugar syrup into the sink to soak before loading the bowl of her mixer with softened vegetable shortening.

Standing a safe distance back, she closed her eyes and flipped the switch. The mixer whirred to life without incident, leaving Tish to heave a sigh of relief. It would be a long time before she didn't think twice about switching on a simple kitchen appliance.

Adding confectioner's sugar to the bowl in one-cup increments, she whipped the mixture until smooth and stiff, then added a splash of milk and a generous amount of vanilla extract to improve flavor and ease of piping. She was just about to scoop the whole lot into a piping bag when she spied Clayton rushing down the aisle toward her booth, two uniformed officers following closely behind him. As they made their way to the front of the exhibition hall, bakers stopped to stare.

'Hey, what's going on?' Tish asked as Clayton drew near.

'That hunch of yours paid off. Whitney Liddell did two years of culinary arts at Boston College while married to her first husband,' Jim said.

'Wait. First husband? She's been married more than once?'

'Yup, that's why the bake-off probably didn't find about it. She was registered under her ex-husband's last name. A simple search for Liddell didn't pull up anything, but when we searched for other names, that's when we found it.'

'So Whitney Liddell, the ideal "family values" Southern housewife, is a divorcee who mastered her cooking skills in Massachusetts? Her fans are not going to be pleased,' Tish asserted.

'Wait until they hear about the Biederman connection.'

Tish gasped. 'I was right?'

'Yep, you're two for two.'

'How did you find out so quickly?'

'When I called identifying myself as a police officer, Biederman's predominantly female office staff was more than ready to spill the tea. They were already sick of Biederman gawking and pawing at them, but when Whitney Liddell came on board as a culinary advisor and started screaming at them and bossing them around over the phone, it was the final straw. The women I spoke with were so fired up I actually had to cut the conversation short so I could come here.'

'What are you going to do?'

'I'm taking them in for questioning.'

'Now? In the middle of the bake-off?'

'What does it matter? They're disqualified from participating anyway,' Clayton snapped back as he hurried along to catch up with the uniformed members of his team.

Tish resumed the task of placing the decorator's icing into the piping bag, but the buzzy momentum she'd experienced before Clayton's appearance had been lost. Looking from booth to booth, she wasn't the only one. Riya stood with her hands on her hips, staring after Clayton, while Dolly kept glancing over at Tish as if on the verge of asking what was happening.

Within minutes, the police returned with David Biederman and Whitney Liddell in tow. Murmurs and gasps erupted from the competition floor, only to be interrupted by the agitated voice of Kitty Flournoy over the civic center public address system announcing a twenty-minute break.

Tish placed her frosting in the refrigerator to chill and set off to the hospitality suite for a cup of coffee. Before she could step foot out of her booth, she was waylaid by a frantic Dolly Pritchard. 'What's going on here, Tish? What's happening? Why do the police have David Biederman and Whitney Liddell?'

Tish sidestepped the question. 'I'm not at liberty to say, Dolly.'

'Well, this had better not mean the bake-off is canceled. I put a lot of work into my dishes.'

Riya arrived just in time to hear the word 'canceled.' 'What is this? The bake-off is canceled? It can't be. Today's dish would have put me in second place.'

'The bake-off isn't canceled,' Tish clarified. 'At least, not yet.'

'Not yet? Do you think it will be canceled?' Riya pressed.

'That's up to Kitty Flournoy. I have no idea what she's going to do.'

At the mention of her name, like a demon summoned by a magical incantation, Kitty suddenly materialized at Tish's side. 'What's going on? Why have you accused Whitney and David of causing your mixer accident?'

'I haven't accused them of anything. The police found something of concern and decided to take action,' Tish explained.

'Action? During the middle of competition? This is the absolute worst thing that could happen right now!'

Tish was about to argue that the absolute worst that could happen was if someone had died at the bake-off, but she was interrupted by a flustered Jules. 'Biscuit and I were out for a walk when I saw David Biederman and Whitney Liddell being taken away in two separate squad cars. What happened?'

'I can't say right now, Jules.' Tish glanced at the circle of women surrounding her.

'You were right!' he exclaimed.

Tish didn't reply. She may have been right about the nature of Whitney and David's relationship, but there was still the matter of the questionable deaths of two women. It seemed nigh on impossible that either Whitney or David could have triggered Lillian Harwood's heart attack or dosed Penelope Purdue with penicillin. Not only were the couple bake-off celebrities whose every move was followed by contestants and fans alike, thus precluding them from getting near Lillian or Penelope without being noticed, but neither of them was particularly liked or trusted by the victims. Even if one – or indeed both – of them had successfully managed to meet with Lillian or Penelope without being detected, their presence would have been received with great suspicion.

Unless – it occurred to Tish – Lillian or Penelope had been engaging in blackmail. A secret meeting to exchange money for silence would have afforded the perfect opportunity for the murderer to strike. Yet both women died after the day's competition, meaning that such a meeting must have taken place during bake-off contest hours – a feat that seemed highly unlikely since their daily lunch breaks were spent in the company of Dolly, Riya, and Gordon.

Tish was roused from her thoughts by a familiar voice calling her name. 'Tish? Tish!'

She scanned the civic center in search of the source, but given the din of the crowd, it was difficult to pick out the direction from which the voice was emanating. 'MJ? Mary Jo?'

'Tish?' Mary Jo's face emerged from the throng of confused fans and bakers. 'Tish! Thank goodness I found you.'

'Mary Jo, what are you doing here?'

Jules soon joined them. 'MJ! You didn't buy a ticket to get in, did you?'

'Didn't have to. There was no one at the entrance to even collect a ticket. I walked right in. What's going on here?'

'Tish solved the case,' Jules boasted.

'We don't know that yet,' Tish amended. 'All we know is that Clayton brought Whitney Liddell and David Biederman in for questioning.'

Mary Jo's brow puckered. 'Clayton isn't here?'

'You just missed him. Why?'

'I came here straight from the dentist's office. I tried calling you, Tish, but I couldn't get through.'

'That's because Clayton has her phone,' Jules said.

'Clayton has it? Why?'

'I'll explain later,' Tish replied. 'What's so important that you felt the need to drive here?'

'Well, it's the dentist's office. That place – that dentist – is really weird.' Mary Jo recounted her experience at Dr Reasoner's office.

'I'm glad you're out of there and safe,' Tish stated at the end of Mary Jo's tale.

'Me, too. Reasoner is creepy and that office is surreal. As I was walking out, I noticed a whole bunch of cars with out-of-state plates parked in the lot.'

'But Reasoner said it was a free clinic day, right?' Jules

mentioned. 'With insurance rates these days, it's no wonder it was busy.'

'Yeah, but the majority of those people didn't even see the dentist. They lined up at the receptionist's desk, got a prescription, and left.'

'Maybe they were refills or prescriptions that had been called in earlier?'

'This isn't a doctor's office, Jules. It's not like you call your dentist to renew your blood pressure or heart meds. Apart from an antibiotic, the only kind of prescription you'd get from a dentist is a painkiller.'

'And if it was a renewal, the dentist would call it directly into the pharmacy. Reasoner's running a pill mill,' Tish deduced.

'Drugs,' Jules said in disbelief. 'This case might have something to do with drugs. Oh, MJ, I hope you didn't leave them your contact info.'

'Of course not,' MJ assured her friends. 'I had to give Reasoner a phone number before I left, so I gave him the first one that came to mind – Glen's.'

Jules and Tish burst into laughter.

'I'm sorry, honey,' Jules apologized. 'I know he's the father of your children, but that just made my morning.'

MJ joined in with them. 'Yeah, once I was safely away from that place, I admit I got a few giggles out of it, too.'

'Tish,' Jules started when the laughter had quieted down, 'do you think the temp at Reasoner's office might have been Desmond?'

Tish bit her lip. 'I honestly don't know. Desmond. Derek. The two sound awfully similar in both name and skillset, but Richmond is a big place. That temp could have been anyone.'

'What if it was Desmond? What if he knew what was going at the dentist's office and quit? Then he came to the bake-off, only to run into Lillian Harwood, who recognized him.'

'So Desmond killed Lillian because she knew he once temped for a pill-pushing dentist?' Mary Jo challenged. 'We've all had a job from hell, Jules. Granted, playing file clerk to a drug dealer is more hellish than most, but I can't see anyone killing to cover it up.'

'He might not have wanted Kitty Flournoy to know about

it,' Jules suggested. 'It might have ruined the reputation of the bake-off. He could have lost his job.'

Tish shook her head. 'If Kitty hasn't fired Desmond for not being able to perform the most menial of tasks, I doubt she'd fire him for a temp job he held as a student. No, the only issue in Desmond's past that might trouble Kitty is if he'd had a social disease.'

'I guess we're still at Whitney Liddell and David Biederman being the culprits,' Jules relented. 'Not that I mind. At all. I just hope they don't get some expensive attorneys to bail them out.'

'Yeah, I don't know . . .' Tish remarked, pensively.

'About Whitney and Biederman or the attorneys bailing them out?'

'About Whitney and Biederman. This dentist connection between Lillian Harwood and Penelope Purdue has to mean something, but what?'

Jules and Mary Jo exchanged puzzled glances.

'Well, we'll pass along the info to Clayton when he gets back and take it from there,' Tish stated. 'You mind if I give him your number, Mary Jo?'

'Please do,' Mary Jo agreed. 'I may not answer right away, because of the lunch crowd, but if he leaves a message, I'll get back to him as soon as I can.'

'Are you OK working at the café? I know you were pretty creeped out by Doctor Reasoner.'

'I'm more than OK working this afternoon. I can't wait to get back to the non-criminal world.'

Tish gave her friend a hug. 'Thanks for checking into the dentist for us.'

'Anytime. Just not anytime soon.' Mary Jo moved from Tish to give a parting embrace to Jules. 'Bye, you two. See you later.'

'Bye.' Jules and Tish waved as Mary Jo disappeared into the crowd.

No sooner had Mary Jo departed than the voice of Kitty Flournoy sounded, once more, over the civic center address system. 'Ladies and gentlemen, the bake-off competition will resume in approximately ten minutes. Ms Whitney Liddell has been removed from the contestant roster and will no longer be competing. All current baker points will remain as they are. Only baker standings will change. Mr David Biederman has also been removed from the competition. I will be taking his place at the judges' table. Thank you for your patience and understanding.'

'Sounds as if Kitty got the memo about Whitney and David's scheme,' Tish surmised. 'The bake-off's legal team must have checked in with the sheriff's office.'

'The heck with that, honey. With Whitney gone, you're in first place.' Jules jumped up and down excitedly, prompting Biscuit, who was still in his arms, to bark.

Tish felt her heart skip a beat. What with the excitement surrounding Mary Jo's recent news and Clayton bringing Whitney Liddell and David Biederman into custody, she'd nearly forgotten where she was. 'First place?'

'Yes, you stand an excellent chance of winning this thing and bringing that prize money home to Celestine. Fifteen thousand dollars! All you've gotta do is focus. Focus on decorating that cake and baking that pie tomorrow,' he coached.

From somewhere behind Jules, Dolly emerged. 'Now I know why you've been snooping around the way you have. Getting Whitney out of the way levels the playing field. But don't you think for one minute that you've got this in the bag,' she threatened Tish. 'Oh, no. I'm in it to win it. Whoot!'

Dolly, still hooting and cheering, returned to her booth, leaving Tish to turn to Jules. 'Just focus,' she repeated Jules's instructions, poker-faced. 'Oh, yeah, that should be no problem. No problem at all.'

TWENTY-FIVE

After a slow start, Tish regained her early-morning momentum and gradually immersed herself in the process of cake decorating. The gentle, repetitive rhythm of piping buttercream roses along the perimeter of each cake layer had a surprisingly soothing effect on her nerves. She had always felt intimidated by the act of piping, but today, filled with the hope that she might actually win the bake-off and safe in the knowledge that whatever errors she might make would be covered with edible cobwebs, she felt confident and relaxed.

Upon finishing her final rose, Tish admired her work and prepared to begin piping the delicate filigree and scrollwork she had outlined in her plans. Removing the star tip from the end of her piping bag, she reached into the top drawer nearest the stove for the small number-sixteen tip she had requested, only to have her fingertips meet spatulas, forks, and servers, but no decorating tip.

Tish rummaged through the other drawers in the booth in case a volunteer had placed it in the wrong spot, but, again, she came up empty. Deeming it quicker to retrieve one from the storeroom, she leaned over the counter and attempted to flag down Willadeane Scott, but she was two booths away, handing a white ceramic mug to Riya.

'You always make a deliciously strong tea,' Riya praised.

'A little too strong if you ask me,' Dolly opined. 'If I left my dentures in your tea overnight, there'd be nothing left of them in the morning.'

Strong tea. Could the penicillin that killed Penelope Purdue have been administered in a cup of hot, strong tea? What about a drug that might have induced Lillian Harwood's heart attack? Could the taste of both drugs have been masked by the flavor of the tea as well?

Tish watched as Riya took a sip of the beverage and then placed the mug on the front counter of her booth before continuing work on her cake. Anyone who passed the booth could have dosed Riya's tea – a baker on a break, a judge watching the proceedings, or Kitty Flournoy making the rounds with Desmond in tow. A quick flick of the wrist was all that was needed and no one would have been the wiser.

As for timing, one didn't need to be exceptionally astute to notice that the majority of liquid refreshments were consumed both in the mid-morning, long after breakfast had been digested and still hours before the lunch break, and in the late afternoon, when lunch was a distant memory and the last stretch of competition seemed insurmountable.

Willadeane Scott spotted Tish and approached. 'Some tea or coffee, Ms Tarragon? Or perhaps some cold water or lemonade?'

'No, nothing for me, thank you. I do, however, need to visit the storeroom for a different decorating tip.'

'Oh? That's strange. I could have sworn we left two different tips at your station last night.'

'I could have sworn you did, too. I thought I saw them here when I arrived this morning. The one I'm looking for probably just rolled away somewhere,' Tish speculated.

'Well, I still need to record that it's missing. For inventory reasons,' the ever-efficient Willadeane explained.

'OK, just so long as you make a note that I lost it. I'd hate for anyone to get into trouble for something I did.'

'There's no room for that in the note field, but I'll let Kitty know what happened when I turn in my log sheets for the day.'

Tish nodded and set off for the storeroom, but something in the back of her brain was nagging at her – something she couldn't quite pinpoint.

Leaving the exhibition hall, she turned right, down the corridor, and then right again, through the heavy, insulated steel door that separated the storeroom from the rest of the civic center. With a keycard lock accessible only to civic center and bake-off employees and volunteers, the door had been propped open with a metal folding chair during competition hours to allow access to contestants.

Outfitted with row upon row of tall racks bearing kitchen gadgets of every description, the storage room was typically reserved for the equipment, luggage, and belongings of conventioneers, but had been commandeered for the bake-off as a supply room. Tish walked down the center aisle, following the signs to the back of the room where the decorating supplies were stored. Spying a rack filled with plastic bins, she found the one that contained piping tips and placed a number-sixteen tip in the pocket of her apron.

Her task complete, she retraced her steps. Walking past the aisle of standing mixers, she paused.

Log sheets. That was what was nagging at her. Willadeane

had mentioned log sheets. Picking up the clipboard that hung from the first rack, she leafed through the pages attached to it. Everything appeared to be in proper order. The log contained three columns – contestant name organized by booth placement, mixer serial number, and a box to be checked off upon delivery.

Tish scanned the top page for row-five contestants and found her name. There were no corrections or changes to the mixer serial number, indicating that she had, in fact, received the mixer originally allocated to her.

Flipping to the last page of the spreadsheet, she looked for an author's name, but there was none. It was no matter. Although the log sheet may have been delivered to the volunteers by Kitty Flournoy, it was Willadeane, and not Desmond, who was responsible for its creation.

Desmond had been incapable of locating the list of past recipes on his iPad. It was doubtful he would have been tasked with the creation of such an important, inventory-tracking document as a mixer log. At least, not when the capable Willadeane Scott was around.

It was Willadeane who had assigned Tish her mixer. It was Willadeane who, armed with this knowledge, had the opportunity to sabotage the mixer well in advance of its distribution, thus rendering the storeroom video footage of distribution day entirely useless. It was Willadeane Scott who had produced two mugs of exceptionally strong tea spiked with the drugs that led to Lillian Harwood's and Penelope Purdue's deaths.

And Tish knew why.

She returned the clipboard to its spot on the rack and reached into her apron pocket for her phone in order to call Clayton.

Clayton. He has my phone, she remembered as she heard the heavy metal door of the storeroom slam shut.

'Hello? Hello, I'm in here,' she called, rushing in the direction of the door. 'Open the—'

Willadeane Scott blocked the exit. 'Yes, I know you're in here. I came looking for you.'

'Oh, sorry,' Tish answered as casually as she could. 'I lost track of time. This place is a treasure trove of cooking gear. I felt like a kid in a candy store but I, um, I shouldn't linger much longer. That cake won't decorate itself.'

'You're not going anywhere.' Willadeane held a hypodermic needle aloft.

Tish took a step backward. 'What's in the syringe?'

'Oxycodone. I already placed the half-empty prescription bottle, made out in your name, in your purse. When you're found here, dead and alone, it will be assumed you were an addict. A tragic consequence of your near-fatal shooting this December.'

'You know who I am,' Tish croaked as she scanned the room for another way out.

'I knew from the beginning. How many Tish Tarragons can there be?' she scoffed.

'So you tried to scare me off the bake-off with a text message and a warning written in icing on my car windshield. And a rat.'

'The rat was a last-minute flourish. I found him near the dumpster at work and knew I had to use him. I also knew your contact details from the bake-off database, just as I knew which car was yours from the list of contestants' parking permits. Most of all, I knew you'd be trouble.'

'Like Lillian Harwood was trouble to the dental clinic?' Tish spied an emergency fire-alarm switch on the wall five feet to her left.

Willadeane looked surprised.

'Yes, I worked out that you're Doctor Reasoner's secretary. Your slavish devotion to your boss, the fact that the clinic just happens to be run by a substitute receptionist at the same time you're working at the bake-off, and the fact that both Lillian and Pen had dentist appointments just before they died led me to you. You killed Lillian because she was going to report your boss, Doctor Reasoner, for pushing pills, wasn't she?'

'Lillian was a long-time patient of the clinic. When she came to the bake-off, she told me that although she didn't want to change dentists, she didn't like how Joel had changed things. She didn't like how long she had to wait to get an appointment and how crowded the office had become. She didn't like the looks of the people who were showing up there. She didn't like how they'd come in and turn right around and leave again. She told me she was going to file a complaint online with the

Virginia Board of Dentistry. I couldn't allow her to do that. It would have raised too many questions. I tried to explain to Lillian how important the work Joel was doing was – how he was helping people in pain – but she wouldn't listen.'

'So you drugged her tea,' Tish surmised, inching ever-so-slowly toward the fire alarm. 'What was it? Epinephrine?'

'Epinephrine needs to be injected,' Willadeane corrected. 'I gave her a common amphetamine. Her blood pressure was already high. It didn't take much to push her over the edge.'

'And then you gave Penelope penicillin in the same manner. What happened? Did she get too close to the truth?' Tish stepped even closer to the alarm.

'She'd scheduled an appointment the day before the bake-off. Supposedly, Lillian had recommended us to her, but how could I be certain of that? How could I be sure that Lillian didn't tell Penelope what she suspected? Penelope was always asking questions. She must have known more than she let on. When I saw Penelope's name in the book just before the bake-off, I wanted to cancel her appointment, but then I realized it might make her suspicious. The office wasn't as busy then as it is now, and the appointment had been in the books for months so, following my advice, Joel honored that appointment. When Penelope showed up, all she did was question Joel about his practice.'

'Of course. How blind could I have been?' Tish rued. 'Whereas everyone described Penelope as nosy, you were the only one who said she was quiet. You wanted me off the scent.'

'Didn't do any good. You're a prying bitch, just like she was.'

'So what happened to Penelope on her visit? Did you threaten her?'

'No. Joel is too gentle for that. He performed the work that was needed and showed her the door, but he told me about the incident.'

'He told you? You mean you weren't in the office that day?' Tish was now four feet away from the fire alarm.

'No, I was here, setting up for the bake-off. I knew who Penelope was from the previous year's contest.'

'But she only knew you as Willadeane Scott, bake-off

volunteer, and hence her guard was down. She didn't know you were Doctor Reasoner's secretary.'

'I'm more than just his secretary, Ms Tarragon. Joel couldn't help half the people he does if it weren't for me.' Willadeane took a step closer to Tish. 'I'm instrumental in his work.'

'His work as a drug dealer?' Tish provoked. She needed to continue to distract Willadeane in order to move closer to the alarm.

'He's not a drug dealer. He's a healer. Joel has dedicated his life's work to eliminating other people's pain. It doesn't matter if they don't have insurance. He prescribes them medication that helps them.'

'And he does it out of the goodness of his heart, I'm sure. Not the hundreds of thousands of dollars in cash he probably brings home each year.' She took another step toward the wall.

Closer. Closer.

'He isn't interested in the money. Helping people is his calling, but I wouldn't expect someone with a mind as small as yours to understand.'

'I may have a small mind, but at least I haven't murdered two women to protect a man who doesn't love me.'

'That's not true! He loves me. He's told me.'

'Then why is he still with his wife?'

Closer still.

'He's waiting for the right time. He wants to let her down gently.'

'And you bought that?' Tish sneered. 'It's the oldest line in the book.'

'Joel isn't like other men.'

'Yes, he is. You're out here killing to protect him; meanwhile, his wife is back in his office, sitting in your chair, working at your desk. My friend was there this morning. She said Joel even leaned over his wife's shoulder and gave her a little kiss.'

'That's a lie,' Willadeane roared and lunged forward, wielding the needle like a knife.

Tish ducked out of the way, pushed Willadeane to the ground, and pressed the fire alarm.

Nothing happened.

A stunned Tish pressed the switch again, but still nothing happened.

Willadeane laughed as she picked herself off the floor. 'That hasn't been working since your unfortunate mixer accident. It's a shame I didn't tell the repairmen about it while they were here fixing the air conditioning.'

Tish felt a cold pit form at the bottom of her stomach, but she wasn't going down without a fight. If the alarm didn't work, she'd simply make enough noise to get the attention of a passing volunteer. 'H-e-e-e-e-e-l-l-l-l-l-p,' she screamed at the top of her lungs, while simultaneously knocking the contents of the nearest shelf to the ground.

'You fool,' Willadeane shouted. 'No one can hear you.'

Tish was undeterred. Dashing to the rack that supported the dozen or so standing mixers that hadn't been distributed in the exhibition hall, she began lifting them, one by one, from their shelves and letting each one drop to the concrete floor with a deafening crash. 'H-e-e-e-e-e-l-l-l-l-l-p.'

Willadeane charged at her, syringe still in hand.

With her back against the shelving unit, Tish picked up a professional-grade baking sheet and brandished it like a shield while simultaneously kicking at her attacker. Willadeane stabbed wildly with her right arm, but the needle only succeeded in coming in contact with metal.

Tish screamed again, this time louder than before. As she screamed, she drew in her leg and released, putting her entire body weight behind the motion. The kick landed in Willadeane's abdomen, sending the woman stumbling backward. Tish followed up on the move by smashing the sheet pan against Willadeane's head, as she doubled over in pain.

All the while, Willadeane's grasp on the syringe remained firm.

Seeing no other way, apart from a lengthy wrestling match, to extricate the weapon from Willadeane's hand, Tish dashed to the door of the storeroom and began banging on it as hard as could.

Without her phone to call for help, all Tish could do was pray that someone, somewhere, would hear her.

TWENTY-SIX

J ulian Davis hit 'send' on the email outlining the details of his coverage of the developing bake-off scandal and drank back the rest of his coffee. The phone call to his boss breaking the news that Whitney Liddell and David Biederman had been brought into custody had been so well received that Jules suspected it might earn him a raise as well as a promotion.

He slid his phone into his front jacket pocket and, reaching down to give Biscuit's ears a quick tousle, rose from his spot in the hospitality suite. It was eleven o'clock and volunteers were already setting up the buffet table with the various plates and utensils to be used during the midday lunch break.

Leaving Biscuit where he was, Jules brought his empty mug to the sink and rinsed it in preparation for placing it in the dishwasher.

'I'll get that for you, Mr Davis,' a kindly volunteer said, snatching the mug from his hands. 'This dishwasher is full, so I'll bring it back to the kitchen.'

'Thank you. That's very—'

Jules's words were cut off by the sound of a distant crash and then another and another and yet another.

'What – what is that?' he asked the volunteer.

She shrugged. 'Construction work outdoors, maybe?'

Biscuit, however, had identified the source of the noise and was off like a shot.

'Biscuit,' Jules shouted, running after him. 'Biscuit!'

The dog ignored his calls and ran to a closed door several feet away from the entrance to the exhibition hall. 'Biscuit,' Jules called, following after him. 'What is it, boy?'

Jules's question was met with the sound of a muffled scream.

'Somebody call nine-one-one!' Jules shouted to the women in the hospitality suite. 'And somebody open this door. Now!'

* * *

With her urgent pleas at the storeroom door unheeded and Willadeane approaching fast, Tish ran for the row of shelving marked *Pots & Pans*, her eyes fixed on the collection of professional-grade brass stockpots that lined the topmost shelf. If the mixers weren't loud enough to garner attention as they hit the cement floor, the thirty-gallon vessels certainly would be.

Using the shelves like rungs of a ladder, Tish scaled the side of the rack until her fingertips could reach the oversized stockpots. She gave the first one a good shove, but instead of waiting for the deafening clamor as it smashed into the hard cement below, she went on to clear the shelf of another pot and then yet another. The noise generated was earsplitting.

'No one's coming for you,' Willadeane shouted. She was standing just below Tish, assaying to inject the syringe into one of the caterer's ankles.

Kicking at Willadeane with her right foot and balancing on her left, Tish swept whatever she could from the second-highest shelf and sent it raining down on her assailant. Willadeane shielded herself, giving Tish a few brief seconds in which she could scramble to the now-empty top shelf and then, perhaps, climb down the other side.

Tish had placed a successful toehold on the top shelf with her right foot and was about to pull herself up when she felt a hand grab her left ankle.

'It's too late,' Willadeane smirked.

As Tish struggled to break free of Willadeane's grasp, her fingertips searched the nearby shelf area for something to use as a weapon, finally coming to rest on a cast-iron omelet pan. Tish lifted the pan high, but before she could bring it down on Willadeane's head, the woman released Tish's ankle with a scream. Tish looked down to see something white and furry attacking Willadeane's leg.

It was Biscuit.

'Let go, you filthy mutt!' Willadeane dropped the syringe and leaned down to pick the dog up by the neck, but Tish, scrambling down the rack, intervened by striking her on the back of the head with the omelet pan.

Willadeane slumped to the ground.

TWENTY-SEVEN

While Willadeane Scott was placed in handcuffs and taken to an ambulance for treatment for a concussion, Tish gave her statement to Officer Clayton. Afterward, she went to sit beside Jules in the hospitality suite. Biscuit lay at Jules's feet, chewing on a dental stick.

'I can't believe he rescued me,' she stated, looking down at the dog while sipping from a large bottle of water.

'Why wouldn't he? You rescued him,' Jules reasoned. 'Then you rescued me, by giving me Biscuit. That's a lot of saving to make up for.'

'Well, let's hope he doesn't need to rescue me again.'

'Fingers crossed,' Jules agreed. 'Although I'm kinda impressed that he went all Cujo like that. You think he might need a superhero costume?'

'Isn't it bad enough you gave him the middle name Wellington?' she teased.

'I suppose.' He laughed. 'How are you feeling?'

'Good. Exhausted, but good.'

'Yeah, if anyone ever tells you that you need to work out, just tell them what you did today.'

'I will,' she agreed with a smile.

'So what's next?'

'After taking a few minutes to decompress, have a sandwich, and drink some water, I'm getting out of here and taking a long nap. And you?'

'Oh, I'll be here for a little while to film some more segments for the five o'clock broadcast. Then it's back to the station. Wanna meet up later for some food?' Jules suggested.

'Actually, yeah. It would be nice to have some dinner conversation that doesn't involve a criminal investigation.'

'You got it. What should I bring?'

'Nothing,' she ordered. 'I'm cooking.'

'But you're exhausted.'

'I'll be picture-perfect after a nap and I'm not fixing anything complicated. Besides, you know cooking is therapy for me.'

'OK,' he said, capitulating, then, looking up to see Schuyler in the doorway of the hospitality suite, bid a hasty adieu. 'Talk later, huh?'

Tish nodded. 'What brings you here?' she asked as Schuyler approached.

'I was in a meeting with Lightbody when he got the call. How are you?'

'Better now that it's all over.'

'Why didn't you call me?' Schuyler's tone was accusatory.

'I was a little busy, fighting a murderer and rescuing Biscuit from Willadeane – I swear she would have killed that dog. Also, Clayton had my phone. He needed to track a threatening text message. A text message he traced back to Willadeane.'

'Does Clayton still have your phone?'

'No, his tech guy downloaded everything he needed and I got the phone back a few minutes ago.'

'And yet you still didn't call me. Instead, you sat here talking to Jules.'

'You're right,' Tish admitted. 'I didn't call you and I probably should have. To be perfectly honest, I thought if I called and told you what had happened, you'd probably reprimand me for being here in the first place or say you told me so or tell me I need to stop trying to be a hero or admonish me for solving a case instead of being on the campaign trail. I really didn't want to engage in that kind of conversation. Not again.'

'I'm sorry you felt as if you couldn't talk to me, but you need to understand where I am. I'm at a critical point in my life, Tish. I can't afford to be distracted from my work, my goals, my dreams. I can't afford to be anything but at the top of my game. I had hoped you'd understand my need for support right now, but instead you're off chasing killers and adding a whole new menu to your already busy café.'

'I don't pretend to be a perfect partner, Schuyler, but I've tried my best to be supportive of your endeavors. I promised, when the bake-off was over, to cut back on weekend hours. I promised to be at your side at your fundraising dinner. I promised to spend the next few weeks with you shaking hands and kissing babies. Considering you threw your hat in the mayoral ring without even consulting with me or giving us the opportunity to discuss how our relationship might be affected, I think I've been plenty supportive.'

'Promises aren't actual support. They're just promises.'

'Says the aspiring politician,' Tish wisecracked. 'I've been living without you for months, yet I haven't complained once. I've brought trays of sandwiches to your campaign headquarters. I've taken over your household chores on the weekends. I drop off and pick up your dry cleaning twice a week so that you always have a clean suit to wear. I've listened to your speeches. I've reviewed your staff press releases. I've discussed policy with you until the wee hours of the morning, even when I needed to be at the café at six. I did all of that – all of that – despite not having signed up for any for this in the first place.'

'I'm sorry, but things change. People change,' he rationalized.

'I understand that, but I haven't changed,' she countered. 'When you met me – when you first said you loved me – you knew exactly who I was. You knew that I was a café owner and caterer who had a flair for solving crimes. Here I am and I am still a café owner and caterer who solves crimes. You knew who I was when we met last August, and you pursued me and acted as if I was the most wonderful woman in the world. And now, suddenly, I feel as though who I am is no longer good enough for you.'

Schuyler took several seconds to respond. 'Because it isn't,' he answered honestly. 'Not anymore. Not for how I envision the rest of my life.'

Tish felt as if she'd been stabbed in the heart, and yet somehow she had already anticipated his answer. She stood up from her chair and set off to get her belongings from the exhibition hall.

'Where are you going?' Schuyler asked, visibly surprised.

'Home,' she answered. 'I'm going home.'

Tish pulled her car into the Cookin' the Books parking lot at three o'clock in the afternoon and removed two suitcases and a trash bag full of shoes from the hatchback. They were all she had brought to Schuyler's condo.

Mary Jo stepped out on to the front porch to greet her friend. Alongside her sat the long-haired black-and-white cat. At the sight of Tish, he meowed loudly.

'Got room for one more?' Tish asked with a melancholy smile.

'For you? Always.' Mary Jo joined her friend in the parking lot and the two women embraced before bringing Tish's luggage indoors and up the narrow staircase that led to the crowded two-bedroom apartment.

The cat followed close behind them.

TWENTY-EIGHT

T wo weeks passed before Tish received a phone call from the bake-off foundation, asking her to deposit her cherry pie at bake-off offices in Richmond for judging. One week later, these instructions were followed by an invitation requesting her presence at the civic center for the awards ceremony.

Tish arrived at the venue at eight o'clock in the morning on the designated Saturday. After passing through the metal detector and the security checkpoint, Tish checked her lipstick and hair, and helped herself to some water from the cooler in the hospitality suite. It was there that she encountered Desmond. He was dressed in his customary dark fitted suit and pastel tie, but he exuded newly minted confidence and calm. 'Ms Tarragon, how have you been?'

'I've been well, Desmond. And you?'

'I've been great, thanks. I wanted to let you know how much we all appreciate what you've done for the bake-off.'

'We? Then you're staying on here?'

'Yes, I've been appointed head of marketing.'

'Wonderful,' she exclaimed. 'Congratulations. And I'm sorry for being nosy. It's just that I read in the paper that Kitty had resigned and I wasn't sure if you'd left as well.'

'Kitty was forced to resign,' he told her, sotto voce. 'She

knew about Whitney's culinary arts training and kept it secret.'

'Oh,' Tish replied, not so much out of surprise but because she wasn't quite sure what to say. Looking to change the subject, she thought it an ideal time to tie up the remaining loose end in the case. 'I, um, I have an interesting question for you, Desmond, if you don't mind.'

'Sure. Go ahead.' He nodded and placed his hands on his hips as if to demonstrate his openness.

'Did you happen to do any temp work prior to this job?'

Desmond looked befuddled. 'Temp work? No, I waited tables while in school, but this is my first job after college. Why?'

'Oh, just wondering. The dentist Willadeane worked for had hired a temp years ago who, er, matched your description.'

'Ah, OK. I get it. Yeah, no. Not me. Shortly after graduating, I answered an online ad seeking someone with marketing experience. Kitty hired me, but she seemed to have other ideas.' He cleared his throat. 'I'm not organized enough to be an assistant, but that didn't deter her. I think she liked the control. I wanted to leave, but she paid me well and, since I have lots of student debt, I stuck around. I'm not proud of allowing her to treat me the way she did, but it was tough to find another gig that paid as well as this one, and when you're faced with paying back loans or eating, it's not much of a decision, is it?'

Tish nodded. 'I'm glad the bake-off decided to give you a chance to put your education to good use.'

'Yeah, I'm extremely grateful. It'll be tough work, of course, but I'm looking forward to bringing the event up to date. It will still be about home cooks, of course, but home has a different meaning to different people. Food can help tell those stories.'

'Sounds like you're off and running. And if you need some help with the organizational tasks, I have a friend with a marketing background who's looking for some extra work.'

'You know, I was discussing with the board the other day how I could use some help. It would be just a couple of days a week,' he warned. 'If all goes well, we might be able to ramp things up, but no promises.

'I can't answer for her, but I think she might be willing to give it a shot.'

'Cool.' Desmond pulled a card out of his jacket pocket and passed it to Tish. 'Here's my number. Have her call me.'

She happily accepted. 'Thanks. I will.'

Gordon Quinn had made his way through the crowd and now stood beside Tish. Desmond said a quick 'hello' to the man before returning to his duties.

Gordon smiled. 'Tish, I want to thank you for not pressing charges and apologize again for scaring you the way I did.'

'That's OK. Losing someone is one of the most difficult things we can face as human beings,' she said.

'Yeah, but that's no excuse for my behavior. I wanted you to know, though, that your kindness and graciousness moved me to take a good hard look at myself. As a result, I've started seeing a grief counselor.'

'Wow, that's a big step, Gordon. How has it been working out for you?'

'Like sunshine after a storm. There are still some bad days from time to time, but I feel better equipped to handle them. I've even started socializing on a regular basis. There's a widow and widower's group in my neighborhood and I've been joining them for a few activities. It's helped a great deal with the loneliness.'

'That's terrific, Gordon.' She gave him a gentle hug. 'I'm so happy for you.'

'Tish,' Dolly Pritchard called from the entrance of the hospitality suite. Seeing Tish and Gordon's hug and not wishing to be outdone, she rushed forward, with Riya following closely at her heels, and enveloped Tish in a rib-crushing embrace. 'Why, how are you, darlin'?'

'I'm good. How are you?' Tish answered once she'd extricated herself from Dolly's arms and caught her breath.

'All hepped-up to find out who won this thing.'

'Yes, the fateful day is here,' Tish agreed, giving Riya a hug and a kiss on the cheek.

'I am very glad you weren't harmed during your scuffle with Willadeane,' Riya said.

'Yeah, who knew that scrawny thing had it in her,' Dolly stated. 'I knew she idolized her boss, but killing for him? I never saw that one coming.'

'People do some crazy things for love,' Gordon observed with a glance in Tish's direction.

The bakers sipped water, tea, and coffee, and exchanged pleasantries for several minutes before an announcement called them into the exhibition hall.

Shuffling into the now-empty hall, the contestants made their way to the front of the room, where a makeshift stage, complete with podium and microphone, had been erected. To the left and rear of the podium, a folding table displayed five bronze trophies.

Tallulah Sinclair and Vernon Staples took the podium to thunderous applause. Tallulah was the first to speak. 'Good morning, bakers. I want to thank y'all for being here today. I also want to thank y'all for your patience. I know some of you gave up work or being with family, and others had to hire childcare to be with us today. Everyone here at the Virginia Commonwealth Bake-Off appreciates your sacrifice and your flexibility during what has been a crazy contest year.

'As all of you know, the bake-off has been beset by problems these past few weeks, the latest of which being that Ms Kitty Flournoy has stepped down as bake-off chair. I cannot say anything further about any of these issues apart from what has already been disclosed in news reports. However, I wish to assure everyone here that we at the Virginia Commonwealth Bake-Off Foundation are determined to see the competition live on, but with a newfound spirit of camaraderie and inclusiveness. It is in this spirit that I am pleased to announce that Mr Vernon Staples and I have been appointed to replace Kitty Flournoy as co-chairs of the foundation.'

As the crowd clapped and cheered, Vernon Staples stepped to the microphone. 'Thank you for your kind support. We hope to make all of you very proud. And in an effort to establish transparency in all our future bake-off dealings, I have an announcement to make. For over a decade now, Tallulah and I have had the great fortune to serve as bake-off judges. We've felt extremely privileged to be able to judge the fantastic dishes you home cooks create. We've also felt quite privileged to be able to entertain everyone while doing so. However, in the past few years we've not been quite so forthcoming about the true nature of our relationship. Although in the beginning, when we started the bake-off all those years ago, Tallulah and I were, indeed, sworn enemies, over time and the course of hundreds of charming and enjoyable public engagements, our antagonistic relationship thawed and blossomed into a friendship of mutual respect and deep, abiding affection. Finally, last summer, Ms Tallulah Sinclair did me the great honor of becoming my wife.' Vernon took Tallulah by the hand and gave her a kiss, much to the surprise, and joy, of the crowd.

'It is this feeling of love that we wish to bring to the Virginia Commonwealth Bake-Off.' Tallulah stepped in where her husband had left off. 'Love is what inspires each and every one of you to cook the meals you do. You cook to celebrate birthdays and anniversaries and weddings. You cook to bring succor to the ill and to console the recently bereaved. This bake-off has always had a lot of heart, but recently that heart has become buried beneath the ruthlessness of competition. Vernon and I plan to get that heart beating again. As always, your recipes are important to the judging process, but equally important are the stories behind those recipes. We want to know if the marble cake you're making for your signature bake was based upon the cake your Aunt Martha used to make for your birthday. We want to know if your curry recipe traveled here with your parents when they left Thailand. Going forward, all bake-off recipes and stories will be published in an annual cookbook, the proceeds of which will be donated to the Square Food Foundation, an organization that provides at-risk youth with the culinary training and skills that will help them find work in the restaurant and food industry.'

The crowd applauded again. Meanwhile, it was Vernon Staples's turn at the microphone. 'In keeping with the theme of love and food stories, the Virginia Commonwealth Bake-Off has established a new award category honoring contestants both past and present whose bake-off stories speak to the power of food in love and personal connections. The first recipient of the "Food is Love" award is Anh Quinn. Born in Vietnam, Anh came to Virginia with her husband, Gordon. A passionate home cook, Anh loved exploring the cuisines of the world, but nothing made her happier than cooking the American dishes of her new homeland, the American dishes her husband loved. It was these dishes that Anh created when she participated in the Virginia Commonwealth Bake-Off of 2002. She did not win the competition – not because of any shortcoming on her part, but because of the bias and prejudice of one of our judges. We cannot take away the hurt, pain, and disappointment caused by their actions. We can only apologize and strive to do better in the future. We honor Anh and her brave spirit, her love of cooking, but, most of all, the love with which she created it. Her story will always be remembered at the Virginia Commonwealth Bake-Off and will, no doubt, inspire cooks for generations to come, including her husband.'

Gordon Quinn caught his breath and drew a hand to his face. 'Oh, my . . .' His voice dissolved into sobs.

Tallulah stepped into the crowd to meet Gordon and bring him on stage to collect the award. Seeing the man was in no shape to address the crowd, Vernon brought the trophy – a brass loving cup with her name inscribed – to Gordon.

'Thank you,' Gordon cried. 'That's all she wanted, you know? To be recognized. To be one of us.'

Tallulah embraced Gordon and then passed him to Vernon, who shook his hand. Amid applause from the crowd, the couple returned to the podium, leaving Gordon to accept the good wishes of Riya, Dolly, Tish, and a bevy of other bakers.

'And now the moment everyone has been waiting for – the winners of this year's Virginia Commonwealth Bake-Off,' Tallulah announced. 'In third place, Angela Burrard.'

Angela, an elderly, white-haired woman with glasses and a radiant smile, went on to the stage to claim her trophy. She thanked Tallulah and Vernon and stopped to pose triumphantly with the cup over her head, before returning to the crowd.

'In second place, Dolly Pritchard,' Vernon revealed.

A displeased Dolly thumped on to the stage, collected her trophy without even a semblance of a smile, and sulked back to her spot beside Riya. 'Second, again,' she said, pouting.

The emceeing duty had switched back to Tallulah. 'And finally, the first-place winner and new champion of the Virginia Commonwealth Bake-Off, Riya Patel.'

Riya shrieked with joy and jumped up and down as Tish and

Gordon congratulated her. 'Yeah, congrats,' Dolly added, half-heartedly.

Riya bounded on to the stage to collect her prize. 'Thank you,' she gushed into the microphone. 'I cannot tell you how much this victory means to my family and me. The cash prize will enable us to expand our business, and the notoriety and esteem of the bake-off will improve my status as a cook and caterer, enabling me to reach more customers. This is a dream come true. Thank you so very, very much.'

There was another round of applause as Riya took her trophy and exited the stage.

'And last but certainly not least,' Vernon began, 'an award for a woman who is truly in a category of her own. Tallulah, the board, and I struggled with how we should thank someone who has done so much. She's dazzled us with her cooking, uncovered a corrupt business scheme between a contestant and a judge, and found justice for two of her fellow bakers. And that is why Tish Tarragon is our choice for Virginia Commonwealth Bake-Off's newest award category, Baker of the Year.'

Tish stepped on to the stage to accept her trophy, shaking hands with Vernon and then hugging Tallulah. 'Thank you,' she said to them.

'Thank *you*,' Tallulah replied. 'For everything. Including that email telling us about Anh Quinn. We're glad we could do our part in setting things right.'

Tish glanced at Gordon's jubilant face in the crowd. 'Me, too,' she agreed. 'Me, too.'

TWENTY-NINE

Tish returned to the café shortly after ten thirty in the morning. The breakfast crowd had dissipated and only a couple of older locals remained in the booths, sipping coffee and talking. Mary Jo was at the counter, adding up the morning's receipts, while Celestine was taking a break, sharing coffee and a muffin with Daryl Dufour.

'Hey,' Tish greeted as the bell over the café door signaled her arrival. She had miraculously managed to cram the trophy into her oversized bag.

'Hey, yourself,' Mary Jo greeted.

Celestine leaped from her spot in the corner booth. Daryl followed. 'So?' she asked.

Tish frowned. 'Oh, well . . . I didn't get the number-one spot.'

Celestine's mouth dropped open. 'Oh, that's OK, honey. I know you gave it your all.'

'Instead' – she pulled the trophy from her purse and presented it to Celestine – 'I got Baker of the Year.'

'Baker of the Year!' she exclaimed. 'I didn't know there was such a thing!'

'It's a new award given to the baker who helps their fellow contestants the most. I guess they figured putting a psycho volunteer behind bars was helpful,' Tish chuckled.

'Well, they'd better. Isn't it beautiful, Daryl?' Celestine gushed.

'It sure is.' He admired the loving cup.

'It is, but there's more.' Tish reached into her bag again and extracted a bank check for ten thousand dollars. The check was made out to Celestine Rufus. 'It's not the fifteen thousand for first prize, but hopefully it will help you through this tough time.'

Celestine took the check in her trembling hands. 'Oh, Tish. I can't take this. You nearly got killed competin' for me.'

'You can take it and you will.'

'Let me at least split it with you. Fifty-fifty.'

'Nope. That's all yours. As for the trophy, we just need to drop it off at the bake-off offices later this week to be engraved,' Tish stated. 'Then it can stand proudly on your mantle.'

'Yeah, I've been thinkin' about that.' Celestine pursed her lips together. 'I know how hard you worked to get that trophy. Fightin' that killer and all, jugglin' things here and at home. I want you to have it. You've more than earned it.'

'But—' Tish started to argue.

'No "buts." *You* are baker of the year. Next year, I'm gonna compete and win my own trophy,' Celestine announced with a wide grin. 'And give the prize money to *you*.'

'I don't want your prize money.'

'Meh, we'll discuss that next year.'

'Well, I think that's a terrific idea, Celestine,' Mary Jo cheered.

'Yeah, Daryl here put me up to it. Built my confidence up. I may not be in the right spot for it now, but I have a year to prepare. And it's always been my dream to compete and win.' Celestine eyed Daryl. 'As you know.'

'Oh, I know.' Daryl sighed. 'It was all you talked about when we were kids. It's about time you started chasing some of those dreams of yours.'

'Well, you couldn't have picked a better time to compete,' Tish approved. 'The new board seems set on making it a fun, inclusive experience. Just be prepared to tell the stories behind your dishes.'

'Honey, when could you ever shut me up from tellin' a good story?' Celestine quipped.

Jules, dressed in a rainy-day ensemble of jeans, striped sweater, sneakers, and trench coat, entered the café, cradling Biscuit. 'Hey, y'all, how'd it go?'

Celestine held the check and trophy aloft. 'Tish is Baker of the Year.'

'Baker of the Year? Whoot!'

'Yes, I was surprised I didn't see you this morning. I thought you'd be at the civic center, covering the action,' Tish remarked as Jules planted a congratulatory kiss on her cheek.

'No, I took the day off. Biscuit and I were exhausted,' he explained. 'I also had an errand to take care of this morning.'

Celestine and Daryl went back to their booth to finish their tête-à-tête, while Mary Jo set about replenishing coffee mugs.

'Biscuit and I went to the cemetery,' Jules divulged, taking a seat at the counter. 'We put some flowers on Penelope Purdue's grave.'

'Aw, how thoughtful of you,' Tish praised, removing her raincoat and hanging it from a hook by the backdoor. 'How did you know where she was buried?'

'Clayton told me.' As if by magic, the young policeman appeared in the doorway. 'I feel badly for her, Tish, having no one to mourn her. All alone in the world just because of who she was.'

'Next time you visit, I'll go with you,' she offered, tying an apron around her waist.

'I'd like that,' Jules said with a smile.

Clayton, in his usual work attire, said 'hello' and sat down on the stool beside Jules. Tish poured them both a round of coffee.

'I've also decided on my new middle name,' Jules announced.

Mary Jo had since returned to her spot behind the counter. 'It's not "a-licious," is it?' she teased. 'Julian-a-licious Davis.'

'Maybe twenty years ago,' he confessed. 'No, I'm changing it to Pen.'

'Hmm, I like it.'

'I do, too,' Tish concurred.

'Good,' Jules deemed. 'As I was saying, I feel so badly for Penelope Purdue, living and dying alone, with no family, that I decided I wanted to pay tribute to her somehow. I couldn't really name myself Penelope – I mean, I guess I could, but it didn't feel right to me. But then I remembered that she always wanted folks to call her Pen. So there you go, Julian Pen Davis. This way Ms Purdue knows that someone here on earth remembers her.'

'It's a beautiful sentiment, Jules,' Mary Jo acknowledged.

'It really is.' Tish's eyes welled with tears.

'Very cool.' Clayton took a sip of coffee.

'Yeah, it felt like fate was speaking to me. Sending me signs that this was what I needed to do. The only problem is that now I need to change my monogrammed towels.'

Clayton laughed out loud.

'Um, he's not kidding,' Mary Jo clarified to the young officer, who promptly returned his attention to his coffee mug.

'What did your mother say? Have you told her yet?' Tish asked.

'I have.' Jules put Biscuit down on the floor beside his stool. 'She said the exact thing you did, Tish, that she didn't care what I wanted to call myself. She'll always love me.'

'Aww,' Mary Jo and Tish cried in unison.

'I know. I'm super lucky.'

'Speaking of lucky, I have some good news,' Clayton announced. 'That's why I'm here, actually – well, that and to bring coffee and muffins back to headquarters. Sheriff Lightbody has been asked to leave. Effective this morning. Apparently, there were multiple complaints about how he handled the bake-off case.'

All eyes slid toward Tish.

'Don't look at me. I'm all about the live and let live,' she proclaimed. 'Even for blustering, big-headed cops who expect freebies.'

As the foursome chatted happily, the bell above the café door chimed. Moments later, a voice came from near the cash register. 'What does a guy need to do to get a cup of coffee around here?'

They looked up to see a tall man with lean, chiseled features, dark, spiky hair, gray eyes, and a day's worth of stubble, standing at the till. He was dressed in a T-shirt, jeans, motorcycle boots, and a lightweight black jacket.

'Sheriff Reade.' Clayton leaped from his stool and vigorously shook the man's hand. 'How have you been?'

Jules followed suit. 'Sheriff! Long time, no see.'

Mary Jo bolted from behind the counter. 'No handshakes from me,' she declared as she threw her arms around his neck.

Tish self-consciously combed her hair with her fingers and followed Mary Jo to the front of the counter. The last time she had seen Clemson was just before she was shot at the Hobson Glen Christmas Fair, and although it was so very good to see him standing, once again, in her café, the experience left her feeling more than a bit awkward. 'Hi, Clemson. It's good to see you. I – we – you were missed.' She extended her hand.

He accepted it and let her palm linger in his. 'I've missed . . . Hobson Glen, too.'

'Are you back for good or just passing through?' A hopeful Tish tried her best to sound indifferent; meanwhile, her heart raced.

'I'm back. If you'll have me.' He smiled.

'It's not really up to me, is it?' She pulled her hand away slowly.

'No. Good thing, then, that I've already called the county office and have been reinstated as sheriff.' His gray eyes danced.

'You have?' She struggled to hide her excitement.

'Yeah, they told me Lightbody didn't work out so well and that no one's stepped forward to take his place. Something about not wanting to work with some "soup-slinging sleuth." Whoever that might be.'

Tish burst into laughter. 'You're joking.'

'I am, but only slightly. You're an intimidating figure.'

Mary Jo chuckled. 'Coffee, Sheriff?'

'Yes, please,' he accepted, as Clayton and Jules returned to their stools and Mary Jo and Tish moved back behind the counter.

'And your usual breakfast sandwich?' Tish asked.

'Um, no,' he declined.

'No?'

'No, I'd like to try whatever you recommend. I trust your judgment.'

Tish looked at him and narrowed her eyes. Was this the same Sheriff Reade who consistently ordered the *Portrait of the Artist as a Young Ham* breakfast sandwich? 'Really?'

'Yes, really,' he assured.

'To stay or to go?'

'Oh, to stay. Definitely to stay. I don't have to report in right away, and I thought you could tell me about your adventure at the bake-off.'

Tish agreed and set about rustling up some poached eggs on toast with creamy avocado sauce, and then she stopped. 'So what prompted you to get your old job back? I mean, apart from the fact that I strike fear in the hearts of law enforcement officers across the Commonwealth.'

Reade replied, haltingly, 'Let's just say a little voice suggested it was time I come back to Hobson Glen.'

'Well, thank that little voice for me,' she said, before getting back to work.

'I will,' he promised and, while Tish wasn't looking, cast a wink in Celestine's direction.

Celestine, facing the till, returned the gesture, but not without being noticed by Daryl.

'What was that for? Who are you winking at?' He turned around in his seat. 'Oh, look, it's Sheriff Reade. He's back. But why were you winking at Sheriff Reade?'

'I was just returnin' his wink.'

Daryl's face was a question.

'He winked to me to say "thank you" for a favor I did.' Celestine grinned. 'A favor for him and a very good friend.'

TISH TARRAGON'S TARRAGON CHICKEN WITH SPRING VEGETABLES

For the bake-off, Tish uses bone-in chicken pieces which are cooked low and slow until tender, but when in a crunch for time, this version using boneless breasts and both dried and fresh tarragon delivers great taste at a fraction of the effort.

For the chicken:

- 4 to 6 small chicken breast fillets
- 2 shallots or 1 small red onion, finely chopped
- 2 garlic cloves, finely chopped
- 160 ml (2/3 cup) dry vermouth
- 125 ml (1/2 cup) chicken stock
- 125 ml (1/2 cup) single cream, soya cream, or half and half
- 1 tablespoon cornflour or cornstarch mixed with 1 tablespoon water
- 1 tablespoon fresh tarragon, finely chopped
- 1 teaspoon dried tarragon
- Salt and pepper to taste

Heat two tablespoons of oil in a large skillet or saucepan over high heat. Season the chicken breasts generously with salt and pepper. Place the chicken breasts in the pan and cook for 3 to 5 minutes, or until they are golden and caramelized, before turning them over. The best way to achieve a nice color on the chicken is to not move the chicken too often.

Once the chicken is golden and caramelized on both sides, remove them to a plate. The chicken does not need to be fully cooked through at this stage.

Add a bit more oil to the pan as needed. Add the shallots (or onions) and garlic. Cook for a few minutes until they have softened. Pour the vermouth into the pan and let it simmer for a few minutes until it has reduced slightly.

Use a wooden spoon to stir the mixture and to lift any caramelized bits (deglaze) from the pan. Pour in the chicken stock and cream, together with the fresh and dried tarragon. Let the sauce simmer gently for a few minutes. Taste for seasoning and add salt and pepper as needed.

Slowly pour in the cornflour slurry, stirring the sauce as you do. You may not need all of the cornflour slurry – use as much as you need until the sauce has thickened slightly.

Return the chicken to the pan and place them in the sauce. Turn the heat down to low-medium, and place a lid on the saucepan. Cook gently for 5 to 10 minutes, or until the chicken pieces have cooked through.

Garnish with more tarragon before serving.

For the vegetables:

- One small onion, diced
- Knob (1 tablespoon) unsalted butter
- Two heads of little cos or little gem lettuce, core removed and cut in half
- 125 ml (1/2 cup) chicken or vegetable stock
- One bunch of radishes, sliced
- Sprinkle of sugar
- 150 g (1 cup) fresh shelled peas

Melt the butter in a medium-sized pan. Add onion and cook until translucent. Add the lettuce on top of the onion and cook until slightly browned. Turn and brown other side. Add stock, radishes, and a sprinkle of sugar. Simmer for 10 minutes. Add the peas and cook for another 3 to 5 minutes.

Remove vegetables from pan with a slotted spoon and reduce the juices by half. Serve vegetables with juice and a scattering of fresh parsley or dill.